THE GREAT GLORIOUS GODDAMN OF IT ALL

Also by Josh Ritter

Bright's Passage

THE GREAT GLORIOUS GODDAMN OF IT ALL

A NOVEL

JOSH RITTER

HANOVER
SQUARE
PRESS

HANOVER
SQUARE
PRESS™

Recycling programs
for this product may
not exist in your area.

ISBN-13: 978-1-335-52253-5

The Great Glorious Goddamn of It All

This edition published by arrangement with Harlequin Books S.A.

Hanover Square Press
22 Adelaide St. West, 40th Floor
Toronto, Ontario M5H 4E3, Canada
HanoverSqPress.com
BookClubbish.com

Printed in U.S.A.

For Haley, who stepped out of a tall tale
and did the rescuing.

THE GREAT GLORIOUS GODDAMN OF IT ALL

MY MORTAL ENEMY

Until Joe Mouffreau, I never thought I'd have a mortal enemy again. Then Joe came back from the Second World War, tearing through the St. Anne river valley in the fancy new car his daddy bought him, throwing around the money that his daddy gave him and convincing his daddy to start in on a fancy new way to just log the holy hell out of the St. Anne. I pegged Joe Mouffreau the moment I first saw him as a lying, foolish, condescending idiot, well worth my bitter spite, and I gotta hand it to him, Joe did a bang-up job as my mortal enemy for most of my life.

Now look at me, lying here in a hospital bed with tubes in my arms and applesauce to eat. Yesterday afternoon I was drinking at the Brothers Swede, watching the soaps. I was ninety-nine years old, sure, but still I was in my prime, full of Rainier and vinegar, fixing to live forever. Then along came Joe Mouffreau, as short-necked, spindle-armed, lite-beer-drinking, milk-chasing, fast-food-smelling, big-talking, nervous-guffawing, flabby-handled, freeloading, sideways-glancing, barrel-chested, jolly-wheezingly poor a substitute for the grim reaper as Fate could supply. Maybe I shouldn't be so gobsmacked. After all, me and Joe were set at odds from the beginning, and over time, the knowledge of his essential wretchedness has come to shape my belief that our mortal enemies can keep us alive.

So despite everything that's happened, maybe I owe him my gratitude. Maybe Joe—with his four Jet Skis, his Harley-Davidson and his hundreds of channels, his house, that enormous, fake log-cabin-style Goliath, more plastic than pine, his whoop-de-do gas barbecue range and his clear-cuts—was keeping me alive the whole time. Still, there comes a time with mortal enemies when you have to have it out with them. It may not be a time or place of your own choosing, but in order to outlive somebody, one of you has to die. There are plenty of ways I could have left this life with more dignity than at Joe Mouffreau's hand. You could search the great-wide supermarket of Human Experience and find a million other fates that would go down easier than this particular brand of humiliation. Still, if you think that I care, you're wrong. Maybe for some it's a scary thing to be small, but I'm not scared. My name is Weldon Applegate, and I've been small before.

And anyway, it's not like Joe emerged from the field of battle covered in glory, either.

Having mortal enemies was one of the ways my father

and I were always different. Tom Applegate never seemed to have any enemies at all, mortal or otherwise. He was always affable, always kept an open countenance, and from the moment we first set foot in the tiny timber town of Cordelia when I was ten years old, he'd been respected as an Applegate, whose father and grandfather had both been famous lumberjacks in their times. We'd made quite a stir, my father and me, when Peg Ramsay brought us to his tiny town to run the general store after Lyle Llewellyn died. All who had heard stories of the Applegates tipped their caps in respect, and of course everyone knew about the Lost Lot, and how it was my father's by inheritance and still untouched. As we walked through the mud of Main Street, Peg had asked my father if he liked Cordelia. My father had said yes, oh yes, he liked it. He was a romantic, my dad.

There had been a time in his youth, before I was born, when my father could have taken to the woods for good. He had worked in the timber around the Montana border with his own father for several seasons and was good at it. His father, Old Tom, had followed the big trees to the St. Anne, and my father would have gone, as well, but for meeting my mother. He stood squarely behind her in their wedding photo, his big hand on her tiny shoulder, his thick, powerful body jammed into wedding attire, looking every bit the caged woodsbeast. There was kindness and humor in his eyes, but also a glint of good-time mischief and hard, hard work. He'd met my mother on a trip to Moscow, Idaho. She was working behind the counter at her family's store. The match was lopsided for sure, her family well-to-do, my father so poor he could barely afford to whistle a tune, but they had fallen in love and you know how that goes.

My mother was no fool, though, and lumberjacking, with its dangers, deprivations and enforced absence, was no way to raise a family if you could possibly avoid it. She promised to marry him if he'd leave the woods behind. So, he made her the damn oath. It couldn't have been easy; jacking was the only life my father (and his father and his father before that) had ever known. Cut those men and they would have bled pinesap. But he said yes, yes of course, and they settled down and I came along.

To my childish eyes he seemed happy and content. He wasn't one of those fathers who seethed or brooded; his face was placid as a bucket of milk. Even when word came that his own father had died working in the tall timber, he took the news in stride. You'd have thought at least that when the deed to the Lost Lot arrived with my grandfather's ax and the rest of his few personal possessions, that it would have had some effect on his self-control, but no. That craggy, tree-covered jut of mountain was just a place on some map to him. He hadn't seen it with his own eyes yet. And anyway, my father had made an oath to leave the woods behind and that was that. At least that's what I thought.

He was an affable, honest guy, Tom was, and he knew his way around numbers, so he helped manage Able and Able's, the general store owned by my mother's family. All day he stocked wares and made small talk, bargained with suppliers and kept the books. He was behind the counter the day that my mother died out of the blue from a stroke at the age of twenty-five, when I was six years old, and he continued to work there for almost four years after her death, but without her shoulder to place his hand upon, he drifted. He dragged himself out of bed each morning and put on nice clothes to work the store, but he tied his apron on loosely, and the thing seemed to hold itself away from his body, as if it no longer quite fit him. He still made small talk with customers, but it was clear that when my mother died the forest that he had cut back from around his heart had begun to edge its wild way in again. You couldn't see the tendrils of that other life braiding themselves into the very stream of his blood, but the breath of the pine trees came out in the lumberjack stories he would tell me at bedtime.

He'd tell how the toppers, men born without fear, would climb hundreds of feet into the air, cutting off branches along the way, removing the top of the pine and attaching pulleys to what was left in order to skid trees. He'd laugh as he told me stories of jacks who'd gotten so rich in the woods that, at season's end, they'd ordered themselves a private train to take them to the rowdy, swirling magic of The Lights, where there were underground bars as long as entire city blocks. "They were so long," he said, "that the men would all divide up into the nations they were from and as you walked down the bar you felt as if you were passing through the countries themselves." Ireland was loud, Finland was silent. My mother would never have countenanced telling such stories to a seven-year-old, but Tom wasn't made for life behind a counter, and at night his heart would wander.

My mother's family were society folks, intent on my being brought up right, so I went to school and Sunday school and learned to read and write and fear hellfire. Even though my mother was gone, things continued on, stable and uneventful enough that the entrance of Peg Ramsay into Able and Able's when I was ten years old was like the appearance of the angels to the shepherds. Peg was wearing his forest-green blazer and he spoke to my father about the St. Anne, about the little town of Cordelia and its dead shopkeep and about the Lost Lot, which was not just a piece of land, but a sublime and terrifying reminder that all men are mortal. He told of drinking Dream, and of the levitation of the soul it brought, of the dances by lantern-light and of Oral Avery, the topper who had recently been struck sleepless by a bolt of lightning while climbing high up in a tree on a bet.

There was no way a man like my father could resist those stories. He wouldn't work the woods, he told me (and himself), but Cordelia was a real lumberjack town, and it had done him good to be raised up in such a place. He told my mother's family about the pretty town and its church and nice little school, but privately he told me that I had had enough schooling and God for now, and that Peg Ramsay himself would give me a job sweeping hair in his shop and doing other jobs around town. What sane ten-year-old kid would say no to that kind of adventure? I mean, here we were, trapped—me in school, my father behind a counter—when we could be in Cordelia, smack-dab in the middle of our own damn *epic*.

Peg Ramsay had talked a long, long time that day he came into Able and Able's, and boy did he have our number. He told immense stories, full of giants. He spoke of the adventures of Serwalter Scott, the Genius of the Great North Woods, who built the Illini incline and the Serwalter trestle. He told of Bud Maynard and the evil claim jumper, Ed Bouley, who had been executed by a posse against the giant tree that now bore his name. He told about the great river drives, the logs five feet across, and of Wandering John, whose pine-board casket was buried too close to the water's edge and washed away one spring thaw so that it had become a tradition to lay a rock or two on his grave each drive for luck and to keep the fucker weighted down good and proper. Then, of course, he told of Linden Laughlin.

MY FATHER WAS HEARING THE TRUMPETS

Linden Laughlin came from Canada, maybe, or sometimes from Maine. He spoke with an accent but of what kind no one knew. A few soupbones said they'd seen him raising hell in Saginaw in the 1880s, but that was decades ago and surely he must have died a long time hence.

Maybe he wasn't a man at all but a graybeard or the kind of forest spirit that the Witch who lived with us was always casting her spells against. Linden Laughlin could kick the ceiling with his spiked boots. He was seven feet tall and had three rows of teeth. He could bite through a hatchet handle, not like he ever used a hatchet. Linden Laughlin's ax could chop down trees all by itself.

One time, at a dance in Vancouver or Aroostook, he got to jigging so hard that he danced right through the floor. One time, someone, somewhere, was skidding logs and got them so mired in the mud that two teams of oxen couldn't pry them free. Linden Laughlin came along and just looked at those logs and started walking toward them. With every step he took those logs got a little smaller and a little smaller, until when he finally got to them they were so small he just pulled them up under his arm and carried them to the sawmill.

And not only that, as a woods boss he could strike fear and respect into the steeliest of hearts and lead a flog of jacks up any mountain with the knowledge that the timber would get taken out and pronto. He knew which way the trees would fall, and his uncanny *knowing* was a comfort to a man as surely as it was a source of trepidation. Some said he'd signed his name in a Black Cat book and sold his soul to the Devil for six hundred and sixty-six thousand years. Some said he was a friend to orphans and women, others that he'd climbed up out of the very cleft of a cloven hoof. No matter what anyone said about him, though, everybody agreed that Linden Laughlin was the best jack that had ever lived.

Whatever he was, ageless, deathless, to my rank disbelief there he was, standing in our store in Cordelia one morning when I was thirteen years old. I had just returned from replacing empty bottles of Dream around town with fresh ones from the cavern under Shorty Wade's. How did I know it was Linden Laughlin standing there? There was no way it could have been anyone else. Good Christ on crackers but he was a huge, great, big fucker. It was a wonder he'd fit in our store at all. The man's hair was black as licorice and hung to his ears like a cavalryman on the cover of one of my father's Custer battle books. His eyes were green as sunlight through alder leaves, and his Adam's apple looked like a half-swallowed fist in his throat. There was something sharp about the edges of him, something that made everything else in the room seem blurred and, if not less real, at least less consequential. It was as if this man had been cut with care from someplace wilder and pasted down here, in our little town. Here was something new. Here was something special and terrifying.

My father was standing, tamarack straight. He had a gut, my father did, but he was holding it in so that he looked husky and barrel-chested. His face was turned up into Linden Laughlin's like it was the sun itself.

"I said to myself," Linden Laughlin was saying, "this was last night I said it to myself, but I've been saying it to myself a long time now, I said to myself, 'If the Applegate that sits behind the counter of Applegate General is Tom Applegate, then the woods are wise. If I can only meet an Applegate once more, I could meet Death whistling when it should come." He barked a laugh and then stared in wonder at my father. "I mean, Tom Applegate? Whose father worked Sitka, the Olympics, Gospel Hump?"

My father laughed a bit under his breath.

Laughlin continued. "Tom Applegate, whose grandfather worked the Spur, Freezeout, Carliss, Unthank?"

"I didn't know they'd made such an impression," my father said.

"Impression? Impression. Why, Tom, they made no impression at all, sir." He bent far over, close to my father's face. "Those men were meteors, sir. They carved canyons, sir. To have met them both at various times in my own time was both an honor and a reaffirmation of the nobility of a life lived in the deep woods. No, I don't think there's a lumberjack from Desolation Sound to the Hudson Bay who hasn't heard about the Applegates. Seems like everywhere I've been they were there before me, doing deeds that cannot be repeated, goddamn them."

I looked at my dad. He wore an apron and sat crammed behind a counter all day as burly, pitch-smelling jacks stomped in and out, bringing so much of the outside in that at the end of the day you couldn't tell the shop floor from the forest floor. He sold scented soap and kerosene, penny candy and all the clothes a jack might wear, plus things for women, as well, like mirrors and fabric, face powder, frilly things, corsets and fans. The girls from the Idaho Hotel usually just dabbed a little of Peg Ramsay's Dream behind their ears and on the napes of their necks, but the shop had a little shelf of perfumes for the gals of the Lady Appleton's. It all seemed so small, so insignificant, next to Linden Laughlin, *the* Linden Laughlin, who was now gilding the great works of the Applegates with the same reverence folks reserved for stories about Linden Laughlin himself.

"Recall a James Jessup?" Laughlin asked.

My father squinted. "Red hair?"

"The reddest," Laughlin said. "Told tale after tale about your father, Old Tom."

"He could tell some whoppers," my father said.

"Oh," said Linden, "the very whoppingest. But then, your father and grandfather were whopping big men, weren't they? Now, I admit that I've enjoyed my own taste of fame from time to time but no, Tom, according to James Jessup, I am but poor moonlight to their summer sun. He spoke of them often on his deathbed." Linden looked straight at me and then swung a finger as big as a wrist in my direction. "Your cub, sir?"

"He's mine. Weldon, meet Linden Laughlin," my father said. He was beaming at me from behind the counter.

"How old are you, Cub?" Laughlin loomed over me. His head alone would have taken twenty minutes to walk around.

"Thirteen," I said, trying to hold his gaze.

"Thirteen." Laughlin sighed. "Do you remember being thirteen, Tom?"

"It's been a while," my father said.

Linden nodded, picking up a can of cold cream and turning it around to read the label. "Sometimes I feel that I'm a thousand years old if I'm a day," he said. "But I'm no soupbones yet, Tom, and neither are you."

"When I met Weldon's mother we decided that there were safer lines of work for a man with a family," my father said.

Linden laughed. "Oh, without a doubt! By God! The woods are a terrible place for a family! Why, I've been in Cordelia, Idaho, for one day and I have counted precisely one child, your cub right here. No, the woods are no place for a family. No place for a wee bairn. In fact, the woods are no place in general, and what families need is a place. I suspect that the Mrs. Applegate would agree with me there, wouldn't she? It must be troubling to her, living so near to roughery and death. It must be…vexatious." He let the word out like a whoosh of steam. "And where is the little wife that I know you have stashed back there?"

"My wife passed some years back," my father said.

"Ahh. But surely, then, the story comes clear," Linden said.

"It does?" my father asked.

"Surely, Tom," Linden said, "you made her an oath."

My father nodded.

Linden smiled. "That you would keep out of the woods, for the sake of your child," he said.

My father nodded again.

"Yet when she died," Linden said, "you left your big, fancy store and moved here, to the dilapidated, splintery edge of the World. By the Devil's black dog, for a man who made a solemn vow, how deliciously close you've managed to get to those woods you swore off! Some would find it puzzling, sir. It is not so to me. No, it isn't puzzling to me at all. That look of contentment that you were wearing when I first stepped into your little shop, I suspect that you put it on each morning with your apron. It doesn't fit your face, that expression. I suspect that you have to convince it onto your face, but that once it's on, like that apron you tie around your big, fat belly, you believe it fits you well enough and that you have not indeed altered the entire course of your living life to make a dead woman happy. My condolences, by the way," he added.

"Anyway, you stay here and tend your little shop and care for your cub and call proximity to the big trees sufficient," he said. "But I know your true nature, Tom Applegate. You were born for those very same big trees. You were destined to be a jack since before those velvet curtains split and the first day was born. Before the first mountains rose in arrow-headed empires of granite and ice, you were chosen out to be one of *them*. A jack. Since before that first white water tumbled down from the reaches into lakes of camas-flower blue, this was your true fate. To think that you ignore that fateful pounding in your blood for the settled and comfortable life! The restraint! But those trees do nag, don't they, Tom? In your bones, they do, and the worst part is that you're the only one that can hear them." Laughlin winked. "Am I right?"

My father sat there with that far-off look in his eyes. "I won't lie and say I don't think of it at times," he said.

"Well, sure you do, Thomas," Laughlin said. "But it's not a deep want, surely. It cannot be the pang at the pit of your stomach. It is not what haunts you in your nighttime hours, unless, course, it finds you in your dreams."

"It comes and goes," my father said. He looked at me a moment.

"Well, let's pray it stays gone," Linden said.

My father nodded, but his eyes were still dull, and he looked sad and diminished for such a big man.

"He's got the Lost Lot," I said, and my voice came out too loud.

Laughlin put the hand cream down carefully on the stack

of others, but he left his hand there, resting on them a moment as if he meant to idly tear them all down.

"Ah, yes. The Lost Lot. I heard correctly, then, that you came into it when your father died." He shook his head. "Well, for that I am truly sorry, Tom. The Lost Lot is not so much inherited as contracted like the flu or a curse. I knew some of the jacks that worked it the first time. Thirty years back. Twenty-two men dead in three winters." He clucked. "Terrible stuff. Terrible to have heard them tell it. Frostbite. Not just toes gone but legs, Tom, legs. And the work! Busted chutes, avalanches, winter storms coming down so quick that men got blown right off the mountain. Blown off the mountain, they said. Why, I heard that even the Illini Match Company gave it up. The hubris of man, Tom Applegate. Imagine, looking at that murderous, glorious ground, festooned with the biggest white pines there ever were, and seeing only a billion matchsticks. They sold it to a soupbones—"

"Who lost it in a card game to my father," Tom said.

"To your father," Linden repeated. "Although perhaps *winning* would not be the word to describe coming into ownership of such a pestilentially difficult piece of land to work, wouldn't you agree?"

My father nodded his head.

"And—forgive me—the capital required to log such a piece of godforsaken rock must be formidable," Laughlin said.

My father shook his head. "I mean, to own a mountain…" His voice trailed away. Silence filled the room as we waited for him to go on.

When he didn't, Linden Laughlin said, "Well, I've never heard the like of such a speech as that. I may never see another Applegate swing an ax, but that doesn't matter a pig's ear to me anymore. Such simple homespun, so sweetly sung, deserves a marble monument." He reached over and laid a hand on my father's shoulder. "I must make confession with you, sir. I did not come simply to commune with nobility. No, like the avaricious and venal spirit that I am, I came to make you an offer. But now I see how strong the pull of the deadly timber is, now that I know you made a promise to your dead wife, now I know that you have a child to succor, I will not further dirty myself by mentioning it again. You need no more temptation troubling your brow, sir. Stay here behind your counter, I beg you. Better yet, move far away from here. Forget the Lost Lot. Move. Go to the Cities of the Great Plains. Forsake the brutalities of the deep woods and sleep soundly on the feathers of visiting birds. Could I trouble you for some peppermint sticks before I go? They're right there next to those pretty lavender soaps you have." He pointed.

My father surfaced from his trance and turned to place a handful of candy in a small brown bag. He shook his head when Linden reached into a pocket of his vest. "I won't be taking any money off Linden Laughlin," he said. "Weldon and I have gotten more fun out of the stories about you than you could get from a year of peppermint sticks."

The giant man broke one of the sticks in his hand and jammed a piece into his cheek. "When I came to see you today, I expected to see a man collared by civilization.

'Imagine the sight of it,' I told myself, 'an Applegate behind a counter.' I simply would not believe it. But now what I see before me is a man who has conquered his true nature and found a safe harbor. It is as if I stand before my own dark mirror—I in thrall to the seasons, to the chomped verdancy of the trees, to the sunsets, to the campfires and fortunes that can be its reward, you to the steady sureties of settled life. To think that I came to tempt you with a time beneath the boughs, with a fortune to be made! To think of you and me actually *logging* the Lost Lot. Think of it! No! Don't think of it! Tell me, please, are you truly done with the woods?"

My father's eyes wandered from the countertop and out the window, over the rooftops, toward the mountains. We'd read a book, he and I, about Custer. In it, Custer was in his tent, the night before the battle was supposed to start with the Indians. He hears bugles way off in the distance, but he knows that it isn't his men, and he knows that it isn't the Indians. He asks some of the other men if they hear the trumpets out there in the dark, but none of them do. So he sits alone in his tent, ten thousand miles away from his pretty wife, listening to the music as the sky turns purple and the burning stars begin to hide their eyes.

Remembering his face now, I think that my father was hearing the trumpets, too.

THE LAST LUMBERJACKS

A few weeks before Joe Mouffreau landed me here in the hospital, I was watching him through my little brass binoculars. The snow that had fallen had melted and then frozen up again, but that hadn't kept Joe Mouffreau from getting out his new snowblower and smashing it around. The fucking blower must have cost ten thousand dollars and already it was making ugly, wrong sounds as he jammed it against a bank of ice. The goddamn thing was so loud, even across the river, that Joe didn't notice Marsha Leeds's pickup coming down his driveway. He didn't know she was there until she came up behind him, screaming at him to turn the thing off and come inside. He finally heard her then, and red in the face from the effort of wrecking his new machine, he switched it off and followed her inside his house. I saw her lay a hand on his shoulder before they closed the door behind them, goddamn it.

It's not like Marsha had ever been what you'd call a nice person. I mean, she wasn't *not* nice, specifically. You couldn't have put her to one side or the other, really. She certainly hadn't gotten nicer since she'd claimed to have found Jesus. She was a couple decades younger than me, but it was also safe to say that she wasn't getting any wiser. Still, she could cook the hell out of a casserole and she could drive and sometimes she was just someone to pass the time with. All that ain't nothing. I won't lie to you and say that I was fucking thrilled she'd taken up with Joe Mouffreau, but we'd had our time, whatever that had amounted to, and anyway, ever since she had found Jesus—to the degree that she'd found Him—she was quite a bit harder to be around. I'd met her back in my eighties, and we'd been done for good by my ninetieth, but still I'll admit it does sting a bit to see someone making a fucking canned-food casserole for your mortal enemy when it used to be for you.

After they went inside, I let the binoculars drift to the mountainside behind Mouffreau's house. The slope was a shaggy, stump-strewn apocalypse. Here and there, slash-piles of branches and trees too small to be milled into lumber sat waiting for Joe to burn. An old camper that had once been fancy now sat up on cinder blocks, a home for the treeless birds. A couple of Jet Skis, uncovered and already crusted over with snow, sat just below it. I've thought often about the ass-kicking that Daddy Mouffreau, who had built and run the biggest sawmill in the St. Anne, would give his no-account son if he could see the lengths to which the family fortune had been squandered. I thought about it again now, just for fun. For all Daddy Mouffreau's tight-assed reputation when it came to paying jacks, there had been a time in the St. Anne river valley when the Mouffreau name was synonymous with riches, power and shrewd success.

Hell, it was Mouffreau money that was on my mind that morning after Linden Laughlin visited our shop. "My father's gonna pay everyone double what they'd get up on Marble Creek or Eagle," I whispered to Peg Ramsay.

We were in the bar of the Idaho Hotel and I was up on tiptoes, unfastening the little brass latch that hooked the naked lady painting to the wall. In my mind those huge Lost Lot trees were already lumber, measured and cut at the Mouffreau sawmill and stacked in a gleaming abundance, the color of wheat. The money was already in my father's hand.

"With the trees they're gonna take down from there, everyone's gonna be rich. My dad is gonna be a millionaire."

Above me, the naked lady was propped up on a fancy sofa. She had a sheet covering one leg but her down-theres were out and a little black cat was curled up at her feet. In one hand she held a fan made of palm fronds. She had perfect, round breasts.

"Anyway, that's what Linden said," I said.

"So it's Linden now, not Mr. Laughlin?" Peg asked.

"So what if it is," I said too loudly.

A couple of the Idaho Hotel girls looked up at us from their chessboards.

"Sorry," I whispered at them.

"Does that mean you trust Linden Laughlin as much as your father does?" Peg said.

I frowned down at him as he passed me a fresh bottle of Dream to stash. "Sure," I said. "I trust him just fine." Jesus. "In fact, I trust him so much that if my dad would let me, I'd go up there to the Lost Lot myself," I said.

"I just bet you would." Peg laughed.

"I bet I would, too," I said, not laughing.

More girls looked up from their games. Someone rang one of their little chess bells.

"Pardon," Peg said to her.

I put the last bottle in its place and then hopped down to secure the latch. "The Lost Lot is a gold mine in timber," I said, "and Linden is the greatest jack that ever lived. He's the only one who can get those trees down off that mountain, is what everyone says. Plus, he's the only one all those other John Johnsons will follow. They're hiring the best jacks out there. The best in the World," I told him. "And they've got Alright Edwards." There were at least six cooks in the St. Anne named Sourdough, and they all hated each other equally, but they all hated Alright Edwards the most because, in skill and stature, he was their king.

"Well now, that is something special," Peg said.

"It is, Peg," I told him.

"I'm sure it is, Weldon," he said.

"Why don't you believe me? When have I ever lied to you about anything at all?" I said.

"I believe you, Weldon," Peg said. "So, your old man is going to pay everyone's hours off after the drive?"

"No," I said, "*double* everyone's hours, I told you that."

One of the girls stamped a heeled foot. More bells rang.

"And the rest for Linden and Tom," I whispered.

"Yes, yes." Peg put the crate of empties on the bar. "Listen, you know how they bring down the big trees, right?"

"They choose them and chop them," I said.

"Sure they do," Peg said. "But they don't just start chopping willy-nilly, do they? They don't cut down every tree they see, do they?"

"No," I said. "They choose the biggest one they can find, take a crosscut ten, fifteen feet up, and two of them stand on buckboards and saw halfway through."

"And then what?" he asked.

"They chop a fall wedge," I said.

"And the fall wedge does what?" he said.

"It decides which way the tree is gonna fall," I told him.

"That's right." Peg began making his way between the girls and their chess matches. I grabbed the crate of empties and followed him.

"Trees aren't the only things that fall one way or the other, kid," he said when we were back out on the street again. "Your father owns the Lost Lot. He made a deal with Linden Laughlin to work that mountain and to hire the last, best lumberjacks there are to bring those trees out. Something is going to fall, Weldon, one way or the other, one direction or the other. It can fall toward the good or toward the bad."

"Linden knows which way every tree is gonna fall," I said, but Peg had started down the street, back to his barbershop. I was just there talking to the back of his head.

"Peg?" I said.

Peg stopped and turned. "What is it, kid?"

"What do you mean 'the last lumberjacks'?" I asked.

"I mean that things are changing, kid," he said. "We've all been around forever, but it's not always gonna be so."

"How do you know that, Peg?"

"Because you're here, kid. Go stash fresh Dream in the church on your own, Weldon. In the altar and up in the steeple. I'm tired out." He turned back down the street and I could swear that I saw his shoulders rise once in a sigh.

My father sat at the table in our kitchen at the back of the store, the map rolled out and weighted down with soup bowls. The route he would soon take was smudged and dirty by the tracing and retracing of fingertips, as if the white of the map were the snow itself beneath the tromping boots of jacks. The Serwalter trestle showed up as a solid black line that emptied onto a trail of semaphore that followed the St. Anne, against its flow, for miles up into the mountains, along gorges, glassy sinks and shallows as sharp as coyote teeth. At the end of the dashed line, at the confluence of the Smokewater and the Flewellyn, Lot C66 (the Lost Lot) jutted up into the sky, just as sharp and splintered as the stump of an avalanche-felled tree.

The Witch, Sohvia, sat there at the kitchen table in the back of the store, as well, burrowing her eyes into the side of my father's face for a long, long time as she turned over her teacups one by one. Her hair, almost blue-black, hung heavy around her high cheekbones. She must have been thirty-five or so, ancient to a kid like me, but ancient in the way that all adults were ancient then. Seems to me now that she had what you'd call a fierce kind of beauty, all frost and rocky outcrops. She had these blue eyes, a pale ring of smoke around black cinders. One look from her was enough to freeze a stranger in his boots.

Yeah, she was beautiful, alright, but it's not like what you might be thinking. My dad might have given her a place to live, but he didn't expect anything from her. It was almost as if she came with the shop. Still, she sure did seem to care about my father.

"Can you tell me my fortune?" I asked the Witch. She could see things in men's lives the way no others could see them, and like no one else, she was brave enough to say these things to their faces. Looking at that map that my father had spread out, I wanted her to tell me that my father would relent and let me go with him to log the Lost Lot. Or maybe I wanted her to tell me in her no-nonsense, witchy way that I was a fool to have such a desire, that my father would never let me contemplate such a crazy idea as taking me along. Either way, I wanted the Witch to say something. She couldn't just go on staring bloody murder at my dad.

"I will not tell your fortune," she said finally, without tearing her eyes away from the side of Tom's face.

"Why not?" I asked.

"Because you have no money," she said.

"I know where I could get some," I said.

"You are a child," she said.

"I could be a man," I told her. "If he'd let me go. I bet you I'd grow a beard for sure. Then I could shave it and you could tell me my fortune." The Witch hated whiskers on any man and would give a nasty fortune to anyone who had the gall to sit before her unshorn.

She leaped up, the backs of her legs knocking the chair to the floor. My father looked up from his map.

"I would never see your Future," she shouted. "Never."

"Sohvia," my father said.

"No!" she said again to him. "I have told you what will happen if you go. I have told you who that Thing is that you've given your life to." She swept an arm across the tea set, dashing the pieces against the wall. "You don't listen, and though you breathe and call yourself living, you are already a ghost." The Witch stared my father down, shaking with rage.

"I'm sorry," I told her. "It was only a joke." Though I wanted desperately to go with him, had been hounding my father for weeks now, to see her face like that made me feel sad and lonesome, as if he was gone already.

I didn't know much about the Witch's people except to say that she'd come from Finland, and all the other Finns, like Unto Sisson, were respectful as fuck around her. What she had been like as a girl was nearly impossible to imagine, but even here in Cordy she seemed to have one foot in another, more fantastical world. It was a world where the mountains spoke to one another low, and the creatures of the forest, visible and invisible, worked with mischievous intent on behalf of the gods who held sway beneath the branches.

Her path to Cordy was as mysterious as everything else about her, and she never talked of her life before, save for that the wind had whipped through her hair one day, caught it up in its fingers and carried her across the water like a terrifying angel only to set her down square in Lyle Llewelyn's shop to tell fortunes. Wherever she was from and whatever it was of the Future that she could see, she sure as shit knew lumberjacks. There was no use in hiding anything. The Witch could see it all, understand it all.

She bucked and planed those gnarly men down to their bare essence, no matter how grizzled the visage: "Your money is gone. Your partner stole it while you were with his wife. This is all your fault. You are stupid with women and stupid with money and stupid with finding partners. Next time don't be so stupid."

Or: "The priest who did these things to you is long dead. He is buried across the sea. You know this already. Nothing will bring back to you what was taken. You have been done a great wrong. I will think of you as I fall asleep tonight. There. Now someone else knows your secret. You have no secrets now. Go live your life and be as happy as you can."

She had arrived at the store one morning, not long after Peg brought my father and me to run the place. She was dressed in a skirt that was blue as nightfall and a fringed

white shirt with long sleeves that billowed out at the wrists.
Her glacial eyes fixed on Tom behind the counter.

"Where is Lyle Llewelyn?" she said.

"Lyle Llewelyn passed on a little while back," my father
told her. "Perhaps I can be of service?"

The Witch looked him over, a flash of anger in her eyes.
"Lyle Llewelyn was a wise man," she said.

"I've only heard good things," my father said.

"He let me stay with him and read fortunes," she said.
"Now I will stay with you and read fortunes. This is a great
honor for you." She motioned at the stack of tea sets. "Give
me one of those."

Since then, she had lived with us in the rooms behind
the shop, sleeping in the spare bedroom while I slept on
the other twin bed in my father's room. When she wasn't
sitting behind a small card table lifting those little teacups,
she was tending to the jacks with her strange liniments or
gathering growing things from the forest. She also helped in
her own witchy way with the cooking and cleaning while
we kept the shop up to snuff.

She looked me square in the face now, with a look that
could have wiped out half the town. "Do you know why
I will not tell your fortune?" she asked.

"Why?" I said.

"Because I need no more sadness in my life," she said.

In the weeks before my father left, the Witch spoke less
and less. My father had made his mind up to go, and store
or no, son or no, Witch or no, he would go. There wasn't
a thing she, or anyone, could say that he would have heard.

The Lost Lot was all that he could think about. He drank his morning coffee over the map as if he were one of the snow-white geese that stretched themselves into V's above it. Even as he worked behind the counter his eyes would soar out over the distant trees before returning, reluctant, to the business at hand.

He didn't care about the money. That much I know. No matter how much Laughlin said the two of them were gonna make together, he just didn't care. He didn't mind the risk of promising double pay for every man on the job. Fuck, he hadn't thought twice about putting everything we had on what many would have called an impossible dream in the first place. The only thing that my father cared about in the days before he left was that the snow had probably already fallen hip-high on the Lost Lot. The only thing that mattered was that the Serwalter trestle was still standing and the great Serwalter chute still held on to the edge of the mountain, ready to carry those monster logs down the cliffs despite years of neglect and the howling elements. I began to understand what the Witch had meant when she called my father a ghost; more and more in the days leading up to his leaving, I could see what it was like for a man to be standing and sucking air in one place, while not really being there at all.

The Witch's anger gave way to whispers under her breath, supper plates plunked down with a drop of the wrist and the quiet, the absolute quiet, of a house long after the light has been blown out but no one is sleeping. Finally, everything was silence. None of it did any good.

Throwing things did nothing, either, and seeing this, the Witch set the last set of teacups on top of the cabinet and took up smoking.

A few weeks prior, Unto Sisson had left a pouch of special black tobacco on one of his ill-fated visits to her. He'd been waiting, head down, in a line of jacks for over an hour. She was returning the cups to their proper positions, shuffling them around and around to reset the fortune, when he sat down. He was a big man, huge in the ass, with tiny eyes that softened only for her and bright sunlight. As always when he sat before her, he wore an expression of wary wonder.

I had pushed my way through the waiting line of jacks and into our little living room behind the store and was now pulling empty bottles of Dream from under the loose floorboards to replace them with fresh ones.

She finally looked up and into his flat, ugly face, his punched-in nose and those hungry eyes, full to the brim with beseeching. "Unto Sisson," she said.

Unto Sisson had been to see the Witch a hundred times. He'd sit there silent as she turned over the cups one by one, gazing at her face as she heaped scorn on him.

"You wish to die sometimes because you are a coward," she said. "Even money, which you think you love, cannot make you happy. You thought that a woman could make you happy, but you were wrong. No man is happy who does not know his own mind. Go, Unto-Sisson-Who-Doesn't-Know-His-Mind. I will not take your money," she said. "Get out of my sight and never come back." Unto sat a few seconds more, his eyes fixed on her face. Then he blinked. Whatever Unto's Future held, from the look in his eyes it couldn't have been worse than the present. He was a brooder, was Unto, and I knew he'd be back.

He stood, then pulled a felted pouch from his coat pocket and laid it on the table between them. The smell of licorice and apricot and warm pine filled the room. He backed away from the table, his hands up like a henchman in a Bud Maynard movie. Only when he was gone did she sit back down again, reach across the table for the pouch of tobacco and casually toss it behind her before grunting at the next jack to sit.

Since then, she had taken up smoking with no problem at all. She took great care over those cigarettes she rolled. She'd pull a leaf from the stack of papers, crease it once, twice with her thumbnail, then dip into the bag for a pinch of the shag. When she struck the match and set the flame to the tip, the smell was like the inside of the grandfather clock where I hid the Dream in Peg's shop. Each time I'd stick my head inside that clock to replace the bottles of Dream hidden inside, the smell of wood and brass workings touched with oil would make my head spin. Just as the hands of the clock would tock and turn, tock and turn, so the Witch rolled and smoked, rolled and smoked, until the morning arrived for my father to leave.

She had been sitting at the table hours before sunrise, tipping ashes into a cup of coffee long since gone cold. My father had been down to the Idaho Hotel for breakfast, and it was so quiet when he returned that I could hear his thumb thrum against the coat hook when he hung his jacket up.

"Cold!" he said, clapping his arms with his hands and looking at her. When she said nothing in reply, he said the same thing to me. "Cold!"

"It's colder than an icicle with frostbite," I said.

"Colder than a bedbug biting a brass bell," he said.

"It's colder than blue belly-helly," I said, but the truth was my heart wasn't in it.

"Thomas." Linden Laughlin stood in the open doorway, his silhouette like punched tin against the bright autumn light coming from outside.

"Linden!" my father said. "I didn't hear you come in."

"It's time, Tom," Laughlin said. Behind him, jacks were gathering in the street to begin the hike to the Lost Lot. He ducked beneath the doorframe as he stepped into the room, nodding to the Witch and unfurling his long-fingered hand in a flourish. "I've come to take your man," he told her. "Could be, I'll bring you back a millionaire."

My father was already throwing his coat back on.

The Witch reached for the purple pouch and began to roll another cigarette.

Linden shook his head at my father's pile of supplies. "I see you've spared nothing in your preparations, Tom Applegate. Is there food, my dear?"

The Witch licked the cigarette and put it to her lips.

"Muffins?" Linden asked.

She ignored him and lit the cigarette with a blue-tip match. The smoke curled into the air, a lazy, gray cat tail.

Laughlin turned back to my father. "No muffins, then—and no love letters, either, I'll wager. Well," he said, turning toward the door. "We burn daylight." He bowed at the Witch again. "Until we meet again, my dear. Unto, help Mr. Applegate with his bags and meet me in the street."

My father went over and placed a hand on the Witch's arm.

"Sohvia," he said, "I'll stop at Peg Ramsay's and shave my beard before I see you again." He smiled down at her where she was sitting.

She let the hand rest there on her arm a moment, then pulled away, looking instead at Linden Laughlin with eyes that could have pounded a log splitter. "You," the Witch said to Laughlin.

"I?" Laughlin replied.

"Yes, you," the Witch said. "Take him away. I have told him all that he needs to hear. The dead have nothing but time and yet they never listen."

Linden tipped his hat at her, gave a wink and was gone out the door. My father followed him to join the rest of the jacks waiting in the street.

Unto came in just then and, somehow, he wasn't the bear-eyed, pig-smelling, whiny Unto Sisson who washed himself once a month in another man's bathwater and ate whatever they fed him in the dismal wreckage of the Rooms Upstairs. With all those bags on his back, in his oiled canvas pants they called tin pants and his spike boots, Unto Sisson was a man. Not just a man, either. Unto Sisson was a lumberjack—tall as trees, straight of back and broad, with a set to his face every bit as fearsome as the Witch's.

She looked him up and down as she drew on the tobacco he'd given her. She held it a moment, then blew the smoke at him. He stood stock-still in the middle of the room, seemingly unafraid of her for the first time, and received it, breathing it in with one deep breath. Then, with a shrug of his massive shoulders, he picked up Tom's bags and stomped out of the shop.

It was a ten-mile walk to the Lost Lot, and the men were dressed warm against the chill of the day, all of them looking several inches taller in their sturdy boots. It was early in the morning, but Peg had cracked a case of Dream and was passing the bottles around to drink a blessing for the coming timber season. Linden Laughlin shook his head at the proffered bottle and began walking down the road. My father watched him go, then took a gulp of Dream and passed the bottle along before hurrying after him.

Alright Edwards's butler, Thorough, stood in the middle of the street, a burlap feed sack slung over his shoulder, a pair of little brass binoculars around his neck. As I watched, he reached into the sack and pulled out a handful of seeds. The ground around his boots was a thick, jabbering carpet of feathers, beaks and black little eyes, and every time he scattered the food, junkos and waxwings, sparrows, robins and wrens would just go nibbleshits.

"Just you wait," he said to me, putting the binoculars to his eyes a moment. "Wait for the forest. You'll see some birds then."

Down the street I could see Overland Sam's team of pack mules, their ears painted white so that they could be seen against the shadows of the trees. Under Alright Edwards's direction, the cookware and other camp equipment was being distributed among the animals, and the rest slung over the backs of the jacks.

"Why the birds?" I asked.

"They make for good camp," Thorough said.

Most all of the men were complete John Johnsons to me, jacks without names or pasts who Linden and my father hired on the promise of exorbitant pay. They were mostly young and, standing in a crowd of them, my father looked old. What if he wasn't able to do the work? What if there was an accident? Who would care for him when neither the Witch nor I were there?

The brothers Otto and Antti Walta were nearby. Otto was so big he blocked out the sun for a whole extra hour when he got up in the morning. Antti was smaller and quicker and always had a laugh and a story about the girls. He was also a bloodstopper, meaning he knew ways to keep all your blood from merrily pumping out of your body when you got cut deep with something. He mostly used his skills on gelding horses, but his presence, in the absence of a real doctor, was a comfort to men who were risking their arms and legs in the woods. I saw an Italian named Cavuto standing next to a Swede who was named Holmberg. The Kaiser I knew by his mustache. Jelly Jacobson, who some said could jump ten feet in the air, had decided to quit a camp on Marble Creek and come along.

His friend, Russian Alex, had convinced him to join them. They shared a bottle of Dream, sipping at it slowly, protracting the moment before the hard work began. They'd watch over my dad for sure. Everything was going to turn out just dandelion dandy, I told myself. Just double dandelion dandy for sure.

"You're a child," Thorough said as we began to walk, "so I'll tell you the truth of it if you really want to know."

We passed by the Rooms Upstairs, and I cast a glance up at the window where poor old Oral Avery was sitting, flour-white and insomniac since being struck by lightning. There'd be no woods for him this year. "I'm not a child," I said to Thorough. "I'm thirteen."

"Then I'm not gonna tell you about the birds. Only children would care."

On the distant slopes, the tamarack trees blazed out, songbird yellow, and in the road, water that had been collecting in the muddy cups of animal tracks had frozen in knife-sharp scrims. Our boots crunched the frozen whorls of mud as we walked down past the Lost Lot cemetery on the way to the Serwalter trestle. I could see five new piles of dirt where the jacks had dug extra graves in grim preparation for the season. In a few weeks, the ground would be too frozen up to dig the dirt without blasting it with dynamite.

Up ahead, Linden's musical growl was telling a joke. "That dog couldn't learn the tricks, boys. Or wouldn't learn them. Finally, he sat down on the floor of the place and said, 'I quit.' 'Well, I said, then I quit, too.' 'Good,' said the dog, 'so can I have something to drink?'"

There were so many birds that I had to walk with my hands covering my face.

"I want to know about the birds," I told Thorough.

"So I fetched him a bowl of fuel oil," Linden was saying, "and he lapped that up and asked for more. Well, he lapped that up like the rest and then he went and ran around town."

"I care about the birds," I said again.

Thorough said, "I like their goddamn voices is why. I like their goddamn little bird faces."

Linden stopped by the lilac glade at the railroad spur to tell the rest of his story. "Well, boys, I was still standing there at the bar when the dog came running back in, wagging his tail to beat the Devil himself. Then he looked at me kinda funny and he just fell down. 'Say,' said the bartender, 'is that dog dead?' 'No,' I says, 'he just ran out of gas.'"

Thorough lowered his voice, and confided in me, "Hearing them each morning, the birds, watching them play in the snow, they make a camp of men feel like a home full of children."

GOOSE TOWN WITH THE GEESE GONE

I know how memory works. I know what happens to it. Some people pine for the past so bad that if you give them even a glimpse of an ear they'll grab hold of it and hang on, telling you stories about the past as if the present were drowning them. Believe me, I know how it happens. Memory comes in to fill the spaces of whatever isn't there. No girl in your life anymore? All the ones you were ever with are up there in your noggin, dancing around in nary a fucking stitch. Memory has a way of growing things, of improving them. The hardships get harder, the good times get better and the whole damn arc of a life takes on a mystic glow that only memory can give it. Go spend a day hearing Joe Mouffreau's stories and tell me that I'm not right. Joe Mouffreau is a grade-A example of the improving qualities of memory.

I say all this because there are some things that defy memory's special magic. There are the things that get stuck in our heads that for some goddamn reason don't improve or grow out of all proportion. Nothing sticks to these memories, nothing accrues to them. Maybe the first time you saw your lover's face is one. Maybe the night you caught the winning touchdown is another, or the cold afternoon you buried your father. You can't figure out just why, but they remain crystal clear when everything else in life is clouding over, turning to long shadows and receding into the mist of fucking unreality and tall tale. I know how memory works. I know how wily it is.

So, you better fucking believe me when I tell you that the Serwalter trestle over the St. Anne was two hundred and thirty-two feet high, a great and ghastly Eighth Wonder of the fucking World. A goddamn confabulation of steel and wood and black magic, it wobbled, a thumb in gravity's eye, so far above the river that the water below appeared to be a line of ragged white yarn pulled through your fingers, wisps of mist here and there like wool that had slipped the darn.

Illini Match Company had ordered their chief builder, the genius Serwalter Scott, to design and construct the bridge to be strong enough to carry a timber-laden train across the chasm, but by the time it was done (built in the same year as the Eiffel Tower, no less) fourteen men had already died on the Lost Lot. By spring, another eight were dead in an avalanche and Illini's bone counters back East had decided that the treasure in trees wasn't worth the price in blood and abandoned the whole enterprise. Serwalter Scott, as fine a craftsman as any Italian who ever chiseled a man's ass out of marble, took it hard. He'd built the trestle and the bunkhouses and the chute. He'd put his whole being and the last of his incandescent genius into that unforgiving piece of land. Drunk, drugged and many-tempered, he gave a tearful toodle-oo to the whole epic story and disappeared across the trestle never to be seen again.

But all that was more than thirty years ago, and although the scrollwork and the intricate carvings could still be made out running between the buttresses, and the great cast-iron portals, adorned with their giant mountain-goat heads, still stood sentry at either side of the bridge, the whole thing was listing with sorrowful neglect. Standing at the edge of it, you told yourself that it was only the trees on the far side that were swaying in the breeze and nothing else, goddamn it, nothing else.

If this was Joe Mouffreau telling you all of this, it would have been nothing for him to do fucking somersaults across it, but I'm telling you how things were, and I had never had the nerve to cross the goddamn trestle. Not on your goddamn life. Never mind that Tom had told me not to, that the Serwalter trestle was in its own way wrapped up in the oath he had given my mother. No, I was afraid of heights. Still, I harbored the secret hope that my father would turn to me, clap me on the back and tell me to come along with him and the rest of the jacks. I would have crossed the trestle for that, even if it had been a thousand feet high.

My father had just turned to me to say goodbye when

suddenly the Witch was there, pushing past us until she was standing in front of him, blocking his way.

"Sohvia." My father put his hands on her shoulders.

"Your ax," she told him. "Give it to me."

He looked at her, puzzled.

"Your ax." She held out her hand.

The other men had stopped, except Linden, who jammed a piece of peppermint in his cheek and continued up onto the trestle with a snort.

"I won't give it," my father said—and then he gave her the ax.

The men moved out of her way as she stepped backward. She struggled to hoist the ax into the air, but when she finally got it up there, she swung it down hard. The ax-head buried itself in the frozen ground at his feet. The Witch pulled on the haft and dug a ragged circle around where he stood.

When she was finished, she stepped back once more and the two looked at each other across the broken ground.

"You will die," she said. "Fool. That is no mountain for men. Up there the meat-birds wait."

What was he to say? He must have dreamed of a better life, if not for him, then certainly for me. There must have been a thousand things he wished for in that wishing heart of his. Against all that wanting, how could a man pay heed to dire prognostications? He looked into those angry blue eyes until they had almost swallowed him up and then, somehow, stepped across the line and put his arms around her. He released her after a long moment and turned to me.

"Take good care of the shop and mind what Sohvia and Peg tell you, alright?" he said.

"I will," I said. My eyes were burning, but it felt as if the rest of me was burning, too. That secret hope inside me burned up in there, turned to ash and whisped away, to wherever the smoke of dead dreams goes. He wasn't going to ask me to come along. Instead, I would walk back to Cordy with the Witch.

"Remember that I'll be home at Christmas," he said. "Six weeks. I'll be halfway to a Rockefeller by then."

He gave me a hug and then stepped between the portals and up onto the trestle. We watched him go, my foolish, sweet father, inching his way across the chasm.

I picked up a stone and threw it over the lip of the cliff. It took a long time in falling, so that you could almost believe that it was floating. When it finally hit the river there was no splash or anything. The stone just wasn't there anymore. It just winked out. When I looked up again, my father, Tom Applegate, had winked out, too, swallowed up by the woods.

After Tom and the rest of them had followed Linden Laughlin into the woods, the whole place felt empty as a goose town with the geese gone. It wasn't empty, of course. Peg Ramsay, who owned the whole goddamn town, after all, was still there, sitting in his barber chair, watching as frostellations painted the window and the silty white powder of the first snow swept up against the hulk of the Rooms Upstairs. At this time of year, with the jacks in the woods, the boardinghouse looked just as depressing as hell on a hard day. The dirty ground that encircled it was whipped up into frozen whorls of sharp-edged mud that sparkled with ice and bits of broken glass. Most of the windows had been papered over with tar paper for as long as we'd lived in town, and whatever light happened to make its way into the place came in through the swaying front door or not at all. It swung to and fro on its hinges, sometimes widely enough that a portrait of the three killed presidents flashed in the daylight before being hidden again. Someone had X-ed their eyes out with charcoal. The only thing shining out from that miserable place was sleepless, white-haired Oral Avery, at a high-up sill.

With no jacks stopping by, the girls of the Idaho Hotel hunkered down and played their chess with the wild abandon of the young and serious. Still, the tinkling bells that marked each move were light and sweet. Hearing those happy sounds reminded me of what Thorough had said about how the birds cheered him up. The gals at the Lady Appleton's hunkered down, too, and spent much of their days reading and discussing novels. I wouldn't see them except when delivering Dream. Pink Mame, who ran the Lady Appleton's, was always cheerful and sweet and strong and she would boost me up to the naked lady painting in the Appleton bar so that I could switch out the empty bottles of Dream behind it for new ones.

The shop was silent and still. There were no laughing, cussing jacks ripping off their shirts and slapping each other's chests up and down the street, no one coming into the store in the middle of a rant, none of that. It was a red-letter day if the Witch put six foreboding words together, and her silence, her black cloud of anger, hung so close to our heads that I grew to miss the way she'd shout at Tom or throw the toy china tea sets against the wall when the jacks pissed her off. She took off the colorful clothes that she wore, her scarves and brooches, and dressed in dark colors that she pulled from the bag underneath her bed. Sometimes she sang in plaintive, jutting melodies to no one but herself, as if mourning a death.

Billy Lowground wasn't taking the dreary weather well. All day every day, he sat down at Shorty Wade's, plinking away at the piano in an endless manner. The notes he played cracked and wavered a little more each day as the weather grew colder, and the sound of each frozen tune carried until you could hear blond-haired, half-cooked Billy Lowground's drag-ass recital all over town. There was no escaping it. No walls were thick enough. Billy was a good sort, you know, and he didn't mean evil by anyone. His music, though, as the World began to freeze, was like a tiny little angel with an icicle, hovering right up against your eardrum all day, and sometimes into the night, and it was hard not to wish him ill. It was a wonder to me that he'd survived as long as he had in Cordy.

"He's been playing the same song for two days," said my friend Annie one afternoon. We were in the cavern under Shorty Wade's. When I say cavern that's just what it was. It was a giant bubble of basalt rock, with a little stream running through it. Light came from a lantern that was screwed into the bare rock of the ceiling. Along the walls were shelves and shelves of mason jars filled with every wild plant that you could gather from the mountain slopes on both sides of the St. Anne. Some jars were filled with pungent, dried petals, wild rose and syringa; others contained tangy mosses, crabapple seeds and juniper berries. Roots looked like tiny figures in the lamplight, while below them a whole shelf was for tree bark of every kind, from the aspen to sugar pine. Annie was brewing Dream, adding pinches of pale river silt to the boiling pot she had going over a stove whose chimney vented in a real ingenious way into the stove upstairs in Shorty Wade's. The music came down the ladder from the passageway and I got an image of the ivory piano keys cracking like pine trunks in the cold.

"For two days," she said again. "He plays the melody so slow that it was hard to tell at first, but it's the same song."

The music stopped.

She drummed the fingers of one hand on the worktable in front of her. It was stacked and packed with all kinds of dried herbs and other foragings saved over from the summer.

"I—" I began.

She pulled her cap off and her long, pretty hair fell in a braid down her back. There wasn't a girl or gal at the Idaho Hotel or the Lady Appleton's that wouldn't have gladly traded hair with Annie if they could have. "Damnitall!" she yelled, and slapped the counter. "How's a person supposed to work like this?"

"He'll—" I tried again.

The music started up once more.

"There it is again," Annie said. "Same song."

"'Some Somewhere,'" we both said together.

Some Somewhere there are mountains topped with snow,
Some Somewhere where the wildflowers grow,
Some Somewhere where I know I'll someday go,
When I finally go Some Somewhere.

Annie wore thick canvas trousers, far too loose around the waist, held up by thick brown suspenders, and a flannel shirt that hung baggy around her thin shoulders and bony arms. She was maybe seventeen, and though her face wasn't beautiful in the same way as the naked lady paintings, it had its own kind of beautiful for sure. Her skin was as pale as one of the Witch's tea sets and her neck was long. There were brown and orange freckles across her nose and high up on her cheeks, like speckles of brown sugar. Unlike everyone else in town, she wouldn't let Peg cut her hair, which caught the firelight when she bent down to add more alderwood to the stove.

The story of "Some Somewhere" was this: an old man once came into Peg Ramsay's barbershop and said in the quietest, most raspy voice that he wanted to get his hair cut and his beard trimmed. The man looked awful, all red around the eyes, with a scar on his cheek and a bunch of other cuts and shit. The man looked like he'd fallen into a pile of forks, he was so poked up. Well, anyone who knew Peg Ramsay knew that Peg was more curious than suspicious by nature. He told the man he'd give him a cut and a shave for nothing except the story of how he'd gotten himself so almighty fucked up.

As Peg cut his hair, the man told Peg the story of how he'd met another man one day on some lonely mountain pass, similarly fucked up and rolled around, and how that man had said that it was all because of a song that was stuck in his head. He'd heard it from someone, somewhere—a real catchy song, you know?—and try as he might, he just couldn't get it out of his head. He said that he couldn't be with people for more than a few hours before his singing it drove them wild. A woman had stabbed him, he said. A man in San Francisco had tried to cut out his tongue. He'd even gone to a priest to see if Jesus could pry that nail out of his head, but even Jesus had had no luck. So here he was, a fucked-up, freezing man on a desolate mountain pass, shunned by one and all and left to die with nothing but this single song ringing in his ears.

"What's the song?" the man had asked.

The man sang him "Some Somewhere."

"I didn't think too much of it when he sang it to me," the man told Peg. "I wished the poor stranger luck, though in truth he was already starting to look better, and I continued on my way. I woke up sometime in the night, sweating by my dying campfire, and that goddamn song in my head. It's been that way ever since."

"Looks like you've had it pretty bad, friend," Peg told him as he put the finishing snips to the man's beard.

"I've been shot six times and my cat ran away."

"How does 'Some Somewhere' go?" Peg asked him as

he dusted the hair off the man's shoulders. That's how Peg
came to get the song stuck in *his* head. Yup. Peg had that
song rattling around in his head for two weeks and couldn't
get a goddamn thing done. Peg's got a lot of jobs, you know.
He has the shop to run and the Idaho Hotel and the church,
plus the Dream and all that. There were too many people
that depended on him for him to just sit around all day and
think about blowing his own head off. So, Peg left town
for The Lights awhile, and when he came back he had Billy
Lowground with him. He plunked Billy down at the piano
in Shorty Wade's. "There," he said. "Have I got a song for
you." Peg sang "Some Somewhere" to Billy Lowground.
Peg said later that he had started to feel better instantly, and
unlike the man he'd given a haircut to or the man on the
mountain pass, Billy didn't give a rootie-toot-toot about
having "Some Somewhere" stuck in his head. Billy had
thousands of songs stuck in his head already.

There was a time before there was so much goddamn
music when it was possible for a man like Billy to know
at least loose impersonations of most songs that had ever
been written. He could get real serious and beautiful, or
slow and painful, or, if he'd had enough Dream, he could
make almost any song sound as if he'd reeled it up out of
the thrashing depths. He played "Some Somewhere," of
course, and "Sally in the Garden" and "Crockett's Honey-
moon," plus all kinds of newer stuff like "Hot Town" and
"Charlie Is My Dandy Man" and "Sugar Boo."

When Annie wasn't brewing the Dream from the spring
water, fiddlehead ferns and forest whatnot, and I wasn't de-

livering it all over town, we would set up and watch Bud Maynard flicks all day as Billy played whatever he was in the mood to play. With few people stopping in, Ed and Shorty never got up until late afternoon, and after years of having Billy around they didn't even hear him anymore. I would do the books for the store in the morning, an easy job since we sold next to nothing to next to no one in the late fall, and then I'd do my Dream rounds for a few hours before meeting Annie at Shorty Wade's. She'd have the stove going and I'd throw my coat down and rub my hands in front of the fire while she asked me how my day was. Then I'd pull an old bearskin over the single window and come sit beside her as she worked the movie machine and laughed at the silly outlaws who tried to put one over on old Bud.

We liked Bud Maynard the best because he once lived on a timber claim on the St. Anne for a year before he headed to Hollywood. Peg Ramsay, unlike fucking Joe Mouffreau, actually *did* meet Bud, and not just met him, but had known him.

Anyway, with that first flash of light from the projector, Billy would launch into "Charlie Is My Dandy Man." With someone to play for, and Bud Maynard and Tony the Wonderhorse careening above him on the wall, Billy would shake his sad-ass torpor like a heavy cloak and the melody would rattle along like a stagecoach on fire. Meanwhile, on the white-painted square of wall above Billy's head, the landscape of the movie world was just as chaotic. Canyons and voids stretched away in every direction and the sky had a blistering, aspirin-colored brightness. Suddenly, across the surface of this other world, there galloped a horse with a pale blaze on his nose and riding him was a man wearing an enormous white hat.

Bud Maynard.

Billy would catch ahold of another melody and stab at it. Above him, a man dressed all in black with the silver star of a sheriff pointed and made bug-eyes at a posse of varmint-y looking types.

The picture disappeared, replaced by words. *Bring me Bud Maynard or don't come back!*

I looked at Annie, who was lost to the movie and laughing as Tony the Wonderhorse, Bud Maynard's best friend, jumped off the lip of a wash and landed on the top of a speeding train. Imagine that! A horse on a train! Bud jumped off Tony and started fighting a man who had a knife between his teeth.

A lady tied to the train tracks cried out silently as the train approached. *Help me, Bud Maynard! Oh, please, help me!*

The music built. The man with the knife in his teeth had gotten the upper hand and was holding Bud Maynard halfway over the edge of the speeding train. Bud's hat fell from his head and bounced away down the rail bed. Bud's hair whipped around his eyes as he and the man with the knife struggled. The train was going to run over the lady for sure. Me and Annie held our breaths. It would be awful to be in a movie where you had to die. You'd never get to make another, and if they paid you, you wouldn't get to spend any of it.

Bud threw the man tumbling over the side, then hopped
to his feet, a big grin on his face. Tony the Wonderhorse
was there—HA!—and Bud threw himself up into the saddle and the two of them galloped down the length of the
train to the locomotive itself and leaped to the ground,
sprinting along the tracks to rescue the train tracks lady.

Annie and I watched those movies again and again, reel
to reel, as Billy slashed and burned his way through whole
forests of musical history. Watching them made me feel
closer to my father somehow—I guess because Bud Maynard was a hero of mine. Ever since I'd first met Peg and
he'd spoken of Bud Maynard the famous movie cowboy
who'd once lived in the St. Anne river valley, the fact that
he'd walked down Cordelia's Main Street, and had taken a
glass of Dream at Shorty Wade's place, made me feel close
to the movie star. Hell, he must have felt the way I felt
about wanting to get out into those same woods I looked
at every morning from the store window. Why else would
he have come to the St. Anne if not for the pull of adventure and fortune, the promise of freedom? So, I guess that
it wasn't that I understood Bud Maynard, but that I felt like
he probably would have understood me. I think that's all
we're looking for in our heroes, after all, the hope of being
understood. When I thought about it like that, it made
me realize how lonely, with all his heroes and stories, my
father had become without my mother. I hoped he was
happy on the Lost Lot, working side by side with Linden
Laughlin. Yeah, I hoped like hell that he was whooping it
up out there.

NOTHING WILL PREPARE YOU

I've never wanted for money, because I've never spent it. I have the things I need. I'm not a fucking mossy rock, though; it's not like I don't have wants. Still, you can't spend your money on the most important things. Some people, people like Joe Mouffreau and Marsha Leeds, know that with enough cash they can make the physical World over in their own image. It's true, too. Joe has rendered his soul as crystal clear as my new glass coffee table. He spent his money right the fuck up, and in so doing made it so that you could see right through him. Marsha may not have inherited a packet from big Daddy Mouffreau like Joe, but she was transparent, too. She thought she was keeping the desperation of her wants a little more under wraps, but I guess that knowing Jesus personally wasn't enough for Marsha.

Like I said, some things that'll make you happy just aren't

for sale, so when I started getting Social Security checks just for sucking breath, I really didn't need the money.

"What are you gonna do with it, Weldon?" Paulette down at the Brothers Swede had asked me as she poured me another beer.

"I'm gonna sit here and drink that beer you're pouring and take the money and not say boo," I told her. "After that, I'm gonna drink one more."

Next month it was the same story, another check with Weldon Applegate's name there on the paper. Well, I wasn't gonna say no to a tit as readily suckled as the government, was I? So, I kept getting them and cashing them. Like I said, I'm not much of a spender. I read a lot of books and I mostly eat canned food or whatever Paulette is heating up down at the Brothers Swede. I just put all the money away in my wallet. You can count it. Over fifteen grand in there.

It gets to be when you get as old as me that people come around and want to hear your whole life story. "What was it like?" is a question they always ask, like that's any kind of goddamn question at all.

"What was what like?" I say.

"You know," they says, "life back then. What was it like?"

"There was less of everything," is what I tell them. Shuts 'em down quick. It's true, anyway. There was less TV, less seasoning packets, less colorful colors and, yes, everything costed less. Besides that, what's the big changes? "Add more crap to the Past and you end up getting the Future," is what I tell them.

A reporter came into the Brothers Swede about ten years

back and was asking me all those sorts of questions. "What was it like? Were you ever on a river-drive? Did you ever want to be anything else besides a logger?"

It was like if I was to go into his office and sit down and say something like "Well?" and he had to account for his every last single second on the goddamn Earth. When you think about it like that, then he ain't looking for nothing else but to make your life into one big goddamn soap opera that he can put into his newspaper. He already knows what he's gonna write, he just wants you to rattle your dentures a bit so's he can say he was there sitting with you over a beer and you rattled your dentures. I didn't want no part in it. I told him to move on. "Now go away and let me drink and watch my soaps in peace," I told him.

So he moved on down the bar with his notebook and his tape recorder, over to where Joe Mouffreau was sitting with some others and a couple of their wives, and he starts asking them the same kind of questions, but goddamn Joe Mouffreau didn't want to let up about me just yet.

"That there who you were just talking to is Weldon Applegate," he said to the reporter. "And he's the fullest bag of shit you're gonna meet if you live to be a thousand." They all laughed and the reporter man didn't say anything, and I just kept looking at the soap opera going on the TV above the bar and drinking my beer. Then he said some stuff that I didn't hear to one of the wives and everyone cracked up all over themselves again, but I just kept watching the show. For a while there was this girl on *The Young and the Rest-less* that had the prettiest face you could stand. Just looking at her on TV was as good as actually being in the same room with some women for real. She was wearing a blue silky shirt, fitted her like it was the luckiest shirt in all of TV, which it was, and she was talking to that villain, Victor, who looked like the goddamn king of the World with his big dumb mustache, and acted like the president of the perfume company, which, for now, he was. Next thing you know a peanut comes flying and hits me on the nose.

"Is that you, Weldon?" Joe says. "That you down there? Come on down and tell us all your life story."

I ignored him and the peanuts kinda sailed around me for another minute until the fucker got lucky and caught me again by chance.

"Weldon, leave off your TV and come tell us a story."

"You tell a story yourself," I says. "You know, how successful you fucking are."

"We all make our own choices in life, old-timer. You coulda made a pretty penny off that land of yours any old time you wanted," he said, all fucking sage and whatnot.

Anyway, like I was saying, the longer you live, the more and more people are gonna come up to you with dumb questions like what's your life been like, and what's it like to live a full life. Fact is, when you live to be ninety-nine, you pretty much got the living part down. There ain't no one else that's lived ninety-nine years that has lived a life that's less full than mine. It doesn't matter if they've traveled the World or stayed in one place. Ninety-nine years is ninety-nine years! Life comes to you, special delivery. Tell you another thing, you ain't gonna live to be ninety-nine years unless you're an ornery fuck, and that's the truth. You can look that up in your book. Hell, I could go on living right now if I wanted to. Wheel me out of here and set me on the street. I always make it back home, that's how ornery I am.

But I wasn't always that way. At least I should say that there was a time before I'd ever seen the ornery side of myself. That night, that long-ago December, all that changed.

The Witch and I had grown pretty used to living with one another without my dad around. She was quiet and saw the Future and bore the weight of that knowledge with her everywhere, so it wasn't like she was a real light-it-up kinda gal, but she took care of our little rooms at the back of the store and we waited to hear from Tom.

But of course we didn't hear from him. I understood. He had promised my mother not to become a jack, and then he'd gone and inherited the most lumberjackingest place on the face of the Earth. After she'd died, that promise had taken on a fearsome kind of oath-ish-ness. I was never to cross the Serwalter trestle. I didn't have to ask Tom why. I knew that the power of his oath extended over me as surely as shadow. He wasn't afraid that I would fall to my death; he was afraid that once I made it to the other side, those fantastic and hungry woods would swallow me up. I would be transformed into a lumberjack and he would have failed my mother in spectacular fashion.

It made sense, in fact, why it had been all this time and my father hadn't been in touch. Every time he thought

of me, he must have thought of the oath he was breaking. Every time he thought of the oath he was breaking,
he thought of me. And thinking of either the oath or me
must've made him think of my mother. Better, he must've
decided, to banish both the oath and the kid from his mind
for a bit. Just until he had the money in his hand, and we
were hat-tipping millionaires. Least that's what I was figuring, after he'd been gone two weeks and we'd heard nary
a peep from the Lost Lot.

I awoke one night to a rapping on my window. I scratched
the frost from the pane and made out the big face of Otto
Walta in the darkness, which was confusing because he
was supposed to be up in the woods at the Lost Lot with
Tom. By the light of his lantern I saw him put a finger over
his lips for silence and motion for me to meet him on the
street. I bundled up and crept out of the store, cursing the
creaking door lest it should wake up the Witch.

"Come with me," was all Otto had to say. I had been
waiting all this time for these words. That they didn't come
from my father was an afterthought; what mattered was
that I would soon enough be going to the Lost Lot myself,
joining my father and Linden and all the other jacks in the
adventure of a lifetime.

"I'll need more stuff," I told him. "I ain't prepared."

"Nothing will prepare you," he said back to me, which
was an odd thing to say. "Come along to Shorty Wade's."

"Are you all back?" I asked as I ran alongside the big
fucker. To think, all those jacks, come back for an im-
promptu kind of party. The girls and gals would be there,

the dogs would congregate for scraps, the bottles of Dream would pass from one hand to the next. But where was Tom and why hadn't it been him that came to wake me? And why were we not waking the Witch? Her anger and dark magic would be awful should she find out Tom was in town and she wasn't made known of it. Even I could see the Future if that happened.

A few men stood about in the doorway of Shorty Wade's place, but not with their party looks on. Jelly Jacobson saw me and looked away real quick. He had a bottle of Dream and he took gulps from it like it was holy water and he was trying to outpiss the Devil.

Inside, men were all kinda just standing around, talking softly here and there, but all of them drinking Dream and looking haunted around the eyes. Tom wasn't there with them. Just a tall, wooden box propped against the wall on the far side of the room from where Billy Lowground played something ancient on the piano.

"Cub," the voice said, and I saw Linden there, a black-clothed blade of a man, an eater of shadows in the corner by the stove.

I looked around for my father some more, but he wasn't behind the counter with Annie or Shorty Wade and he wasn't guzzling Dream and he hadn't come to wake me up when he got back to town, so where was he? Of course I knew. I went to stand in front of the box.

"Now, Cub. Best leave things as they stand and well enough alone," Linden said. The room had gone quiet. The lid hadn't been nailed shut. "Do you understand me, Cub?"

"I want to see him," I said.

"You don't," Linden said.

"Fuck you, I do." I pulled the lid away from the box enough to see what it was I had to see. And what did he look like, my poor, sweet dad? There was nothing left of his face, is what he looked like. The only thing recognizable as anything was his mouth, which was wide open, and a tooth, which had somehow popped through the flesh of his cheek. Nothing else remained of his features. It was like God had reached down and just kind of smudged out his face with His gigantic wetted thumb.

A REAL
DRY-MOUTHED LAWMAN

Like I said, old Weldon has been getting Social Security
for a while now—a check in an envelope, addressed to me.
Just a few days ago I got another. I looked at it for a while,
as I stood in the snow at the mailbox, then I hitched a ride
into town to the Brothers Swede. Fuck you, yes, I hitch
rides. Since they took away my driver's license earlier this
year, you know what gets picked up more than pretty girls?
Ninety-nine-year-olds, is what. I fought to keep that license because I knew that if they took it I probably wasn't
gonna be able to get it back and there's an age when folks
start taking stuff from you and not giving it back, goddamn
it. There's an age when God starts taking stuff from you,
too. Hell, God's first in line.

I went to the doctor's office not long ago. Young guy.
He was looking at his fucking clipboard.

"You've been pretty banged up, Mr. Applegate," he said.

"I didn't know that we were checking *your* eyesight," I told him.

"Broken bones, herniated discs, lacerations," he said. "You could have been a candidate for hip replacement twenty *years* ago. I can't even guess what it was that...did *that*."

"Bit me?" I said.

"Bit you," he said. "There, on your upper thigh."

"Fucking wild dog," I told him.

"How is your eyesight?" he said, changing the subject.

I said, "What?"

He said, "How is your eyesight, Mr. Applegate?"

I said, "You're the doctor, you tell me. You put me inside a bunch of boxes today and then you took the rest of my blood that I had saved up and took off all my clothes and you couldn't find out how my eyesight is for yourself?"

He laughed a little at that. Young people like to think that old Weldon has a good old sense of humor. I let him laugh a bit more. "Well?" I said when he got done with laughing.

"How's your driving?" he asked.

I said, "Let me pull my pants up and get out of this fucking place and we'll find out." So, he let me go and I pulled out of the hospital and I was thinking I might go to the Slurp 'n' Burp, which is a good afternoon place on the road to Cordy. I was thinking about a hamburger and wondering what a doctor looks for up an ancient ass like mine. He knows how old I am. It's on my goddamn chart. He doesn't have to go looking for tree rings.

I was thinking along about that kind of stuff when a cop pulls me over and, sure enough, I was driving the complete wrong way down a one-way. They don't give you tickets for that if you're ninety-nine years old. They just take your license away.

So that's how I ended up hitchhiking.

"You really get everywhere you want to go like that?" fucking Joe Mouffreau asked, down at the Brothers Swede.

"I'm here, ain't I?" I said.

That's how, after he crashed his new, fancy car and the bank wouldn't give him a loan for another one, Joe Mouffreau started in on the hitchhiking, too.

It's a funny thing that Cordelia had a church. It had been designed and built by Serwalter Scott, so of course it was gorgeous, though, like the trestle, more than a bit worse for wear and neglect. I won't speak for all jacks, and I won't speak for God, either, but I can tell you that the relationship between the two parties was strained, to say the least. So, it wasn't strange that Tom's body spent its last night aboveground in Shorty Wade's place. Next morning, I carried his casket, along with Otto and Antti, Nearing and Dollar Edwards, leading Peg Ramsay and Annie and a bunch of sad-looking motherfuckers, shuffling off their drunks and each of them squaring their own ledgers with the grim reaper in their minds, as we all made our way up the frozen street to the frozen stretch of ground by the edge of the trees that marked the Lost Lot cemetery.

Peg Ramsay wasn't a minister, but the jacks wouldn't

have wanted a minister to put Tom in the ground. He talked plain and told jokes on Tom and generally showed him for who he was. He said Tom was good, plain salt who had loved his family and always made a square deal. "I'm sure there's nowhere else he'd rather be laid to rest," Peg finished.

Then we were all quiet as Death itself, and listened as Billy Lowground, back in Shorty Wade's, played "Some Somewhere" low and slow, the notes carrying and dark as mahogany.

> I love the World but if I gotta leave it let me go,
> Some Somewhere where a man is free to roam.
> Cut me loose to wander where a man can be his own
> When he's on his own Some Somewhere.

The rest of the words I can't remember. That's another funny thing about memory. It gets sometimes, even now, lying here in the hospital, that I think I'm about to remember how that goddamn song went. It's like trying to remember a taste. It's in your head, but it ain't on your tongue, you see what I'm saying? Everyone standing over that hole is dead now, but when I die, that song ain't just gonna die with me, is it? No fucking way. Songs last forever. You might know that song Billy Lowground played. It might be stuck in your head right now. I know that it's bouncing around somewhere inside my brain like a bottle fly that can't find the open window.

Where Tom was buried would have mattered a lot to my

mother. She wasn't much for Jesus Christ, either, believe it or not, but she always liked those fancy, broad-leafed trees in the fancy cemeteries elsewhere. It was where she imagined holding hands with my father forever, which was pretty sweet, goddamn it, and I would have liked to have made it happen if I possibly could have. My father had lived most of his life outside Cordy. There were plenty of folks that lived elsewhere that would have missed him and would have come to his funeral out there by the ragged tree line, if they had known. No, it wasn't a big funeral or anything like that, but Peg was right: if my father had to be dead somewhere, it probably felt good and comfortable to be surrounded by other jacks who had all died on the same piece of ground as he had. I tried to think of my dad in a cemetery full of bankers and Sunday school teachers instead, but the image just didn't fit.

The sole salve to the whole goddamn shebang, I thought, was that his body would be buried a lumberjack. He would have appreciated the Witch being there, but I'm sure that his spirit would understand that she had gone out into the woods and was doing her own kind of mourning, keening and spitting, pissed as hell at him. I suspect Tom would have been hurt, though, to see Linden Laughlin, like I did, standing alone in the doorway of the Rooms Upstairs as we walked the casket down the street. You'd think the man that had tempted my father into the woods in the first place might lend a hand in carrying him to his grave, but no. Course, I didn't know then what I fucking know now, goddamn it. Linden had eaten his fill for the time being. All of the Witch's prognostications, all of Peg's warnings, they were in a language I couldn't understand yet. They were in an adult tongue, I realize now. And they were warning me that Linden Laughlin was a monster, that his belly had been filled by the deaths of lumberjacks since before anyone could say. The world of the jacks was shrinking, and Linden Laughlin lived on their demises, made a meal for himself from their sorry deaths. If I'd been able to understand what the Witch, what Peg, had been telling me, maybe then I would have...

I don't know what I would have. Sometimes in life there are monsters. It was just my luck that the monster in question was Linden Laughlin and real life was Cordy and the Lost Lot. Before we lowered his box into the ground, Otto pulled my father's ax—my grandfather's ax—from where it had been stuck into the lid and handed it to me across the hole.

Otto and Antti walked me back down the street after we'd thrown the dirt down on Tom. The store had murk for light and the rooms behind were about as dismal as wet blankets for breakfast. They sat down around the table and pulled the stopper from a bottle of Dream that I fetched from under the loose floorboard. The Witch, wrapped in a shawl and looking apocalyptically sad, came out to join us. I went out and dug around in the sticks for pieces of wood small enough to jam into the stove. By the time I rounded up the last of them and was back inside, the bottle of Dream had a dent in it about half. I left the stove door open so the heat would pour into the room and maybe a bit of the light, as well. The firelight on that bottle looked like the sun going down. Otto pulled out a chair and I sat down. My shoulder hurt from carrying Tom's splintery box. I drank the Dream that was in front of me and the Witch rolled us cigarettes with Unto Sisson's tobacco and we sat there quiet and smoked and drank that first bottle down. As she smoked, the Witch tipped her ashes on the floor. Antti did his trick of blowing the smoke out of his bad ear, but only once for me and even at that it was just a little puff of smoke. For some reason that really got to me.

"Did you see it happen?" I asked him, and I didn't try to keep the edge out of my voice when I did.

"No one saw it. Not even Tom himself," Antti said.

"Course *he* didn't see it. If he'd'a saw it he'd'a moved out of the way," I told him.

"The snow is deep, Weldon," he said. "Up to the hip. Even if—"

I interrupted him, "He'd'a gotten out of the way. Are you saying he didn't know enough to step out of the way of a falling tree?"

"It was too late," Antti said. He held the glass of Dream to the table like it was trying to fly against the wall and he wouldn't let it.

"And speaking of too late, where were you with all your bloodstopping stuff?" I said. "You think you got all the rest of those big, stupid fucks fooled with all that nonsense? I bet you don't. I bet they laugh at you behind your back.

When my dad caught a log in the face, didn't that seem like a good time to work your magic?"

"Weldon, it was too late. And the tree," Antti said.

"Oh, I *saw* what the tree did," I told him.

"I can stop blood, but I cannot stop a tree," Antti said.

I grabbed another bottle of Dream from below the floorboard and popped the cork to pour myself another goddamn drink.

After a while Otto and Antti got up from the table and the Witch followed them. At the door, Antti put his hand on her arm.

"Careful on your touching," I told him. "We don't need no accidental bloodstopping here."

The Witch stood at the door watching them head up the street in the muddy light, then she came back to sit down heavily in her chair at the table. Her feet barely touched the ground, she was such a small woman.

She said nothing but took the bottle and poured real correctly till her glass was full up with Dream once more. She went to set the bottle back down but held it real close to the tabletop without actually setting it down, before finally setting it down.

"Your father is the frost now," she said.

"Beneath it," I corrected her. "He's *beneath* the frost. There ain't no frost down there." I had never, ever seen the Witch drunk before.

I opened the flue to draw the fire, then I came and sat down with her and opened the tobacco pouch once more. She was a kind woman, the Witch was, underneath it all, but I bet even when she was a little girl out on the rocks and in the ripping wind she wasn't a talker. I pinched the shag out into two papers and rolled the first one, then lit it and handed it to her. I could feel her regarding the side of my face. I felt hot all over. If I'd been out there, I would have been with him. I could have warned him. That's what the Witch was thinking, I knew it. That I should have been close to him.

"We buried him in a good place," I lied, and felt the tears rise up all hot. "He'll be happy."

She shook her head. "There," she said, and jammed her finger through the thin clapboard wall, through the hidden rows of Dream all lined up, through the snow and wind, through the miles and miles of white pines and Douglas fir, toward the outside world. "There is where he was happy. There is where he had a wife. Not here in some field for dead men. Not as a meal for that fiend."

You've seen someone getting drunk with a purpose before. Maybe it was your father or your sister. Maybe you've looked in the mirror once or twice late at night or on one of those awful mornings when you started in early. There's a cone of darkness that comes spiraling out from the middle of your forehead. It's like black water, or like cold, cold space, like a black hole. It'll pull you in. It wants to pull you into yourself through that hole in the middle of your forehead.

Have I told you yet how blue the Witch's eyes were? Well, they were, each one pale as the silty glacial flow that came down off the mountains every spring. For a moment there, a real terrible one, the cone got larger, larger, larger until it blotted out her eyes and the whole room started spinning around us, pulling us down. Then just like that it collapsed and there were tears coming down her face. I heard one drip on the table: *plit*. I went and stood behind her and put my arms around her and felt how small she was. I was already bigger than her, and one day soon I was gonna be as big to her as Otto Walta was to me. That made me feel all alone in the strangest way. She didn't go and put a hand on my arm or nothing, just sat there putting the cigarette to her lips and taking it away. When she was done, she stubbed it out on the bare wood of the table, and poured another glass of Peg Ramsay's Dream, and then, like she'd forgotten all about it, she stood up in all directions at once and I had to let go my arms from around her shoulders. She turned and without another word went into her bedroom and closed the door. I heard the bedsprings squeak as she sat down on the mattress. A moment later I heard them squeak again as she got up and latched the lock on her door. I relit my cigarette and sat back in my seat, trying to stare down the glass of Dream she'd left. The twirls of smoky silt in there just kept coiling around themselves, paying me no mind. I felt their tendrils snaking their warm way through my veins. I rolled my aching shoulder and thought about what the fuck we were gonna do.

Much as we'd all lived together and it was all sweet in its own weird way, I didn't know too much about the Witch, and I never learned much from her stories, which were all about the bird-white way, and the singers who traveled to the spirit worlds. She'd talked a few times of a sister, though where she lived I had no idea. And who even was the Witch to me, now that Tom was gone? I hadn't even known her to pay rent of any kind, and yet she had lived with us. She was far from being a mother or a wife, but she had taken care of my dad in her own, stern way, I supposed. Something about her presence had helped anchor him to the shop for three years after we moved to Cordy. The only thing that the Witch wasn't stronger than was Linden Laughlin. Where would she go now that he was gone?

Peg Ramsay owned the whole goddamn town and was king of the St. Anne. Maybe he could have helped me sell the Lost Lot to Rutledge Timber or the Mouffreau Company. The Illini Match Company had tried to log it, had even hired Serwalter Scott and built a trestle to get back in there, and still they had thrown up their hands and called it a wash, abandoning all of it—the bunkhouse and cookhouse, the chute, the splash dams, all of it—when enough men had died that even the cock-stupidest jacks wouldn't have anything to do with it. No, it didn't seem like there was much chance any of those timber companies would touch it with a peavey pole. That left me with trying to sell to someone as crazy, or foolish, as Tom had been, or trying to sell off to Linden Laughlin. Anyway, considering I even *could* sell it, what was I supposed to do after that? The Future was as a blank, snowy field.

I couldn't just keep the land, could I? No, I would have been able to do even less with it than my father had. I discarded the thought. I looked at that bottle of Dream and knew that it was gonna have to be me who did the land selling, and it was gonna be me having to make the blank, snowy field into something new. I finished my cigarette and threw the butt in the sink, then picked up the Dream and took a sip. It was like a hawk lifting its wings. It made me cough and my eyes water and I squeezed them hard against the misting and opened them again. I wondered what Bud Maynard would do. A man like Bud, who could ride and rope and shoot, had all kinds of resources to fall back on, of course. Still, Bud had owned a timber claim in the St. Anne, and he'd managed to sell and make an alright new life for himself. I thought of Bud sitting here with me, leaning back in his chair like only a true cowboy hero could, his boots up on the table, his white shirt immaculate and his coal-black eyes glinting with good humor as he toasted me with a bottle of Dream. "Worked for me, partner," he'd say. "Worked for me."

Something about that vision was all wrong, though, and I knew what it was. I'd never seen Bud Maynard take a drink in any one of his movies, now that I thought about it. I filled my glass and tossed it back, trying to summon how Maynard would have done it if he ever did do it. I poured another and sat back to stare it down as I rolled another cigarette. "Nope," I told myself, "Bud Maynard didn't ever take a drink, did he?" Not one drink. He was history's soberest cowboy. A real dry-mouthed lawman.

I poured another drink and carried it forward from the firelight and into the darkness of the dirty shelves and through the front door, onto the street. It was cold enough that the whips of frozen mud thorned up beneath my boots. There were some folks out still, mostly jacks, and those that noticed me walking along down the middle of the street nodded their heads in passing on account of Tom. I nodded back, the fucks. About halfway to Shorty Wade's a big knot of them hove up alongside me heading in the same direction, and when they saw it was me they all quit their yapping and said good evening to me and the glass of Dream in my hand.

"Evening," I said back to them, 'cause it was. It was goddamn black *nighttime* is what it was. They all murmured, like they hadn't been drinking, too, and wasn't on their way to do a lot more.

Shorty Wade's place was a whole lot wilder than the night before. Dogs running around between legs, men yelling at each other friendly or unfriendly, a few sitting off to the end of the bar with cones coming out of their foreheads like I told you about, gals and girls laughing. Shorty and Ed Kleinerd were behind the bar and Annie was there, as well, picking up empty bottles and replacing them with fresh Dream that she pulled up from the cavern below. I brought all those jacks in trailing behind me like a tall, dark cloud. People looked up and saw me, Tom Applegate's scrawny kid, in the door with an empty glass in my hand, framed by a stand of solemn lumberjacks. Silence washed over the place from the door until it reached the piano, which was all fine with me. I had the courage now. I went right up to Ed Kleinerd and jammed the glass over the bar at him.

He looked at me and then he looked at the empty glass

in my hand, then back at me, and then out at that whole crowd who were all looking back at him. He handed me a full bottle of Dream and everyone shouted so that the quiet in the room was broken like a sheet of ice. Well, I expect not everyone shouted. Annie probably didn't shout, but that didn't make no difference to me. If you decide to be drunk, you might as well go all the way. I had a good enough reason. I held the bottle to my lips and took a sip, real nice, to show Ed that I could do it, then I turned around and people were busy trying to get back to having a good time, but the place had changed. Whatever had been there before I got there wasn't coming back. I couldn't do nothing about that, and the idea of going back home, with Tom gone and the Witch locked in her bedroom, sounded worse to me than being buried.

I wandered around between the tables and the people talking and didn't say a word or return anyone's nods or looks or words or nothing. I just moved among them in Shorty Wade's like I was a ghost. Like I was Tom's ghost come back for a drink or two.

The projector was in the back, on a wheeled cart in a dark corner where no one would knock it over. I grabbed ahold of it and pulled it out but after a few feet it couldn't go no farther because it ran up against a big man's chair back. That didn't make any difference to me with the shape that I was in. I got behind the projector cart and gave it a hard push and the big guy jumped up and spun out of his chair like he was about to fight. When he saw it was me, he said something under his breath and moved his chair out of the way. Next to move was a table of jacks and gals, and by now people were looking at me kinda funny. At least I thought it was funny. They were making *me* laugh, anyway.

"Weldon, honey, we can't be looking at movies tonight," Annie said. She was standing in front of where I wanted to roll the projector.

I looked at her a second, standing there tall and lovely, and I wanted to stop. I knew that she was right. But then she tried to put a hand on my shoulder and that twisted something in me and I shrugged away from her and tried to give the projector a hard shove to get around her, but the wheel of the cart got caught on a floorboard and instead of the cart moving, all that happened was that I slipped and fell to the ground at her feet. I was really feeling that Dream. I stood up again as fast as I could, which wasn't all that fast. People were getting up and moving out of my way now, and it was real silent as I got the movie machine pointing against the white painted square above the piano. By the time I had it all lined up I had forgotten all about Annie. I loaded the first reel, and then, because I felt everyone's eyes on my back and also because I wanted the lights down, I stood on a chair and turned around to face them all.

"I want to know if Bud Maynard—" and I thought about it and added "—or Tony, his Wonderhorse, ever took a goddamn drink of liquor. I expect to find out tonight, so turn off the fucking lights."

Well, folks started bringing the lights down. I began to crank the machine and on came *Sky High*, my and Annie's favorite, the one where Bud's investigating a gang

that is sneaking across the border. Bud Maynard is riding
Tony out into the road to stop an old Model-T filled to the
brim with gangsters. He's got on a blazing-white shirt and
his face is blazing white, too, with charcoal eyebrows and
those charcoal eyes. He had this face, Maynard did, a real
dark-eyed face, like a lean snowman. He maybe had a bit
of an underbite, but it was hard to tell with all the bouncing around on Tony. Anyway, he was riding and roping
and shooting but he wasn't taking a drink. Next thing you
know he has two ladies out of the car, and he's got a gun
pointed at 'em and whips off their bonnets and it's two
fellas with big, long beards! They're pointing and gestur-
ing and making all kinds of fuss, but Bud Maynard is just
standing back, laughing, and having a hell of a time. He
thinks this is just great.

I was watching and watching, and it was nice to be in the
dark where the whole room wasn't spinning and the figures
were moving across the screen in the silence like blazing-
white ghosts. Then the reel flapped over and the first part
was done, and I turned around to see where Annie was,
but she wasn't there. In fact, nobody was there at all. The
place'd just emptied out somehow while I was watching
Bud stay sober. Even Billy Lowground was gone from the
piano. Well, I didn't care. I slipped the next reel on and let
it rip. Bud hadn't taken a sip yet. Then I felt a hand on the
top of my head, real light so that I thought it was Annie
coming to say that she was sorry, that I'd been right, that
my father had died and any way that I wanted to grieve was
just dandelion dandy and was there anything she could say

or do to help? I was feeling pretty damn aggrieved toward the whole fucking World in that moment. Then the hand moved around to my forehead and my chair got yanked backward on its back legs and I was looking up into Peg Ramsay's face, lighted up and flashing with the pictures on the screen. He wasn't happy.

"You wanna sit here and watch a movie? You wanna sit here and have a drink?" He yanked me up and pushed me across the room, up onto the piano bench and over the top of the piano, to the white square that was painted on the wall above it. He jammed my face into it.

"You wanna sit around and feel sorry for yourself?" he said.

"You got any better ideas?" I said.

He pressed my face harder and harder into the wall. "You've got plenty of time to feel bad," he said. "I know for certain that you will later when you're drying out, but I'm gonna be gone by then. I need you to quit the ninny-ing and listen."

"I don't feel bad," I told him. "I was just trying to see Bud Maynard take a fucking drink." I struggled and pushed back against the wall and tried to kick out at him behind me, but Peg was strong, never mind that he was old. Then, like how it starts to rain, I did feel bad, and I didn't have any more to give him in the way of kicks and bites.

I guess he felt that, and he eased up a bit and then he let me go and I turned around and slid down so that I was sitting on the floor by the piano. Peg reached over and grabbed the bench and slid in front of me. "Sit like a man," he said. "Fuck the floor. The floor is for kids and dogs and scraps."

"I'll be going now," I said. I rose, and made to walk by him, but he grabbed my arm and pulled me back to face him.

"You're not leaving until I say so." He reached across real fast and slapped me. "You and I have words to speak, and we don't have much time."

"Motherfucker," I said. His big knuckles had really stung.

"Quit your whining," he told me.

"The Lost Lot is mine now," I said, rubbing my cheek.

"I suppose it is," Peg agreed.

"I need your help to sell it," I told him.

"That isn't going to happen this time, Weldon," he said. "You're such a big man, you do it yourself. I'm not gonna sell your land for you, kid. I already buried your father for you. I thought you were a good kid. Then, tonight, Ed comes down to the shop and says that Tom Applegate's son is drunk as hell and he's making six kinds of scenery down at Shorty Wade's and what is he supposed to do about it? I told Ed Kleinerd, honest Ed Kleinerd, that he was full of jackshit, and I don't like to swear, Weldon. I don't believe in that kind of thing. Then Annie comes down and tells me the same thing, only she's more upset."

"At me?" I asked. I saw Annie's face again, saw how she had tried to lay her hand on my shoulder, tried to comfort me, and how instead I'd shrugged away from her and fallen on the floor. What a fool I had been.

"I'm real sorry," I said. I wasn't feeling too good now.

There was a lot more spinning in the room and my head was confused-hurt from the drinks and then from the getting my face run up against the wall and getting slapped around. I mean to say that there were at least six kinds of pain going on. "I'll talk to her. I'll apologize."

"Too late for that, Weldon," Peg said. "You missed your chance."

"What do you mean?" I asked. "Where is she?"

"Listen to me now, kid," he said, looking over my shoulder out the small window by the door. "I suggest that you go and sell that land for whatever you can get for it and clear out of Cordy. This town is changing. I can't say what's going to happen here anymore. I can't promise that I'm gonna be around to save your ass, and I sure don't want to have to bury it."

"Peg?" I asked.

"Shut up and let me finish. Right here, in Cordy, things are the way they are for old, old reasons, you know that?" He swept his arm behind. "Out there? The World is coming. It's been coming for a long, long time. Cordy was the best place for our kind to end up. That's why I founded it. And that's why the jacks came. That's why Serwalter Scott came here, that's why Bud Maynard and Alright Edwards and Otto and Antti Walta and your father came. Or I brought them here, or whatever. There was nowhere else in this Modern World for them. You think you're a jack, Weldon?"

I thought about the Lost Lot, which was now mine. "I could be one, if I wanted to," I told him.

"Bullshit," he said, dismissing me entirely. "You're no jack, Weldon. What about the rest of your family?" he asked. "Can't you go somewhere? I can't have a kid and a fortune-teller running the shop forever."

I understood that. Now Tom was gone, the scenery was fixing to change. I thought of my mother's family, back in Moscow. There would be school and starched collars. There would be churching in a high fashion. Fact, now I thought about it, things were looking to go from worse to worser, faster than fast.

"I haven't got any family left," I lied. There was no way I was going back to Moscow.

Peg just looked at me. "Well, then, I guess you're in a pickle, kid."

He stood up, walked behind the bar and got up on a stool to reach the naked lady painting. "You're not a jack. You never will be," he said. "The jacks are dying. They're dying out. Their time is done. For a while, I made it so that they could live and die like they always have." He pulled a bottle from behind the canvas and stepped off the stool to hold it up to the light of the projector. "For a while," he said again. "But I'm an old man. My world is passing away, too. Maybe for a time, maybe forever." I looked at the bottle, there in the light. At the bottom, tilted there in the corner, was a patch of blackness as dark as nighttime in the Rooms Upstairs. "Dark Corner," Peg Ramsay said.

"What is it? What does it mean?" I asked.

"It means you're on your own for a bit, kid." Peg grabbed the back of my shirt and the back of my pants and dragged me through the front door and out into the frozen night, where Jensen and Webb and a load of prohibition agents were waiting, the headlights on their paddy wagons blazing. They'd come for Peg Ramsay, and for Peg Ramsay's Dream.

RAPTURING ANGELS

Marsha was telling us about the Rapture just the other goddamn night, driving us each to our homes from the Brothers Swede. Meaning she was gonna drop old Weldon off at his trailer and then go on to stay at Joe Mouffreau's house. She was saying about the Rapture that we'll all be going about our work or raking pine needles in the yard or making a Spam sandwich, all la-di-da about life, and suddenly we'll look up and everyone will be gone up to heaven, except for the bad people. The moon will turn to blood, she says. The dead will rise and Satan will rule the World for a thousand years. Marsha hasn't come into the Brothers Swede since she found Jesus. She just picks us up in the parking lot. Suits me. People believe all kinds of crazy things, from teetotaling to religion, but I try to spend as little time as possible listening to the ones that trumpet their virtues from the mountaintops. I just watch for her truck from the window.

That night, the prohibition agents roosted on the buildings of Cordy like God's own avenging, Rapturing angels come to clean things up. Jensen and Webb didn't take me in because I was just a kid.

"What kinda kid is this, Jensen?" the one named Webb said.

"He looks like just the worst kind of kid," Jensen said. "Think we oughta take him in, book him, too?"

"I think we get him to tell us where his little friend is," Webb said. "One way or the other." He popped his knuckles.

"Who's his little friend?" Jensen said.

"You know," Webb told him with some exasperation in his voice, "the girl. The one who actually makes the stuff for the old man."

"Yeah," said Jensen. "Where is she, kid?" His voice was flat. "We know she's around here somewhere. Unless she took off through the woods."

"My dad just died, and I already got my drunk ass kicked around once tonight, so whatever you got planned for me when I don't tell you shit, I hope that it's memorable," I told them both.

The two probie agents looked at one another.

"You say your father just died, kid?" Webb asked me. "How, if you don't mind my asking?"

"Tree," I told him.

"I don't know what kind of fool would be a lumber-jack," Jensen said.

They didn't even ask me word one about why Peg Ramsay was kicking my ass when they showed up to raid the town. They just locked him in the back of the paddy with Shorty Wade and Ed Kleinerd and drove them all away with nary a tip of the cap, but the rest of the probie agents stayed around and just tore the town apart in darkness straight through to dawn. Once they found the Dream hidden in the walls of the Lady Appleton's, they knew to look for it everywhere. By everywhere, that's what I mean. It took a whole lotta Dream to keep Cordelia satisfied, and it wasn't for nothing that I spent so much of every day hauling bottles and stashing them all over the place. In the altar of the church, between the roots of the Bouley Tree in the middle of town, up and down the street, under every floorboard and filling every hidden (and frankly, half-hidden) space big enough to stick a bottle. They ripped the facades off the barbershop and off the front of our store. They pulled up our floor, and they found the false back of the Witch's wardrobe. She cursed them in old languages as they threw her few possessions in a pile in order to get at the Dream. They demolished Peg's grandfather clock, took every bottle that they could lay their hands on, put the whole she-bang in the back of four trucks and drove to the edge of the Serwalter trestle. Then they dumped it over the edge, and all those milky-blue bottles of swirling magic crashed down into the St. Anne. The only reason they didn't find the cavern below Shorty Wade's place is that Billy Lowground just sat there at the piano, pounding away the kind of slapstick movie soundtrack that woulda made Bud Maynard proud, and hiding the passageway behind the piano from discovery through the force of sheer sonic irritation.

And the jacks? Gone back into the woods the moment they got wind that Jensen and Webb were in town. Probably cleared out into the trees and back to the Lost Lot while Peg was kicking my ass and chewing me out. It was almost a magic trick how that shirksome bunch of motherfuckers could disappear at the very moment that the emissaries of the Modern Fucking World showed up.

So, Peg and Shorty and Ed were gone. The jacks were gone. Annie was gone. All of them gone, as if Raptured away, leaving me alone to stand in the middle of the empty road lined with skeletal buildings, blown through by a skeletal wind, surrounded by the bones of long-dead lumberjacks who had lived and died beneath the spreading boughs of ancient, fragrant, fading magic. It was almost winter, and I was on my way to a roiling, boiling hangover.

I walked home weavingly and pushed through the open front door into the torn-up shop. I went back into the dark. The stove had gone cold and I pulled my father's blanket off his bed and on to my own and lay down beneath both of them to keep off the chill. Still, when I awoke my bed was damp with sweat. Outside, the sad afternoon light was beating its weak little fists against the frosted window.

I breathed on the glass and rubbed the fog away to look out. The creek had a cataract-colored skin of ice across it and the Idaho Hotel looked dreary and cold and devoid of the merriment of chess. The sky was full of snow, but it hadn't started coming down yet. I think it was probably waiting on me. I pulled myself off the bed and stepped into my boots and went out the back door to the privy. I sat there in the frozen dark and I swear I nearly emptied my entire self out through my own asshole. You know the feeling, those little beads of sweat you get after the real hard type of drinking? I had those beads in spades. I was sore all over—my arms, my legs, high up on my thighs. God, even my goddamn finger joints felt like they were a hundred years old, which is a comparison I expect I have the authority to make now. Part of the pain was probably from getting thrown against Shorty Wade's wall and then dragged out onto the street, but the lion's share was from all that Dream I'd drunk the night before.

When I came back out into the yard, the first flakes of snow had started to come down and the whole town looked even sadder and emptier for it. Even the dark, piney mountains that were always so full of adventure before seemed like they'd farted and rolled over to try to sleep out the day. All Creation looked about as special as a pile of sucked chicken bones.

Back inside the fire'd gone out and there was no more wood. The Witch's door was still closed. I went and stood in front of it to listen for her but there was nary a sound. It wasn't long before it was set to get dark again, and with the woodpile in the deplorable un-split state that it was, I realized that I was gonna have to get down to it if we weren't gonna freeze in the night. I put on my pants and

I picked up my grandfather's ax. The haft was of oak and stained deeply over time with pitch and sweat and blood and whatever tears a lumberjack might shed. Where the axes my father sold in his shop were teardrop-shaped, heavy and blunt at one end and sharp at the tip, my grandfather's ax-head was shaped like batwings. The freshly sharpened blade running along each edge popped out from the dark metal. The thing felt a fair shade heavier than a normal ax, as well.

I could have gone back in the shop and picked out an ax of my own from the ones that my father sold, but that wouldn't have felt right to me in that moment. It was true that as magic axes go, it had done a pretty poor job, but still, I couldn't just toss it aside, into a snowbank to rust.

I somehow got the thing above my head where it wobbled a few long seconds before I brought it down, into the ground, remembering the circle that the Witch had dragged around Tom for protection. It took almost everything I had to get it up there, and once it was up there, balanced perilously above my head, it wasn't easy to get the heavy thing to fall where I wanted it to. Finally, though, I lugged a big log of wood up onto the stump and brought the ax down on it. The wood took the blade, but it didn't split. After some gracefulness I got the bit out of the log and set it up again. This time when it came down, the pieces split enough that I could pull them apart the rest of the way with my hands. I went up into the store and got some gloves. The next piece split for real.

I worked away like that for a while, with the snow falling all around, feeling the ache in my hands go from that hangover kind to a different, better sort. The sweating I was doing was surprising, too, and not bad, neither. I got these big circles under my arms from the sweat, which felt like a different kind of sweat than what a kid would sweat. There was maybe a hundred pieces of green-sap ponderosa, all told, and I split about twenty of them down to where the billets would fit into the stove. I caught myself thinking what it'd be like when Tom came home and found all this wood split and he didn't have to do it himself, and got that sweet-sad feeling in my stomach like when something happens to you in a dream that's so good and perfect that you're so happy when you wake up but then you realize it was all a dream. I knew Tom wasn't coming home, now or ever again. If it was how the Witch thought it would be, then he was wandering around the Lost Lot graveyard at the end of town, making calls on a few old friends whose luck had been as bad as his, maybe meeting folks he didn't know so well but had heard of from his father or grandfather, looking up every so often in confusion in the direction of the Lost Lot. Winter must be a hard time for ghosts, too.

I stacked the wood under the store's porch awning where it would be out of the snow, then took some pieces inside and made a fire in the store stove and then in ours in back. Then I did the dishes in the sink and I straightened up the store a little and by that time it was hot in there and I was still warm from chopping all that wood and from my drink fever, so I went back outside. It was really coming down now, but I don't mind telling you I felt real good all of a sudden. My grandfather's ax was good and sharp, I thought to myself, but it didn't split that wood on its own. It was me that split the wood. I also knew and could feel how fucked up my face was from the booze and the wall and the slapping and the run-in with the frozen road. I'd certainly earned all that the lumberjack way, hadn't I?

I went back in the store. The display of hand lotions had been strewn across the floor. The jars of candies had been smashed, the perfume stolen. Of course the bottles of Dream were ransacked and gone. I got out a block of beeswax from the floor and ran it up and down the haft of the ax like I'd seen the jacks do. Since Peg wouldn't let me run the store, I'd have to go elsewhere—The Lights or the Cities of the Great Plains—and make my way as a man. Hell, maybe I'd go to Hollywood and get myself a goddamn Wonderhorse.

Course, no matter where I went people would see me as a kid and treat me as a kid. They'd make me go to school in kid clothes. I could already feel the wind pulling through the thin fabric. I could see the looks on all those teachers' faces when they saw I hadn't been learning my lessons, the little kids sitting all around me, laughing in their hands as I sat there trying to multiply, the bigger ones waiting for me in a pack at the noonday siren, when everyone piled out of the doors and into the yard. "Let's see any of those fuckers split the pile of logs that I just split," I said to my-self. Tom wasn't here anymore, but I didn't need him to split the wood. Let's see any of those kids, whoever they were, take the kind of beating Peg gave me and walk away from it. He wasn't knocking no kid around Shorty Wade's last night, no, he wasn't. That was a real lumberjack's ass that he'd been kicking.

On top of all that, there was the Lost Lot. I needed to see it through, one way or the other. Like the ax, it had been my father's and his father's before him. Now it was mine. I tried to think of what they would have done, but my grandfather had won the Lost Lot by chance in a card game, and my father had died for it, and I wasn't sure that there was an object lesson in either of their examples. Now the Lost Lot waited, ready for me to sell or abandon. Well, I wouldn't be *abandoning* it. Linden Laughlin, my father's partner, would still be there. If I walked away, he'd take it, and, by law, once I'd been gone six months it'd be his by rights. That just didn't feel right to me, either. They had been partners, Laughlin and my dad, but that didn't mean that they'd been brothers. Tom wouldn't have wanted Laughlin to walk away with that whole magnificent mountain of trees. He wouldn't have wanted me to go into the World with nothing, even if I decided that I wasn't a lumberjack.

That's when the thought first came to me that I could stay and be a lumberjack and keep the land. I couldn't go back on my father's deal with Laughlin, but maybe I could log it with him, side by side with the Waltas and Cavuto and Holmberg and Unto and all the John Johnsons right through the winter and into the river drive, come spring. Hell, I thought, look what I had just done with the woodpile. I could stay. Yes, I'd work my way through this winter and, come spring, I'd ride a monster log down the St. Anne to the sawmill. That'd show Peg. If he ever came back. Blisters had risen on the palms of my hands. I reached into the hollow of the old apple tree and pulled out a bottle of Dream that the probies had missed, but the black shadow in the corner of the bottle put me off drinking it. Dark Corner.

There came a knock at the door.

A SCREECH AGAINST ALMIGHTY GRAVITY ITSELF

When Marsha and I had been more companionable, back before she got all wild-eyed about Judgment Day, she used to cook me casseroles like you wouldn't believe. She made green bean casseroles with the green beans all soft and salty and the cream of mushroom bubbling up between those little bits of fried onion, and she made tuna casseroles that would steam up the windowpanes. My favorite of hers was called Train Wreck, and it was a fucking mess. Elbow noodles and stewed tomatoes and ground beef, all seasoned up and baked. But all those casseroles were in the past and we both knew it. So, it was real odd to see her come over one afternoon with a bag of groceries.

This was right after I bought the color TV. It was her that gave me a ride to the store to buy it. She came with me into the store and she tried to flirt with the man who sold the damn things. "Weldon's entering the twenty-first century," she was going on and on. "He's figuring that it might be time he got rid of the black-and-white and moved on to a flat-screen." Then she and the man selling the things, who was wearing a blue vest, started walking up and down the rows and rows of TVs, him explaining the "options" and the "features" to her. "Look at this, Wel," she said, like buying a TV together means you're married. "The buttons on this remote are big and light up so you can see them easier. His eyes," she said to the blue vest man. "They took away his license, so he's spending a little more time at home these days."

"Don't get me started on the fucking buttons," I told her.

"Weldon!" She put her hand over her mouth.

"Alright," the man said.

"We ain't buying a fucking fifty-inch flat-screen TV," I said.

"We can deliver it to your home, if that's convenient," the man said. He was trying to be helpful, but he was only fifty years old.

"You deliver out to Cordy?"

"Where?"

"Cordelia? My trailer's about ten miles outside Cordy, across the St. Anne."

"We can't deliver there. I'm sorry," he said.

"Thank the good Christmas Lord," I said, and pointed at the littlest TV they had.

"Weldon!" Marsha said again, clucking her tongue at me. Then she said, "Weldon, you'll barely be able to see that."

"That's the one," I said. "Now get me the fuck out of here."

It was when I was paying for the goddamn television, almost two hundred bucks, that she musta gotten a peek inside my wallet. I don't go to the bank and I don't leave my cash buried in mattresses or nothing like that. Plus, since I'd gotten the trailer, I had a nice fucking mattress. I mean, it was fucking *nice*. No way would I have cut it up to stick my filthy bills in like some kind of burrowing forest rat. Nope, I carry my money with me, and I don't own credit cards. I had about fifteen grand in my wallet, and I guess she got a peek in when I opened it up to pay the blue vest.

Anyway, she showed up the other afternoon and turned on the TV and told me to sit down on the couch and she was gonna make us a casserole. I made sure that I had my money on me, good and safe. Then I sat there flipping through the channels using the remote controller with the hundreds of little buttons, and I waited for her to fucking poison me.

"The elbow pasta looks like elbows," she said. She took the switcher from me and turned to a channel where a woman was showing off bracelets and that's what she wanted to watch and I was fine with that 'cause, and this is a fact, I was really enjoying that meal.

I've never lived much with women, and it ain't because I'd be all that fucking hard to live with, either, in case that's what you're thinking. It's not like I wouldn't have tipped my cap to a schoolteacher if she'd come to the St. Anne, unattached. I ain't a hermit. There ain't nothing wrong with me. If I had to say why I never much lived with anyone, it's probably because of *where* I live. You don't get a lot of dewy young things out in the woods ten miles from Cordelia. Not even now. So yeah, when I was in my eighties Marsha and I found each other the last ones in the Brothers Swede more than once, and if I got to say it, even now, even after the Jesus stuff and how she got into cahoots with Joe Mouffreau, even when it was plain as fucking daylight that she just wanted my damn money, that didn't mean it wasn't real nice to spend time with her, watching my new TV and eating that Train Wreck casserole that she made.

I wonder if it was all her idea, or if the two of them were dreaming up plans together. Whether Marsha put him up to it or not, though, like every scheme that Joe Mouffreau got mixed up in, something ended up getting cut down.

It was Laughlin at the door, hat in enormous hands, fresh flakes of snow on enormous head. He had a bottle of Dark Corner in his hand, a black shadow stuck like tar to the bottom. Behind him, a tree trunk, bucked and trimmed, lay by the side of the road, like magic. It woulda taken a team of horses to skid that thing from the woods, and yet here was Linden Laughlin, pretty as you please, come out of the cold, black night with nary another soul, man or beast.

"It's getting cold, Cub. I thought Tom's unfortunates would appreciate some wood." He stepped inside.

"I already have wood," I told him. "I just chopped some."

"We're partners, Cub. You and me. Your father and I had an agreement. I would help him log his show, and he and I would become rich men. Now I expect it's you and me who must come to terms. So, consider the wood a toast to goodwill." He threw himself into a chair by the fire. "Mighty cold in here with the walls ripped away," he commented, and took a swig of the Dark Corner. "But this is nothing to the Lost Lot." He swept a hand across his brow and my heart bumped a bit at the look on his face.

"Yeah?" I said.

"Oh, there's trees up there, Cub," he told me. "You could build Noah's Ark with the trees up there. We could be hat-tipping millionaires if we could figure a way to get them out. It's just that there's no way to get them out."

"What about the chute? Serwalter's?"

"Ravaged by the elements. It'll never hold. No, we could work, day and night, with all the Devil's elves and the ghosts of every single jack that ever died and not be able to get enough board feet out to buy a shave and a shoeshine. The ground's too steep, the snow's too deep, the rocks are too big." He offered me the bottle of Dark Corner. The fumes off it gave me an uneasy feeling, as if I was sitting before a fire that gave off no warmth. I shook my head and he took it back and took another great gulp. "Cools the core," he said.

"Maybe I could sell," I said.

"To who, Cub?" He leaned toward me, out of the chair, sharp elbows on sharp knees.

"Rutledge? Mouffreau?"

"Mupwidge? Moofwo?" he burst back at me out of nowhere. For a second there it looked like his eyes were about to bust out of his head.

The Witch opened the door to her bedroom and stepped out, took one look at Laughlin and spat on the ground.

"Sohvia," Laughlin said, "you are welcome to our confabulation."

She gave him a look that woulda murdered a softer man, then strode by him as if he was invisible to her, opened a can of mandarins off the shelf and went back to her room.

"I'm sorry, Cub. I'm sorry to make fun of you like that," he said when she was gone. "You don't deserve that kind of treatment. I'm tired, is all. I'm tired and feeling foolish. I was drunken on fantasies of the money to be made, drunken and careless. Now your father is dead and I'm the cause. It was me who tempted him with the woods, at last, and I am responsible for your present hardships." He pounded his fist on the table so that the bottle fell and shattered on the floor. "I am sorry," he said, surveying the shards.

He seemed set to drunk-cry and the fumes of Dark Corner swirled around us, all oily in the heat of the fire. He slid out of the chair to the floor and sat there a moment in the glass and the liquor, then he pulled off a boot and began picking up the shards and dropping them in. He took a while down there, his shaggy, black-haired head peering out the bits and pieces and putting them into the empty boot. The pieces tinkled away merrily as he stuffed his toes back into the huge thing. He pulled another bottle of Dark Corner from his jacket and stood, crunching the glass in his boot. "Are you a man of sense, Weldon? Because if you are, you'll leave the Lost Lot and what's left of this town. You're not a jack, Weldon. It's no faltering of your own blood, it's just that times have changed. You don't need the woods and those woods don't need you. Go somewhere comfortable. Get on a train and leave all this behind."

"Then what am I supposed to do? You say I won't be able to sell to the timber companies."

"I was thinking," said Linden. "But no," he added.

"What?" I asked.

"Well, imagine, Cub, imagine that I bought the land off you, as a favor to your old man." He examined his long fingers. "The place isn't worth the dirt beneath a fingernail, but I feel warm toward you, Cub, and don't want to see you enter life shiftless as well as brokenhearted."

"I thought you said the land was worthless," I said.

"Oh, it is worthless, Cub. As worthless as an empty hole, and yet what kind of beast would I be to let you leave town with nothing at all. I'll give you fifteen hundred for it, minus fees."

"Minus what kind of fees?" I said.

"Minus the modest ones," he said. The room had suddenly gotten very small, or should I say that Linden Laughlin had suddenly gotten a whole lot bigger. His shoulders, shrouded in black as ever, seemed to melt into every crevice of the room. His legs stretched longer and longer and thinner and thinner until they were like the spikes of a spider's leg and black as cinder. His head bent forward until his chin was on his chest and the bones at the back of his neck cricked against the rafters.

"To be honest with you, it's not the money that I care about, Cub," he said. "It's not the money that I need, but because that is the tongue we are forced to speak in, I will again restate the sum. Fifteen hundred. Take it."

The room was beating like a big, black heart all around us, about to explode us all into the night sky. Suddenly, like I'd made it all up in my mind, he came back down to his normal fucking size, wiped his mouth with the sleeve of one arm and turned toward the door. "I'll give you the night to think it over," he said.

"I need to see the land," I said.

"You don't need to, Cub. It's no place for you. Children are bad luck in the woods," he said.

But I'd never even seen the Lost Lot. I'd never even been across the goddamn Serwalter trestle. I'd been a boy, and my father had kept an oath. Then I thought of Tom out there in the Lost Lot cemetery. Him and all the other jacks that had thrown themselves up against that great big frozen, rocky crag. I thought about them all, shivering and talking together out there in the dark, their eyes drifting always toward that place whose true and drastic outlines I might never fucking know.

"My father died on the Lost Lot," I said. "It's all that I've got left of him and it's all I've got left in the World. I can't sell without ever laying eyes on it. I need to see it."

I made sure I was waiting for him in the blue light early the next morning. I had scooped some cans of beans and mandarins off the shelves and put them in a rucksack, grabbed my grandfather's ax, told the Witch where I was going through her keyhole and then waited at the window to see him come weaving down the street from the Rooms Upstairs. By the looks of him, whatever dog-piss Dark Corner was left in town, he'd found it. He was missing his hat.

I went out and stood in the middle of the road so's I was blocking his path. He was off somewhere in his own head, pickling. He pulled up short when he looked up and saw me. He didn't like it that he was getting stopped. He burped and then started around me. I let him go—he was moving pretty circuitous and it wasn't hard to catch up with him.

"Good day to you, Cub. I'm headed back into the bleakness," Linden said.

"I'm going with you, then," I said.

"Little Cub, Cub, Cub," he said. "Little Cubby, Cub, Cub." But his eyes were wandering like he wasn't even thinking about what he was saying. The words were just falling out of his mouth like pebbles of sheep shit. He started walking again. I picked up my bag and balanced Tom's ax over my shoulder and followed him, past Shorty Wade's place, past the Lost Lot cemetery and down the hill, past the brackeny lilac grove that marked the railroad spur, whose train tracks went all the way to The Lights and then fanned out beyond like aspen roots between the flowering Cities of the Great Plains. I walked alongside him, that tall, ominous figure from my father's campfire tales and the Witch's dark forebodings, and I thought about what in Almighty Hell I was doing.

"It's good to be getting back," Laughlin said, out of nowhere. "To the trees, I mean. There's so little in town. For me." He flourished his long-ass fingers in the air. "Friends

I have not, though of companions I have had many, and all of them, every haunch and hulk of them, have been jacks. You are not a jack, Cub. I wish you were, but you are not."

"You don't know me," I told him.

"Your father and I spoke often about you, Cub. He was proud of you. This is not what he would have wanted," Linden said.

The great rams-head portals loomed up, all majestic and glowering, in front of us, and I stopped to take in the Serwalter trestle. I hadn't been to the trestle since the day Tom and Linden and all the rest had headed across and up to the Lost Lot. It was crusted over with snow, but you could see where it had been tromped down by men. Against the backdrop of forest, the trestle seemed to list in the breeze, held together with sorcery and perilous mathematics. I thought of Bud Maynard and Tony the Wonderhorse galloping up and down the Grand Canyon and not worrying about it a bit.

Linden swept his arm and stepped aside, motioning like I should go in front of him. I didn't want to, but I sure as hell wasn't gonna let on to him that I was any more scared than he thought I was, so I went first. The water level was way down, what with all the snow being frozen high up on the mountains. Without the white water, you could get a good look at the rocks below. I swear I could make out all kinds of broken bones, mixed with the glittering galaxies of smashed bottles of Dream, but I told myself they were sticks and such and decided to keep my eyes ahead of me and made my way slowly out over thin air.

After a moment I heard him following me, muttering along drunk. Goddamn but it was quiet on that bridge in the middle of the chasm. Maybe if I'd refused to go first across the trestle I coulda pushed him off, part of me thought, but another bigger part told me that there was no way I could have done it even if I tried. There was too much Linden Laughlin and he was too quick. It occurred to me to wonder what would happen if I disappeared. The Lost Lot would be up for the taking, and no one pays dead boys a dollar. I looked back over my shoulder at him and he was looking right back at me like he could see my thoughts through the back of my head. I tell you, I was goddamn relieved to step down off the trestle and onto the far side.

The fir trees before us were immense, the biggest things I had ever seen. I craned my head back as far as it would go but I couldn't see the tops of them, they were so lost in cloud. They stood in a straight wall, one to one to one, their boughs sweeping over each other as if the only thing they were made to do was keep the sunlight out and keep the nighttime in. The morning rays that struck them just got eaten up and disappeared. There weren't even any ice crystals on the needles to glint out at me. Those trees were just as huge and dark and terrifying as you can imagine. Nothing like them now. A road just big enough for a train track or a team of horses snuck through the only gap in their armor, and it was down this tunnel in the trees that Laughlin walked. He was maybe ten steps into the forest before he disappeared completely. I found that I was wet through with sweat. My hair froze solid the instant I took off my hat and wiped my arm over my forehead. The morning light felt good on the back of my neck. I stood there, in between the trestle and those dark woods, and I was of more than half a mind to go back. If I was to turn back now, I'd be in town by the time the Witch had boiled her coffee and cast an angry glance out the window. I'd have to pass by my father's grave, and I wondered if he'd leave off his hobnobbing with all the other dead jacks to stand at the churchyard gate and watch me pass by. He'd understand, I thought.

The snow got deeper. It was that hole-punch type of snow with the crust on it that you can walk on top of sometimes and other times you just kind of crunch down through and have to struggle out of. It wasn't graceful walking, and I had to work hard to keep up with that long-legged devil. It got so deep, and the trees got so thick, that it was hard to tell in spots where the road actually was. There's only one way to get around when the snow gets three or four feet deep and you lose the road. What you do is let your eyes go out of focus a bit and wait for some kind of magic in your head to point out the path where maybe you couldn't see it if you were looking directly at it. We were heading uphill now, hard up into the mountains that I'd been looking at since my father had inherited the Lost Lot and we'd come to Cordy.

I was tired and hungry as hell, and watching Laughlin drink and muse darkly along into the desolate foothills, I cursed myself again and again for being so goddamn stupid as to come out here with him. It began to get colder and darker around noon, and I was getting worn out and wet. My boots were soaked, and my wool socks had balls of snow on them the size of crabapples, but above my waist I was sweating through from the exercise of punching in and out of the snow. I was thirteen and all, but I hadn't done much but deliver Dream around Cordy and sweep up hair in Peg's shop on occasion. I wasn't in the way of making ten-mile mountain hikes. Finally, we came around a bend in the road and he threw his arms wide as if to encompass the great, glorious, goddamn of it all. I'd never seen it with my own eyes, but I knew it like I knew the moon.

There, where the Flewellen and Smokewater converged to form the St. Anne, a jut of rock rose from the ground like the partially submerged prow of some immense and rock-hulled boat, like a mackinaw of deep green and granite, hanging from some invisible coat hook in the heavens. Its cliffs were ludicrously festooned with icicles, the shortest as long as a man's leg, and its outcroppings were spiked with impossible trees. The whole thing was a screech against Almighty Gravity itself. The slope went up so steep that I had to tilt my head all the way back to see the top of it, and even then, it was hard to do. I'm telling you now I ain't never in my whole life ever seen anything as big as those trees holding to a slope like that. There wasn't any explanation for it. It was a cliff. You could cut a tree a thousand feet up that thing and, if it fell wrong and toppled off the cliff, it would whoosh down through empty space for a few minutes at least, before smashing to pieces on the rocks of the riverbed below. Even if you *could* cut it right, and the tree landed so you *could* keep it, it would take some fearless, gravity-defying wonderhorses to skid it to the Serwalter chute. Then you'd be praying that your chute could actually carry those big fuckers down a slope like that to safety and the splash pond by the banks of the St. Anne without shattering into a bajillion busted matchsticks.

I don't mind telling you that my heart went out of me just then. It was as if not only the elements but Insanity, as well, had somehow crafted a malicious craggy monument to their continued, wild existence—all encroachments of the Modern World be damned. But it also—and I want you to take this right—it also had a goddamn kind of *beauty* in the same way anything is beautiful when it is beyond all scope of sheer tremendousness.

"You see what we got ourselves into, Weldon? You see?" Laughlin sat down in a messy heap in the snow as I took it all in.

I didn't answer. "Where's the bunkhouse?" I asked, though just as I asked I realized that I could hear it. Or at least I could hear the birds that Thorough kept around the place. I made my way beneath the cover of trees to the Lost Lot camp.

Yeah, Memory has a way of improving on things. But Time has a way of actually turning them to shit. So standing there, taking in the bunkhouse and the outbuildings and the cookhouse, it was easy to see the kind of care and wildflower whimsy that Serwalter Scott had put into the buildings, but it was also pretty damn clear that those buildings had been deserted for almost thirty years. This

wasn't your typical timber camp, and it was as if the Genius
of the St. Anne had been drinking Peg Ramsay's Dream
as he sketched out the plans and built those scrollworked,
strange-assed structures for the jacks to live in. Windows
of all kinds, some broken now, some grimed over, were set
at odd levels, and chimneys jutted from the roofs at crazed
angles. The bunkhouse sat near the bank of the St. Anne,
far enough up from the riverbed that, come spring, when
the river rose high and white as Christ on the cross, the
whole shebang wouldn't get washed away with it.

Linden just sat there in the snow, drinking. He finished
the bottle and threw it onto the frozen rocks of the river.

Otto stepped out of the bunkhouse. "Weldon, what are
you doing here?" Goddamn, it did my heart good to see
him.

"Otto," I said, the relief a bit too real in my voice. "Everyone else is up on the mountain?" I asked.

Laughlin was rolling snowballs in between his out-
splayed legs. "All up there," he said, ignoring Otto's presence. "Bringing out what wood we can for you." He tossed
one lazily at my chest. "Satisfied?" His eyelids just came
down to that steady drinking place on the middle of his
eyeballs.

"You're gonna log it and just give me the money?" I
asked. Whether Linden Laughlin was a world-famous jack
or a monster from the deep woods, that part of the deal
didn't add up for shit with me.

"You have but to provide me with an address," he said.
I looked at Otto, as if he could vouch for Linden, but

Otto just looked quietly on, inspecting Laughlin's face for something.

"How do I know I'm getting a fair deal?" I asked Laughlin.

"Tut, tut, Cub," Laughlin said. "So you scampered along with me all the way out here to question my honor?"

"How do I know what kind of honor you have?" I said. "This is the ground my father died on. This is all I got in the World, so I guess that I should—"

"I'll give you a thousand dollars for it," he interrupted.

"For what?" I asked him.

"Don't toy with me, Cub," he said. "For the ground we're standing on. For the ground and the trees. One thousand dollars, right here, and you'll leave."

I looked at Otto and he shook his head slightly at me: *No, don't take it.*

"You told me fifteen hundred last night," I told Laughlin. "Anyway, that ain't near what it's worth." Truth was, I had no idea what the Lost Lot was worth, but my father had placed his hopes upon it, had died on it, and for that alone I guessed that made it a whole lot more valuable than the thousand bucks that Laughlin was dangling in front of me.

"I beg you to see reason, Cub." Laughlin took on an aggravating, beseeching tone.

"Shit in your hand, a thousand dollars," I told him.

"Now, Cub. You have no money, you have no men," he said. "You're a boy. You're not a jack. I'll give you eight hundred for it."

"You just fucking told me a thousand," I said.

"I'll buy it off you for six hundred dollars and you'll call yourself lucky," he said. "Some of those up the hill might care about you, but I am not one of them." The day seemed to follow his voice off into shadow, and all around me I could feel the light beginning to draw inward on itself. I became aware again of Thorough's birds, peeping their good-nights from the trees. Laughlin just stared at me with that level gaze he'd gotten from the bottles of Dark Corner.

Otto came to stand beside me. "This is Tom Applegate's son. The land is his now. We work with you, Laughlin, but we work for the boy as long as the land stays his. Nothing will happen to Tom's boy, or I will know about it. I will come for you. My brother will know. He will come for you. Every single other jack on this mountain will come for you if anything happens to this boy."

It was big talk, and I appreciated it coming from Otto, but I also knew that most of those John Johnsons up on there on the mountain didn't give the tippy-tip of a rat's tail whose land it was as long as they got paid the exorbitant wages my father and Laughlin had promised them. "It's my land," I said again. "You ain't gonna just take what's mine by law."

Laughlin pursed his lips and gave a little kiss to the air. "Legality is your concern, Weldon Applegate? Out here, alone in the woods with a creature like me before you? Does the wind follow laws? Does the paper wasp? No, Cub, you had better just get home and get out of town. You've seen what you came to see, a spit of unforgiving rock that became your father's headstone. Now, I'd hate to send you back into the howling elements empty-handed, so one more time, three hundred dollars." He stuck his ginormous hand out for me to shake.

"The boy isn't selling," Otto said.

"I ain't selling," I agreed. I stepped around the two big men and made my way through the snow to a tiny green sapling poking up through the snow. "Before now," I said, "nobody wanted to touch this land. But I'm working the damn thing, so the claim isn't abandoned." Then, just so's Laughlin knew that I was serious, I took my father's ax and severed the top of the little tree where it rose from the snow. "Now I've been up here myself and brought a tree out, you can't say I left it all behind."

Suddenly Laughlin seemed to be getting bigger and bigger again, just like he had when we were at home the night before. His legs lengthened out until they looked as thin as spider legs, and his face got longer and thinner beneath his mop of hair. Against those deep green trees with their darkened skirts and with the sun sinking behind the Lost Lot, I can't say for sure if he was actually getting bigger or if it was just some trick of the blue shadows. If Otto could see the changes, too, he might have showed some reaction, but he just stood there, looking from one to the other of us.

"I'll be heading back," I said to both of them as nonchalant as I fucking could. A fog had rolled in as the temperature dropped. The sun still shone golden high up on the face of the Lost Lot, but down here in the valley at its feet, the day was turning deep blue. It'd be well past fucking dark by the time I'd made it back to Cordy.

Laughlin smiled. "Go home, Cub. Bid good riddance to this place that killed your father. Leave it alone, with me."

"It ain't your land. Those trees are mine. The chute's mine. Those men working up there are getting paid with my timber," I said.

"Other arrangements can be made, Cub," Linden Laughlin said.

I didn't like the way that sounded, but there was nothing that I could do about it, so I didn't say anything but, "I'm going now." I summoned all my goddamn will, turned my back on the two men and walked back down the lumber road and into the gloom, pulling the tiny tree behind me. When I finally looked over my shoulder for them, they were gone.

THIS IS YOUR FORTUNE

Joe Mouffreau took out half of the Japanese army himself during the War, for you to hear him tell it. A real killing machine, if you believe him. For all his heroism, though, he musta done his great acts of valor completely in broad daylight, because I never met a man more afraid of the dark than Joe. I remember the last night I ever spent in total darkness. This was before I got my trailer and window curtains, back when I was still living in the old bunkhouse. Joe had just built his big, new, fake-ass log cabin, right across the river from me. The night he moved in, he turned on every goddamn light fixture in the place, outside as well as in. I mean to say that that house was blazing with light, positively crammed with it. And on top of all those lights, he also had motion-sensing ones out by his garage that would turn on every time they registered a fucking mouse on his fucking patio.

I was sitting in my lawn chair under the stars, drinking a beer and just hating Joe Mouffreau already, before he even turned on all those lights. But when he did turn them all on, all at once the stars just disappeared, the moon lost its bone-glow, the owls quit their hooting in the trees, and the crickets and frogs tore their attention from the sheet music of Creation to cover their eyes against the goddamn glare. That's how it got to be goddamn *daytime* all the time where I live. I mean to say that *no one* was more afraid of the dark than Joe Mouffreau.

I'm not some fucking sage hermit at one with the Universe or anything like that. I'm just used to the dark, is all. And I've walked miles alone through the guts of it when I've had to. And everyone knows, it ain't ever the dark that's the scary thing. It's the scary thing that's in the dark with you.

So, I'll just say that it was an even tougher walk down from the Lost Lot after that first visit than it had been to get there, though not because it was dark. No, I was soaked through and frozen and exhausted, dragging a tiny tree and my grandfather's ax behind me, and just because I wasn't walking side by side with Linden Laughlin doesn't mean I couldn't feel his malevolence in the fog all around me. On top of that shit, there was the wondering what the fuck I was gonna do. I dropped the spar of the little tree that I'd cut. What was I gonna do with it, put it up in our torn-up shop as a Christmas tree? I was crossing the ice of the trestle; I was passing the lilac grove at the turnoff to the spur. I was trudging by the Lost Lot cemetery, past empty Shorty Wade's and the darkened Idaho Hotel, past Oral Avery in his high-up window. I was fumbling at the latch, stumbling through the store and into the kitchen. I was looking into the Witch's fury-laden face, there at the table. She had a rag stuffed in her mouth and the last china tea set was before her. Linden Laughlin sat across from her. He had somehow beaten me home. He smiled at me, turning one of the little cups idly over and over in his giant hand as if I had interrupted him in the midst of telling the Witch her own fortune.

My grandfather's ax didn't do anything but hang there in my hand. I couldn't even lift it before Linden reached over and, with a great, spidery arm, knocked me back against the wall. I dropped the ax. Linden didn't even have to stand up. He kicked a chair against me and blew the lantern out. Next thing I knew the kerosene was running down my face and I jammed my eyes shut from the burning. The ringing in my ears was getting louder. Something sifted down onto me where I lay, and I heard the crinkling of a heavy paper sack. Laughlin was pouring a bag of salt down on me.

And here's a secret. Blinded, covered in salt and kerosene, bone-tired and frozen through, I still could maybe have gotten up, grabbed the ax and taken one good swing at that devil. But for a moment there, for the most important moment there, I didn't want to. I didn't want to do nothing. I didn't want to stop what was going to happen. I wanted it all to happen to us, to the Witch and me, all at once. No more of this slow hurt that comes day by day, drip by goddamn drip, from loneliness and consternating grief. I wanted him to do what he was gonna do so that he wouldn't have no more he could do to us. I tasted that thought in my mind and it was every bit as bitter as the taste of kerosene in my mouth; still, by the time I'd tasted how bad it was, it was way past too late to do anything about it. She shrieked as I heard him kick her chair over, then the tacking-tromp of his spike books as he walked over to stand above me.

He grabbed me up off the floor by my hair, though I twisted and tried to bite him while he was doing it. He gave me a fist in the side of my head that knocked something loose so that I couldn't have stood anymore, even if I'd wanted to. I heard the Witch crying from behind the rag, and I hoped that she could see me, could see I was still alive and that I was fighting.

He rolled me over and tied my hands to my ankles from behind, which is the worst way to be tied, if you can't imagine it for yourself. "Oh, Cub," he said over and over again. "Oh, Cub, Cub, Cubby! It's time for you to leave this place! I want you gone, cleared off that land. Run, Cub. But first, listen and remember what is about to happen." Then he picked me up and carried me into Tom's room and opened the closet door and dropped me in there. I landed on my knees, everything all bent backward and twisted and to this day, even with all that's happened between Joe Mouffreau and me, I've still never felt a pain as bad as when Linden Laughlin dropped me on my knees, with my back all bent backward like that.

He slammed the door on me. Pain bloomed in dirty yellow flowers against the lids of my eyes. No matter how tightly I kept them shut, the burning salt and lamp oil snuck through, anyway. It felt like my eyeballs were bleeding. The pain crawled in circles around my wrists and ankles where the rope had rubbed the skin off.

Out in the kitchen the Witch was trying to make sounds around the rags in her mouth. You didn't have to be able to understand her to know that she was laying six kinds of curses on Linden Laughlin. For a few moments it sounded like maybe he was listening to what she had to say, then came the tinkling smash of china and I knew that the Future was over for the Witch. I heard her muffled curses above the thrashing of her limbs as he dragged her across the floor. I thought then that he was gonna kill her. I thought that it was already happening. The Witch started screaming beneath the rag. I couldn't hear Linden Laughlin, though. Whatever evil he was working he worked as quiet as shadow.

The dirty yellow flowers of pain behind my eyes rotted red and then brown and melted black as new ones bloomed in their places. Pain trickled over me in centipedes of kerosene and sweat and blood and salt and melted snow; and Time and God, those useless, lazy fucks, sat down under an apple tree some somewhere and rested awhile.

A curse is a birdlike thing. It is meant to fly. Once uttered, it hovers, it travels, it roosts. I imagined our little kitchen full of all of the Witch's curses, a cloud of beating black wings and voracious beaks, like Thorough's camp birds but dreadful. It felt like a year or so later when, like birds fly off all at once and all together, the Witch stopped her cursing and was silent.

I heard Linden Laughlin's boots crunch through the china and pass out into the shop, pausing there. After a few moments the front door closed politely and from that moment on was the quietest time of any time I can remember in my life. I didn't hear the Witch. She wasn't crying or making any other sounds, either. She was dead for sure, I thought, lying there in the dust of broken china and tromped-in snow. She was dead and he was going to come back inside and kill me, too. But he didn't come back. I guess he coulda come back in and just done it, just killed me. There was no one who would have seen him do it. But Linden Laughlin was a monster and the worst monsters take their time. If he aimed to kill me, he wasn't aiming to do it at that moment. And something about his particular brand of Evil told me he'd get more happiness as a thorn in an old man's memory than he would from the momentary bliss of killing a tied-up kid.

I saw on a program once about how it takes light from the sun ten days, or something like that, to land on the Earth. It makes you think about what each one of those little pieces of light is thinking when it finally lands on what it lands on. Maybe it gets to land on the hood of an old red pickup truck. Maybe it lands on a trout fin or a pile of old coffee grounds in the yard. Maybe it lands on a piece of glass and gets reflected back up into space. You wonder whether it's happy landing where it lands, after coming all that long, long way.

After a long, long while I tried opening my eyes, just a little, and I could make out a thin line of blue light, so thin it was like imagination, starting to glow up from under the crack in the door, and whether or not it was glad to see me, I was glad to see it.

When I heard the bedsprings creak, I knew she was alive. I called out to her, but she didn't answer. I kept calling out to her, goddamn it. I heard her walking around a little bit. Some chunks of wood got piled into the stove and the stove door closed. A pot got moved on the stove top. Finally, I heard her footsteps come into the room and saw her shadow come to stand in front of the door and hover there long enough for me to wonder why she was waiting as long as she was. When she opened the door, I fell face-first onto the floor at her feet. There were speckles of china dust on her little black shoes as she untied me. Her shirt was wrinkled and ripped at the collar, but she'd pulled her hair back, not a strand astray. There was a welt the size of Linden Laughlin's open palm rising across one of her cheekbones, and her lip was split. She didn't say anything, just made those little sounds that people make when there aren't any other sounds that will do, and words don't mean anything anymore, anyway.

And that's how it was. That's how it was.

The Witch untied me, unbuttoned my overcoat and pulled my flannel shirt off. Then she untied my boots and pulled them and the wool socks off my feet. I'd been in those wet boots for so long that the skin was all wrinkly and white and awful under there. She stood up and went away while I took off my pants and underpants, and when she came back she grabbed up the whole fucking mess of clothing and carried it into the kitchen. She was melting snow in the big pot on the stove, and when it was melted, she threw my clothes in. She did all this without saying a word to me the whole time. She didn't even look at me.

I was fine with that.

I was thirteen. I thought I knew a few things. I knew about how jacks visited the women of the Lady Appleton's or the Idaho Hotel. Men being men the world over, I knew that there were places like that everywhere, where a man could pay a woman and receive something in return. I'd heard the jacks' stories of visiting The Lights, where a big, big boat called the *Miss Giggles* was docked at the water's edge. I knew about marriage, too, and how it leads to children and a settled life. But I didn't know the things then that I know now. All I saw was the Witch's face. The feelings in it were raw as a stripped sapling: the bark ripped off, the branches, the needles and the knots, all of it, everything just planed down until all that was left was a painful, fresh essence so alive that it hurt you to see it exposed to the air. That was terrible enough. But I was just a kid—I didn't know then how much worse Linden Laughlin had really hurt her.

She went to stand at the stove with her back to me, waiting for the water to boil and jamming the rolling pin in there every so often to stir the clothes around. She went out once and got more snow, then she stood there some more, not looking at me, just looking at the pot. I was sitting there, with burning eyes and goose pimples, trying to decide what to do, when she turned around and walked past me and into the bedroom and ripped the sheets and bedding up off the bed and dragged the heap in her arms into the kitchen and used the rolling pin to jam all them into the fire. She closed the door and stood up, turning to look at me in the wintery morning light with my hands cupped over my little pecker and my eyes burning from old kerosene and salt.

She gave me a rag dipped in warm water for my eyes. "Bed," she said, and I went. I crawled into my bed and pulled my covers up around my face so's only my nose stuck out. I watched the steam from the boiling water settle on the windowpane in heavy drops and then I slept. A lot later I woke up and she was there lying in bed next to me, her arm over my shoulders. Her arm had all those fine white hairs, and I looked at them while she slept. They flew every which way, those hairs on her arms, like they didn't know where they were going. Some were flying this way and others going that way and it made me so sad and so lonely to know that it was me she had her arm around and not someone else. My father would have protected us. Otto or Antti could have protected us. Otto would have been big enough to fight with Linden. Antti—with all his weird knowings—coulda done something. Peg Ramsay, Shorty Wade, Ed Kleinerd. They all coulda done more for the Witch than get themselves tied up in a closet. What if it was Bud Maynard lying here instead of me? I thought about what her arms, with all those little white hairs, would look like next to his black-haired ones.

The fire had burned down while we slept. I pulled on some fresh clothes and relit it. Then I took the clothes that had been boiling out of the pot and laid them on the stovetop to dry. You know that moment immediately after someone breaks something like a chair or a beer sign over your head and you know you've been knocked out and just haven't fallen yet? That's the feeling that I was having. I knew the real hurt was coming, but in that time before it did come I was just doing what I needed to do. I would go to The Lights. I would take the Witch with me. I would sell the Lost Lot to whoever would buy it and, like everybody else, pick up and leave this raggedy-ass town without so much as a final "fuck you."

I didn't have to go to school. Maybe Peg and Linden were right, goddamn them. I wasn't a lumberjack, but I could work, and that's just what I'd do. I'd work my way through the Cities of the Great Plains. I went forward, into the store, and pulled some cans off the floor and put them in a bag, then came back into the kitchen and ate some canned ham while I waited for my clothes to dry. When they mostly were, I folded them and put them in my bag, then went into the Witch's room. I picked my way quietly through the bits of china and splintered cabinet glass so she wouldn't hear me from my room where she was still sleeping and wake up. I pulled her old bag from under the bed and set it out on the stripped-bare mattress. There were a few pictures at the bottom, the first of a woman I took to be her sister. Her eyes were the same color as the Witch's, all ivory and shimmering in the black-and-white portrait.

The Witch woke up at my moving around and came out of my room to stand there in the doorway behind me. "Now I will read your fortune," she said.

We sat at the table, the Witch quiet, careful, as she placed the fragments of broken cups from the final tea set each upside down, covering the diviners as best she could. How she'd learned the things she'd learned only she knew, and the rules were such that only she understood them. Who could say the meaning of the items beneath the cups? A length of red string? A nail? The power in her magic had something to do with the Future, sure. But it also had something to do with the power she had to speak the truth of the World plainly.

She turned over a cup. A feather from some snowbird, and beneath another cup a ribbon of aspen bark. She took a long time in turning over the cups. Finally, she said, "He will not kill you."

"Do you know that for sure?" I asked.

"No one ever knows for sure. You will leave here. You will leave with me. You will go your way. Go to the Cities of the Great Plains," she said.

"And then what?" I asked.

"And then you will be alive. He will not kill you because you will not be there to kill. This is your fortune," she said.

"And what about you?" I asked.

"I will go back to my sister and her husband." She pulled a wad of bills from the pocket of her dress, money she'd made from prognostication. "For the tickets," she said.

"We won't be needing tickets just yet," I told her.

Even now it's hard to get to Cordy in the winter. But back then, once the real stuff started coming down in late fall, the road was impassable. Hell, Jensen and Webb had probably been the last ones to be able to make it through on their quest to bring Peg Ramsay to justice for bootlegging. But the Witch and I weren't gonna take the road. After the Witch was packed, I put on most of the clothes I owned and put some cans and a can opener into a burlap sack. I took my grandfather's ax, and the map and deed to the Lost Lot, and pulled the door shut behind us.

I couldn't help but take a last look up and down that deserted street. Shingles had been ripped from the roofs and snow now piled in. The facades had been torn away in search of Dream. Here and there a few dogs made their way back and forth across the road on dog business, but even that seemed to be mighty slow these days. All of it—the grim deprivation, the solitude, all set to Billy Lowground's pining melody. I thought about taking him with us to The Lights. Surely someone would have him. But Peg Ramsay had brought him here, like he'd brought everyone, and it didn't feel the same to take him as it did taking the Witch. Fuck me if I was going to be the one to turn off the music on my way out of town. That would have been too much to bear.

When we came to the Lost Lot cemetery, I walked out into the middle of the field. The ground that my father lay beneath had not yet sunk back level with the earth. The snow was mounded up on his grave like a mountain so that I felt like a bird soaring high above it. I let the ax fall from my shoulder into the snow, where it lay, waiting to rust and rot into the earth with the passing of the seasons.

I could have said sorry to my dad, but he was a ghost and he woulda known how sorry I really was, anyway. It wouldn't have done no good to speak it.

The Witch and I continued on until we stood at the spur, surrounded by the brackly branches of the lilac grove, and waited for the sound of the Ponderosa Express rolling down the line. A lone pine stood near enough to the tracks that the sweep of its boughs shadowed the rails. I went to the base of the tree, by an old oil drum, and brushed the snow away to expose a root. I felt under the root and pulled up a bottle, but knocking the dirt away I could see that it had turned to Dark Corner. Still and all, I wasn't planning on drinking just then and I wouldn't have drunk that evil stuff, anyway. I put some sticks and snapped branches into the drum and poured the Dark Corner all over and lit a match and set the fucker burning to keep us warm. Then we waited.

Hadn't the Witch seen this all coming? Hadn't she known it all, the whole goddamn story, the moment she'd set eyes on my father standing behind the counter of the shop? Hadn't she realized that all of this was coming down the tracks at her, like the train tracks lady in a Bud Maynard flick? Most people would say that fortune-telling is a load of garbage, but not me. To me, the Future is just a thin skin of ice on a frozen lake. No one can go stepping out onto it without it shattering all around them. The Future breaks around those who see it, and the Witch had seen the hell out of it. She was bruised-up pretty bad, lip all swollen and her right eye bloodshot.

"What's your sister's name?" I asked her, but she shook her head.

"Not here. I will not speak her name here. Not until we are far from here, far from The Lights, not until the Cities of the Great Plains will I speak her name," she said.

I could understand why. Linden Laughlin wasn't standing before us, blocking our passage. In fact, he wanted us to leave more than anything so he could steal the trees off my land. Still, his absence at this moment felt like a mouse-breath between cat paws. We weren't gone yet, weren't yet far enough away from those shadowy trees and that shadowy demon who made a game out of misfortune.

I felt something in the World change and went to put my ear to the track. You could hear it coming.

"We should climb," I told her.

She went up the tree first, her bag over her shoulder, using the boards nailed to the trunk and then climbing until she reached the great limb that overhung the tracks. I followed, quick as I could, behind her until we were both standing on the limb, holding the branch above us.

The Ponderosa Express came into view through the trees, and the rumble assembled itself into meter and music as it approached. We began to inch out along the giant branch. As we did, the train let out a scream so loud that snow drifted down all around us from the branches above. I felt our perch begin to shake from the force of the wind as the engine passed beneath us. After that, car after car after car whooshed by.

It had been my idea to catch the Ponderosa, but it was the Witch who jumped first, her feet swept out from under her as she landed on her back on the roof of a boxcar. She lay there a moment, being carried away from me, before I let go of the branch above my head and let myself fall into an open-topped car full of Christmas trees. I pushed my way through the trees and came to the coupling and then, like Bud Maynard himself, jumped across the gap to the ladder on the far side and climbed up on the roof of a boxcar. Far down the train I could see the Witch sitting there on her own boxcar, her hair blowing back in the wind, her face set away from Cordy, from me, toward the Cities of the Great Plains and somewhere beyond them, toward her sister.

LUST AND SKIPPING DEGRADATION

Oh, it's all gone now, The Lights. You won't find it and you'd be a fool to look. Sure, you could find the old Skid Row, but now it'd be a bank or a mattress store or a Greyhound station. It's all gone now, and I'm not saying that Magic is ever created or destroyed by this World, only that if you're looking for Magic don't go where The Lights used to be, because that shit is Gonesville. However big it had once been, however glorious and carnal it had once flowered before I first laid eyes on it, only soupbones and jack songs could say, but The Lights was still ornery and magical enough to be The Lights when the Ponderosa Express slowed to a stop near the outskirts and we climbed off and escaped into the night.

I didn't know much about The Lights that wasn't hearsay, goddamn me, but whatever hearsay I heard said told me that The Lights weren't the kind of place my mother would have wanted me walking around. I'd never been. But if Cordy was hell, The Lights were heaven. It was where the jacks, and not just jacks but seasonal workers of all stripes, would go at the close of their labors. After months at the bottom of a mine or cleaning fish guts, The Lights held the promise of laughter and forgetting. Imagine circling that flame for so long, feeling its warmth, and never once tipping a wing into its blazing core. But up until recently, I told myself, I had only been a kid.

Annie, who had grown up in The Lights and had met Peg when she was making rotgut at the Top Notch, said that there were underground rivers just beneath the street, and that you could float from card tables to T-bone steaks on streams of whiskey. She said that a person could walk through certain doors, give the sign or say the word, and the whole shitty World would fold back before their god-damn eyes and a new, golden World would wrap itself around them for a while.

Above the ground, where the businesses weren't trying outright to sell liquor, everything was lit up bright and colorful. These days I can look in my refrigerator and see every color that's ever been invented, but back then it wasn't like that. Back then, if you lived in a place like Cordy, you didn't get to see all the colors that a kid did who grew up in the Cities of the Great Plains. The Lights—with its lit-up theaters, flashing signs, restaurants, lunch wagons, its very fancy women, its cards sharks and its music—had more color all at once than I'd ever taken in at a single time.

Those colors swam around us as we yanked our stuff down the street, past street corner preachers and Wobblies, draft horses and stray cats, just an orphan and a Witch, spit out of the woods and mixed in with a river of other souls all headed somewhere else, among them all a moment as they drank and chased and fluttered around the flames of their own free choosing before heading off to work the silver mines, or to pick in the orchards or go back into the trees. I felt the deed and the map, folded up and safe in the inside pocket of my coat. The Lights was also the place to do business, and I had some business to do.

We found a boardinghouse that was nominally more hospitable than the Rooms Upstairs. I held the door for the Witch and followed her up a steep flight of stairs. Her head was down, and she was moving slow. Her hair had come undone from its loose braid and it fell around her shoulders all messy and unheeded. She dragged her sack of possessions behind her down the hallway. It made me so goddamn sad to see her like that, and not just sad, either. It made me angry and scared, too.

Our room was tiny, with two little beds that looked out on a muddied-up alleyway.

"I'll go and fetch us something to eat," I said, but she was already pulling off her clothes and making to get beneath the covers. They were pulled up over her head when I left her.

The land office was above a shoe factory with the words If You Can't Buy Shoes, Don't Buy Booze written in blue along an outer wall. "He's just closing now," a man in a brown hat and brown all-over suit said when I came in the door. He was reading a paper, had it all spread out in front of him, and didn't even look at me when he said it. "Suit yourself," he said when I walked by him.

"We're just closing up," the man behind the counter said. He was a skinny guy, with a sharp nose, looked like a minister.

"I got land to sell," I said. I slipped the deed under the slot for him to see.

The land office man wouldn't even look at it. "Come back tomorrow," he said. "We don't rush things like this."

"I'll take this, Harold," the man with the brown suit said, stepping up beside me.

"We're closing, Meeker."

"I know, I know, the horror. Let's hear the boy out, Harold. Be a Christian."

"There's nothing to hear out," I said. "I got prime timberland to sell." I pulled out the map and the deed. The man named Meeker leaned in closely to see. After a bare instant he straightened again. "That?" he said, like he was offended. "Kid, I wouldn't give you two middling-sized turds for that parcel. Everybody knows that land is cursed."

"*And* we're closed," the land office man said again.

"There's trees on it bigger than anyone has ever seen," I told Meeker. "Whoever logs it will be a hat-tipping millionaire."

"Whoever logs the Lost Lot is a fool and a dead man, kid," Meeker said. "At least twenty men died the last time that someone tried to log that parcel. The best jacks there are. Everyone knows that ground is all cliffs and avalanches and heartbreak. You're not gonna find a man breathing with a brain in his skull who would buy that land from you—you can't even give away a lot like that. You think that if Illini Match Company can't get the trees out that anyone else can? Get away from me with that nonsense. I don't even want to touch your filthy map, and don't tell anyone I ever saw it. That place is cursed."

"I said we're closed," said the land office man. "Now get out, both of you." And he pulled shut the wooden partition over the window of the office and that was fucking that.

I went back to the boardinghouse, but the Witch was asleep, and the room was dreary and cold. I noticed that the Witch hadn't taken off her shoes before climbing into bed. I untucked the blankets and pulled the shoes off her feet, then I sat on the edge, in the curl between her knees and chin. She looked up at me from the corner of her eye, but when she knew I was going to say something she closed her eyes again. Still, a tear puddled up and ran down the side of her nose. I wanted to wipe it away, but I felt too dirty to do it. I let another tear roll by, and when that one was gone, I left the room and headed back down to the street. I was starving.

Tomorrow I'd go back to the land office early, I told myself, but I already had a sick feeling in my guts that it was hopeless. The man, Meeker, had laid it out squarely enough. To hear his superstitious ass explain it, the Lost Lot was cursed, and I was cursed for owning it, and anyone else nearby was cursed by association. I shouldn't expect to get anything for the land. So, there it was, the Lost Lot was mine to keep or to abandon. I fished around in my thoughts, looking for a way that I could somehow do both, but there was none. Whether I kept the land or whether I gave it up and let Linden Laughlin take it from me, the Lost Lot would be with me forever as the first, irrevocable decision I would make as a man.

I was wandering down the street like this, thinking thoughts like that, when a bunch of filthy silver miners came piling out of a doorway, all elbows and shoulders and piggybacks and laughing. I got knocked and tried to catch my balance on a cart handle but no luck. Next thing I knew I was down on the ground and mad as a hornet.

If I was to title my life story up to this juncture, I could have done worse than calling it *On the Fucking Floor*. I had been on the ground against my will so many times in the last several months that one more shouldn't have mattered, but it did. It just fucking *did* matter. I had barely hit the ground when I was bouncing back up again, figuring how I was gonna take on five or six full-grown men. I figured I could get two from behind by kicking their knees out from under them, and after that I'd improvise, but then something flashed on the ground. It was a thin golden crack, and when I looked closer the crack rippled with light. Some people passed me on either side as I got back down on my hands and knees and put my eye right up to the crack. Far below were tables and tables of men and women drinking, laughing, playing cards, crowding around one another, swaying to music. I looked up and down the street to see if anyone had noticed me noticing what I'd noticed, but people just rambled on by me without a second look.

I put my eye back down to the crack in the paving stones. A group of pretty women wearing top hats were fanning out between the tables. I saw the flash of firelight against some kind of brass horn. I looked up at the doorway I was kneeling in front of. The Top Notch. Some of the window glass had been knocked out of the front window and been replaced with boards. Whatever windows were left were grimy and grease-stained and everyone inside looked the color of a smoker's thumb. There was a pile of chicken feet by the door. It didn't look like the kind of place that Annie would have ever gone to work in.

Annie.

People who tell you they're disappointed in you are full of the worst kind of shit and you can always ignore them. The stuff they say only means that you're doing what you want to do, not what they want you to do. It's the people who really *do* care about you who will never tell you when you've hurt them. Annie hadn't said a word to me after I'd shrugged away from her. She'd tried to comfort me, and I'd turned away. Well, I hadn't turned away, I'd fallen on my ass, but it amounted to the same thing. Goddamn it. I woulda made it up to her, explained myself the next day, something like that, but then Jensen and Webb and the other probie agents had come around and Annie had taken off to who-the-hell-knew-where before they could nab her.

So, I went inside and found a place at the counter.

Maybe once upon a long, long time ago, the Top Notch hadn't been such a terrible-looking place. The tile that lined the countertops and the walls had been white at one point, and maybe still could be again, but whoever had once fought that battle had given up and tied a white flag to a mop stick years ago, judging by the level of disgustingness all around. You coulda killed a pig in there and the place would only have gotten cleaner.

I was looking at an ancient man gumming his way through a piece of ham that appeared old enough to be his own son. He was looking about as awful as everyone else in there, maybe a shade worse. It looked to be a fucking unforgiving piece of meat, so he wasn't paying much attention to anything else. I asked the guy behind the counter if he knew a girl named Annie, but even as I said it, I knew that it was a stupid question. The guy didn't answer me, just went on cooking whatever it was he was cooking.

"Hey," I said. I was thirteen, goddamn it, a man by anyone's standards. "Hey!" I said again. The cook turned around and threw such a mean-ass look at me that it discombobulated me, and I forgot about asking him again if Annie was around and instead put the dime on the counter. "I want a cup of coffee," I said.

The coffee was yellow and tasteless but at least it was hot. I sat there warming up, watching the soupbones gum his ham and feeling generally miserable. It wasn't long before I heard shouting and laughing coming from the back of the restaurant as a door swung open and some men came out. As they passed, I caught a glimpse into a small room with a nice little chandelier hung way up near the ceiling. The crystals danced against each other with the sound of the music and dancing below. There was one of those statues that's just a man's head, and someone had glued some sparkly pieces of glass to its eyes. The eyes were looking down into the darkness at the bottom of a long flight of stairs. Whoever was playing the piano down there knew how to play and had half an orchestra with them.

I left the counter and headed back through the door. The music grew louder. I started down the steps, holding on to the banister as it began to get real dark. Below, the stairs just seemed to fall away into a pit of blackness and laughter. It got darker and darker until I was testing with my toes for each new step as the laughter turned to laughter and music, turned to laughter and music and shouting and dancing and stomping. I wondered if there really would be a bottom at all or if I was gonna keep going down, down, down forever, down to the kind of hell that birthed villains like Linden Laughlin.

At the bottom of the steps I turned a corner and a blaze of a hundred fucking colors washed over me. I'd seen some things before. I'd seen a stockade full of labor organizers. I'd seen two dogs get stuck together fucking. I'd seen half the girls at the Idaho Hotel more than half-naked, and I'd seen men get so drunk that they thought they were Jesus Christ's next of kin, but the confusion and lust and skipping degradation now before my eyes made me realize I'd been living through one long church picnic.

The hall was large and vaulted, with brick pillars and a

springy wooden dance floor. Through the mist of liquor and sweat and smoke I could make out the very far end of the hall, where not one but two pianos and piano players sat up on a large stage, flanked by what must have been ten men to either side, all dressed up like millionaires, and all playing whatever they were playing as loud as they could play it. Running outward from the stage were long tables, and down those long tables kept traipsing all these beautiful women, stepping between the drinks and card games. As I watched, one girl pulled a bottle from behind her back and, without even bending over, poured a long stream of liquor down into a glass on the table. The men nearby her cheered, but the sound was drowned out by the music and the clamor of a boxing ring to my right. A long bar stretched the other side of the room, and above it the largest, most nakedest painting of a woman I've ever seen. Barrels of apples were everywhere, and barrels of peanuts, too.

I tried to picture Annie in one of those top hats I'd seen, pouring liquor into glasses, but I just couldn't. Then, all at once, I was afraid that I *would* see her. What would I say to her then, after how I'd treated her? *Help me? I'm sorry?*

I felt a tap on the back of my head, and I knew it was her. I turned around, looking for words to tell her all that had happened, how much more had gone wrong since the probie agents had come, how sorry I was, how terrible Linden Laughlin had turned out to be, how I'd stumbled on the Top Notch and then found my way down here and was she happy to see me?

The woman who met my eyes was shorter than I was

and very, very old. She wore a wide-brimmed white hat with a splash of purple flowers in it, and her dress was light purple, too. She had white gloves on and carried a little white purse. If it wasn't for the rolled-up newspaper that she had clutched in her hand, she could have been coming home from a church service.

She whacked me good with the newspaper. "How old are you?" She whacked me again. "How? Old? Are? You?"

I put up my hands to cover my face. "I'm thirteen!" I said.

She poked me in the guts. "You! You're thirteen and I'm twenty-six! Get out of town that you're thirteen." She poked me again, "How old are you?"

"I am thirteen, ma'am," I told her. "I'm looking for a friend."

"Everyone is looking for a friend," she spat. "That's the story of the World. Do you know how old you have to be to even set foot down here?" She grabbed me by my ear.

"No, I don't know!" I yelled. She really had me by that ear.

"Sixteen is how old you have to be." Men got up and moved out of her way as she began dragging me back toward the door. "Even so, you're thirteen if I'm Napoleon Bonaparte." She kicked a chair out of her path. "Move!" she snapped at a big lug biting into an apple. She pulled me through the doorway and into the dark stairwell, leaving the big, noisy hall behind. "Do you know why they hire me to watch the door? Because they think no one will hit an old woman. And you know what?" I was heading up the staircase, ear-first. "They're right."

"I'm just looking for Annie!" I shouted through the pain. "Tell me she ain't here, and I'll go."

"Which Annie?" the woman said. She was still dragging me up the stairs. "Honeysuckle Annie, Dynamite Annie, Switchblade Annie or Kitchen Annie?"

"I'm looking for the one who brews rotgut," I said. My eyes were watering from the pain. The old lady stopped hustling me up the steps.

"Why are you looking for Rotgut Annie?" She whacked me with the rolled-up newspaper until I answered.

"Stop!" I yelled, trying to shield my face. "She's a friend of mine. I came to tell her sorry."

"Lordy, is she already old enough for men to start telling her 'sorry'?" the old woman asked. "I remember when she was still small." She began to fan herself with the newspaper. "I must be getting ancient," she said. Then, "Is she still working with Peg Ramsay, that no-account, good-for-nothing charmer?"

"Peg got picked up by the probies," I told her. "Annie disappeared, and then…a lot of stuff happened. I know that she worked here before. I'm trying to find her."

"Well, she's not here, or I'd know," the old lady said. "If she was in The Lights at all, then you could taste it in the booze. They might call it rotgut, but even a minister could pick out Rotgut Annie's work by the taste. And you," she said, looking me up and down. "What do you have to apologize to Annie about? I'm very fond of that girl, fonder than I am of most who consort with Mr. Ramsay, anyways."

"I was a fool to her," I said.

"I'm sure that you were," the old lady said, grabbing my ear again, and started walking. The glass-eyed statue watched us hustle by. She kicked open the door to the diner and swung me through. "Now get out for three more years," she said, making a big old show of clapping the dust off her gloves, "and if you *do* find Rotgut, tell her that the widow Estelle always has a spare room for her."

The door slammed closed and I stood in the middle of the dingy desolation of that shitty diner. Men with heads bowed low slurped soup and coffee, or else scraped forks on metal plates.

"It's alright, bub," the old guy said to me over his ham. He gazed wistfully at the back doorway. "At least she's gonna let you back in someday."

I took one last look at the soupbones. To this very day, to this very fucking hospital bed some eighty-odd years later, I can still picture him as I left, working on that piece of ham. Jesus, he looked rough. I know that lying here I'm nothing to get exactly dewy-eyed over, either. Now that I've been shot in the head and in the fucking hip it doesn't look like I'll be getting any prettier anytime soon. Oh, sure, some folks could look at me here, shot in the head and in the hip and with all these tubes for jewelry, and think that old Weldon is entitled to have some sympathy for himself. Well, maybe that's true and maybe it isn't, but I can tell you for a fucking stone-cold surety that I look healthier now than that old-timer in the Top Notch.

I felt the map and the deed, crease-worn and thick in my pocket. Through the grime of the window and across the street, the marquee of a movie theater pulsed. A smiling picture of Bud Maynard hung above the ticket window.

The girl who sold me the ticket was pretty, but she wasn't as pretty as Annie, and the girl who tore my ticket in two wasn't as pretty as Annie, either. I'd never been in a movie theater before. As I waited in the dark for the show to begin, I tried to imagine that Annie was sitting there right next to me, right by my side like she used to when we'd watched Bud Maynard movies back in Shorty Wade's. I knew she wasn't actually there with me, but it was nice to think that at any moment she could lean over and whisper something funny or tell me to hold on to my seat because Bud was gonna get in some real trouble this time. Like I said, I knew she wasn't there, but it was still a little sad when the first reel came on and the theater began to dance with light, and I looked around and there was no one in the whole place but me and the organist.

The first reel that went up seemed to be a biographical film about Bud himself. Bud came galloping across the screen on Tony the Wonderhorse, the two of them being chased by an angry crowd. It was a silent movie, but you could feel Tony's hoofbeats in your guts above the organ music if you tried. The first letter board came up.

The life of Bud Maynard is just as full of adventure as the characters he has played in all of his Stereogram pictures.

Bud had jumped on a truck and was fighting someone. He looked like he was having just a grand old time.

As a young man he was a noted frontier scout and rode up San Juan Hill with Teddy and his celebrated Rough Riders.

Bud and Tony the Wonderhorse were in the corral doing tricks, Bud going up and over Tony, then under and around him, Tony all the while lifting one leg and then the next, twirling around this way and that as Bud showed off.

From 1907 to 1911 he served in our nation's army in the Philippines, where he was badly wounded.

Well, now, I was taken aback a bit by this. Here was Bud Maynard, who said he was in the Philippines when actually he was in the St. Anne, trying to work a homestead. I knew that was the case because everyone said he was there—Peg, Shorty Wade and Ed Kleinerd, all of them—so unless Bud Maynard could be in two places at once, and unless Peg Ramsay and everyone I'd ever known was lying to me, then Bud Maynard had some explaining to do.

It was Bud who was lying about where he was and when. It was like he cut a ragged patch the size of the St. Anne out of his life as if it had never existed and then sprung, a fully formed American Hero, onto the screen in front of me. He wasn't in the Philippines getting shot at with arrows or hacked all over with machetes and he wasn't riding up San Juan Hill on Tony the Wonderhorse next to

Teddy Roosevelt. He'd been out on his homestead claim, sitting there trying to stay fed and keep from freezing his pecker off, I bet, eating whatever food folks threw his way.

What did he do when he realized he wasn't gonna get real rich, real quick off his piece of land? Well, he'd sold it. He'd sold it like all the rest of those homesteaders that were just sitting there and waiting for the timber companies to come and buy it up off them. Maybe he took the money and bought a train ticket that would take him as far as he could go. The screen in this theater was enormous, and Bud's face was glowing so white that you could see that it was some kind of powder they put on his face. His hands, too. His eyebrows were black. His eyes were black. He looked like a ghost. He was a ghost, is what he was, just a shadow on a screen and not a real man anymore. He walked around on ground that wasn't real, rode on horses that weren't real, jumped on phantom trains that rolled away on phantom tracks, rolled around in the dirt fighting men who were paid to let him win and protected phantom girls who got hired to fucking phantom faint in his fucking phantom arms every time he tipped his hat in their direction.

Goddamn it, the only thing he had that was real, really *real*, was that piece of timber in the St. Anne. But that hadn't been real to him, either, had it? He wasn't like my father, who died working his own piece of ground. I knew what was gonna happen to Bud Maynard. He was gonna one day get his head stepped on by Tony the numb-nut Wonderhorse while he was showing off. Or he was gonna fall wrong and sprain his wrist and die of it. But where would he be when he was taking his dying breaths? Who knew? I knew *how* he was gonna die, you know—the smallness of it, the triviality of it—but I didn't know *where*. He didn't have no piece of ground. Not like my father did. Not like I did. I closed my eyes to the screen and saw my grandfather's ax, my father's ax, my ax. I saw the Lost Lot itself, that deadly, impressive fucker, biting at the sky. My grandfather's land, my father's land, mine.

I didn't look back as I left the theater, but the flickering light of Bud Maynard doing something ridiculous guided me up the aisles. The air outside was as sharp to breathe as crackled bits of glass, but it was better to be out here with the rest of the living, hunching up the cruddy, slushy street in froze-through boots and an empty stomach, than to sit for one second more in that theater. It had been the worst, most terrible day ever, but somehow, through the pain, things had suddenly gotten real, real clear.

I slammed into the Top Notch like a grizzly bear. I banged my hand on the counter and ordered half of the menu. I ate it all and stood up and banged my hand on the counter again until the cook turned and gave me another piece of his stink-eye.

"Pencil," I said. I gave him that stink-eye right back and waited for him to tell me no. He shrugged, left the grill and tossed me over a pencil. "Coffee," I said. He gave me coffee. I took the map out of my pocket, turned it over and began to write.

Annie,

Before you left, I wanted to tell you how sorry I am if I hurt your feelings that night in Shorty Wade's. That is not what I wanted to do or ever would want to do. You had every right to be mad at me and disappointed, too, but you always treated me good and you didn't deserve how I treated you back and that almost breaks my heart. I came in here looking for you but you weren't here so I will just tell you that I'm going home to work my piece of land that Linden Laughlin is trying to scare me off of. Anyway, like I said, I'm real, real sorry and I hope that we are still friends.

—Weldon

"If Rotgut Annie comes in here, you give her this," I told the cook. I put the map under the money for my meal. "You could throw it away, or you could not be an asshole. Me and her are friends."

YOU'D NEED A DOUBLE ISSUE

"You wouldn't know 'cause you weren't there," is how fucking Joe always starts up, cranking away at one of his yarns like he's trying to start his snowblower. A lot of people thought Joe Mouffreau was a hero, just the cat's ass, but I was never fooled by him, not even in the beginning, when he was fresh back to town from the War, got a fancy car and drove around spending his daddy's timber mill money. Still, I let him talk. It didn't take but a few months of him telling his war stories before the numbers of killed and wounded had grown to a considerable enough size that most folks stopped giving his estimates quite the fucking credence he thought they deserved. If you think Joe Mouffreau was sharp enough to realize it, though, you don't know Joe Mouffreau. Most people who found themselves telling a worn-out story like the ones Joe told would notice that folks' eyes were glazing over and they'd decide that maybe they'd hold off on recounting the same goddamn story for the thirty-seventh time.

Joe took the *opposite* way of thinking, and whenever he saw anyone's attention start to wander off toward something more exciting—a saltshaker, maybe, or a busted neon sign—he'd add a few more bodies, a few more tanks and some of those kamikaze pilots the Japanese had so many of.

Only last year they did a story on Joe for the *Spokane Daily News* and he got to tell his story in full, don't you know? He came into the Brothers Swede with about ten copies under his arm and put them out on the bar for Paulette and everyone to gawk at. I didn't even need to read it to know what it said. Joe had fought off the entire Japanese armed forces and saved the American Way, more or less. Yeah, Carnage and Desolation and Joe Mouffreau walked hand in hand everywhere he went through that conflagration. It was a merciful goddamn miracle to all that we had him on our side. "You weren't there so you won't know this, Weldon, but..."

My God, it's not like I ain't seen enough death just living in one place my whole life. Jesus. You live long enough you see 'em die all kinds of ways you can imagine. I saw three, *three* men killed by getting electrocuted, and only one of those was by lightning. Colum Sullivan, who was from Canada, got crushed between two heavy-loaded railroad cars. They weren't moving hardly at all; they just kind of drifted together while he was walking between them, smooshed him like a screaming grape. The Keltners, they were a real nice family that moved into town about ten years ago, burned to death, all of them in a fire. A man I worked with one season by first or last name Moses got swallowed up and run down by a river full of logs after he busted up a jam with dynamite. I've seen men with perfectly good guns knife each other to death like assholes when they coulda gotten the job done quicker, just because they were born plain ferocious. Measles, mumps, polio, flu and fucking drink. Trees falling the wrong way, logs jumping the chute, donkey boilers exploding, dead falls, hypothermia, broken bones. The list of unfortunate fucks that I've seen die is at least as long as that fucking article they wrote about Joe Mouffreau. You'd need a double issue. No, I'm not afraid of dying.

And anyway, I have a plan.

If you don't think the Witch was pissed enough to spit fire when I told her I was going back to my claim, then you don't know the Witch. When I say that she cursed, I mean that she was actually cursing—Tom, Linden Laughlin, the Lost Lot, the fucking cold, the fucking torn-up store, all of it. She went back into her old language to do it, but I got the gist. She didn't curse me, though, at least I don't think she did. And I didn't change my mind in the face of her fury, either.

"You said he wouldn't kill me," I reminded her.

"Because you will not be there," she said.

But I was going to be there, and I suppose she saw it in my eyes and in my Future. I went with her to the train station and stood there mute while she bought her ticket and waited for her train. Then she was gone away, and there were no long goodbyes or waving from the window or nothing like that. I could just make out her face through the frosted panes of the passenger car as the train pulled away, but I could no more read those plumes of frost than I could read the Witch's teacups. Finally, I was standing alone on the platform before a set of empty tracks, waiting on my own train.

I slipped down the railway line to the outskirts of The Lights where I was out of sight. The Ponderosa wasn't long in coming, and when it did it was already picking up speed. With no Tony the Wonderhorse to help me, I ran alongside the train, full-sprint, and pulled myself aboard, into an empty boxcar, being really damn careful the whole time not to get caught and pulled down beneath those razoring wheels. I found a place in the corner of the car where the wind from the open door wasn't whooshing quite so hard, and I fell fast asleep.

When I awoke, the heavy sky outside the speeding train hung in the doorway of the boxcar like a stone wall going all the way up to heaven and all the way down to hell, ready for me to bash my brains and bloody my fists against. I'd lost that angry, hungry feeling, though. I was just tired. Tired and sad and missing the Witch, missing Tom and Annie, and even crusty, mean Peg. The tired and the sad swirled around inside me like cold coffee in a porcelain bowl all the way back to Cordy, through the hemlock and fir and ponderosa, along the endless, bending river. I rolled past logged-

out ghost towns, where the broken-down buildings that I
saw were dark and their few windows rattled in their sills to
the beating wind. Gnawed-down old soupbones peered out
of them, sucking their toothless gums and worrying their
swollen knuckles with ancient thumbnails as I rumbled past.

The train tracks stitched the ragged, stump-ravaged fabric of the land to the dense, shadowy forest that remained
beyond. As the Ponderosa Express tunneled back into the
trees, the wall in my mind loomed larger and larger, so high
up that it seemed as if it might be leaning over me. Whether
I was to scale it or beat my way through it I couldn't have
said. Whether that wall was Linden Laughlin or the Lost
Lot or something inside me I couldn't have said, either. I
almost jumped off the train a dozen times on that trip back.
But maybe, I thought, Linden Laughlin could hear the train
coming across all those miles, too. Maybe he knew that I
was coming for him and he was scared, deep down. I told
myself all of this, hoping it was true, but still the only thing
I could feel was sad and tired, and that hungry anger was
gone. I wasn't big like Otto and I couldn't stop blood from
flowing out of a wound like Antti. I wasn't a knower like
the Witch. I couldn't read the stars that made the bird-way.
I was only Weldon Applegate, thirteen, with cold fingers
and a bruised-up face. Then I saw the grove of lilac trees,
naked, scraggly and finger-boned, and it was time to jump.

Bud Maynard jumped on and off trains every chance
he could get; it didn't matter how much extra trouble he
had to go through to do it. For a man with the best horse
on Earth, he just couldn't sit in the saddle when he saw a

puff of smoke coming up over the horizon. No, he had to climb up on the roof of that train and ride there awhile, if possible, fighting with whoever wanted to climb up there with him. I'd like to say that since I'd made up my mind about him, I wasn't looking up to Bud Maynard for anything, but when it came to jumping off trains, I couldn't help but think back on him for clues as to how it might be done best. I woulda thought on it for a while longer, but the grove was coming up fast and I took a deep breath, as if about to plunge into ice water, and jumped.

I was in midair, high over the embankment, the ground rising slowly up to meet me, when it came to me all of a sudden that Bud had never jumped off a train and landed on his own two feet. I'd seen more than a dozen of his movies, and as I floated along through the air, I searched my memory for one paltry instance in which he'd ever jumped and *not* landed square in the saddle of Tony the Wonderhorse, who had been galloping along beside the train, smooth as silk, the whole time. Well, I didn't have any old horse at all, so right then and there I began to resign myself to, and prepare myself for, a rougher landing than was in Bud Maynard's movies generally.

And a rough landing is what I got. Somehow, as I was thinking back on all those movies, I'd gone from being upright to being in a more lying-down position. For a while I was flying on my stomach and then I turned over and was going sidestroke through the air for a bit more. I might have gone on gracefully like this, but at that moment I hit the lilac trees and scraped through their skeletal branches, landing hard in a crusty bank of snow. I lay there and waited for my breath to come back, listening as the wheels of the train disappeared into the wilderness. It wasn't how you'd ever see Maynard land, but then in real life Maynard was a coward and a clown and there was probably someone in Hollywood who he paid to carry around a silk sheet for him so his ass cheeks would never get outhouse splinters. "Fuck you, Bud," I told him as I lay there. "You'd still be on that train."

I tried sitting up once, and then decided against it and gave it a few more minutes. When I finally did get to my feet, though, I was surprised that I didn't seem to hurt any more than I had before I jumped. I seemed to be getting used to having the shit knocked out of me. Maybe, I thought as I climbed up into a lilac tree to grab my bag, maybe I was even getting to like it a little.

I walked back toward town only as far as the Lost Lot cemetery. I stomped out through the deep snow, the juts of wooden crosses guiding my way between the graves, until I came to my father's mound. For a moment I was afraid that the ax was gone, but I scraped away a crust of snow and it was there. I pulled it from the snow and held it up in the cold winter light. It was dark-handled and silver-tipped, still sharp from where my father had cared for it before he was killed. Then I looked past the ax and out at the mountains. They were greeny-black and foreboding as fuck. I could have gone back to the lilac grove at the spur and waited on the Ponderosa Express again, but I had the ax in my hand. My ax. I had put it down once. I would not put it down again.

MUST HAVE BEEN GRAND

Nowadays no one knows anything about what those days were like back then. Somewhere back around 1930 or so, near as I can figure, some jackass in a suit invented the idea of fucking pushing a button to do whatever you wanted to do. Maybe it wasn't real obvious at the time what that kind of shit was gonna lead to, but someone musta been paying attention, because by the fifties there was buttons every-fucking-where. It got to be so that for a thing to work it had to have lots of buttons on it for people to push. Used to be that the only things with buttons, and ivory at that, was pianos and fucking *brassieres*, but by the time Joe Mouffreau was settled back in the St. Anne and helping his daddy clear-cut every stand of trees he could lay his hands on, there was so many different types of buttons that they started to be all types of colors, too, arranged all together like flowers in a flower bed. And to complicate things more, there were some buttons that if you *didn't* push them, they'd do something. Some buttons needed pushing.

So, what you ended up with was a bunch of people sitting in front of a bunch of buttons, pushing them in all kinds of orders and combinations, just trying to keep the goddamn things happy. It was overwhelming. It's no big wonder someone got the idea to have one button to do everything. That's how you got the situation we have now where you can press one button and you get your soup hot, one button to run your car, even one-button chain saws. I can press this button here in my hospital bed and it gives me the fucking medicine to keep the fucking pain out of my fucking hip. I've been pressing it like crazy, I don't care. I press it, and the drip comes out of that bag. I guess that I could hold my thumb down and let the medicine just wash through my veins until it carries my soul bobbing away with it. I get a rushing in my ears when I hold the button down, like white water, but warmer.

What I'm trying to say is that stuff got to be easier gradually, over time, and no one noticed it happen. It even happened on the soaps I watched during the day at the Brothers Swede, now that I think about it. There used to be all kinds of folks doing stuff on those shows. Now, though, they just walk around each other and stand here by the lamp and stand there by the big leather sofa and say stuff like, "Do you want it, Victor? Do you want it all?" and there's never any cooking going on, or people parking their fucking cars or standing in line or any of the rest of the human condition. The commercials are all for cooking and cleaning stuff, all on the same one-button system. That mop that you tie little towels to, that cake mix where the only work is cracking three eggs into it. Christ, the chickens work harder to make that cake than the cook putting it in the oven and pressing the one fucking button. "Did you make this?" one woman says to the other while she's eating cake. The other one rolls her eyes and smiles to herself because she knows all about the one-button cake.

If I'm gonna tell you about logging back then, you ought to know that there were no fucking buttons nowhere. I can tell you it was dangerous and you'll say, "No shit," and you'll be right and I'll let you nod your head and say, "Old Weldon is a real blowhard with the improving type of memory," but unless you spend a winter pulling logs off a snowy mountainside you won't ever know just how dangerous it was. This here is where I broke my arm top-loading on Flewsie Creek in 1953. I had narrow misses a hundred times, and I've broken bones that I've forgotten about breaking and only remember when I start to feel them in the fall. Part of it was the terrain. The St. Anne is huge fucking trees on steep fucking mountains, cold fucking rivers, hard fucking rocks and all of it a long, long slog from anyone with morphine and a bone saw. Oh, there were plenty of blades around, mind you—axes, crosscut saws, splitters, all that. All that stuff could cut you way easier than it cut wood. So there was that.

But let's say you do a good job and cut through a tree without cutting your own leg off, then you have to worry about which way the goddamn thing is going to fall. Maybe it knocks down some other trees when it falls, maybe it throws one of those big knife-y splinters of greenwood up into your eye as it cracks free from the stump. Or you might end up like my father did, with two hundred feet of white pine in your face. Then, once the tree is down, you've got to get it to the river, which of course is at the total bottom of the mountain. You don't just pack it a lunch and say, "So long, you big fucking fuck, and don't forget to write." A tree falling in the forest don't mean nothing to no one; it's a tree floating in the river that gets you paid, so you've got to get it down the mountain gently. If you just roll it down it'll get battered up by all the other trees and rocks it hits on the way, and every little ding it gets, the less money goes in your pocket. Believe me, there isn't anyone in the World tighter than a fucking sawmiller counting board feet. Go dig up fucking Joe Mouffreau's daddy and ask him, the stingy fuck. The only way you'd get a nickel out of him was if you stuck your own spoon up his ass and he pressed one for you, and even then, he'd take two cents off the top for labor. So, you've got to get the tree down to the river some other way, which is where skidding and chuting come in.

Skidding was where you'd stick some big hooks into a log and drag it somewhere behind horses or oxen. That's why Paul Bunyan had his big ox—to drag the trees around. "Go with fucking God," I always said about oxen. First of all, they're fucking stupid is why. Stupid and stubborn. It's a tough job, of course, and they're not getting paid and they're getting whipped up and down a stupid mountain all day, so they got a right to be stubborn, but still that don't change the fact of how stupid they are. The only way to get them to pull a tree is by teaching them to do it new every fucking time. Oxen need a lot of grass and hay. They don't do good when you give them grain. They eat too much and swell up and die. Plus, they tip over on steep hills. Otto was good with oxen. I wasn't ever any good with them. I liked horses.

Horses are more artistic about the whole enterprise. Jenny, who was a horse I had for a while and took around from job to job, got to be so good at judging trees that you could point her up into the woods and say, "Get on, now," and she'd just climb ahead of you up the mountain until she came to a tree that looked about right to her and she'd pull up and wait patiently to the side so you could cut it down. Then she'd move a bit more, so you had plenty of room to strip the branches. When she judged that you were just about done with the stripping, she'd mosey on down the hill a piece and wait for you to set the tie-hooks to the downward end of the tree, and after that all you had to do was give her a click of the tongue and she was off, pulling the whole thing wherever you needed it pulled. Good skid horses could get to be almost legendary. Belle and Blue were two that were like that. They were Corkboard Corrigan's team and by the time they were worn out with mountain work they'd become so famous that the president got to meet them when he came through The Lights one year.

I don't remember who it was that had for a while this big, black horse that everyone called "Little Sugar." I was there one morning when Little Sugar came to stand near the fire and watched us eating our lunch as we stomped around in the cold. For a joke, someone poured him a cup of coffee with a little sugar. That goddamn horse drank it down, hot, and looked up for more. Over that drive, the cook took to putting aside a whole extra pot of coffee and some sugar lumps, all for Little Sugar.

So, horses were great and if logs had only needed to be dragged on flat ground that would have been the end of the story. Mountain work was dangerous for horses, too, though. The log could get snagged on another tree and swing around, roll out of control and drag them down the mountain. The horses could get stuck in the snow and get plowed under by the log behind them. They could break their legs in the underbrush beneath a drift or chip a hoof on the jutting rocks. Still, you needed something to take those trees from the place they fell and either pull them slowly down the slope to the river, which was time-consuming and risky, or pull them to a log chute.

Once you'd cut the tree down and bucked its branches, leaving only the trunk, you pulled it to the chute however you could and then gave it a push down the mountain. The chute was made with spruce or fir, in a kind of U-shape so that the logs could rest in them. If the log needed help to get moving, you'd slick up the chute with icy water. You wanted to make sure that there were no nicks or knots in the chute wood because anything that might catch the logs could end up marring the whole bunch of them or might even send a log jumping out of the chute and end-over-ending down the mountainside. Besides being a waste of a good piece of timber, it was also a good way to get killed. That was the same reason you didn't build a whole lot of curves into your chute, either. Sometimes, once they got going, the trees would shoot down the chute so fast that they'd smoke. That was how fast they could go. You know what doesn't make a lot of sound? A fucking tree jumping a chute and flying like Fate itself through the air toward the back of your head.

Once you got them down to the bottom you didn't have no gravity helping you to move the logs, so the chute would empty out into a holding pond, like cattle in a pen. You'd put the big old pile of timber there, and then, when you were ready for a true bitch of a time, you started to build a dam in front of those logs with the aim of accumulating enough water behind it that you could float those fuckers into the river and guide them to the sawmill to get paid.

"That doesn't sound bad," you're saying to yourself as you cut the crust off your little fucking sandwiches. "Working in the great outdoors and all that. Must have been grand." Oh, it was, it was. But you weren't working out there in the summertime, were you, because there was no water coming down the mountain in the summertime, was there? By then all the snowpack had melted. The time to float the logs out was the fucking middle of March to the middle of April when the river was running high enough to carry your logs over the river rocks. If the thaw came early and your trees weren't down the mountain and ready to be rolled into the river you were fucked. And if the thaw came late and everyone went off to work other jobs you were fucked, too. And if there wasn't enough snow that year and not enough water came off the mountains, you were fucked then, as well.

Finally, if you got your timber to the river you still had to drive it, keep the logs from centering out in the middle of the current where it got more shallow, drive the way-ward ones from the edges of the flow where sweeper trees could snag up a whole shit ton of timber and pull it off into the marsh ground and gum up the whole works, and finally, when the works *did* get gummed up and you had a big log jam, someone had to go out there with a spike-ended peavey pole and slow-fuse dynamite and try to blow the jam away. If you lived through all of that and didn't get exploded by the dynamite, crushed by a big wall of tumbling logs, drowned in the river, dashed against the rocks, frozen to death, impaled by your own peavey, lost in an avalanche, crippled by a widow-maker snowfall or killed by any of the other ways that are too numerous and creative to even try imagining, if you lived through all of that and got your trees to the sawmill, you had to take what they were gonna give you for them. Sometimes the price was good and sometimes it was worse than fucking terrible, straight-up down-by-the-riverside murder. Still, by the time you'd gotten the timber there, what the hell else were you gonna do with it—float it back up the river, push it up the mountain and prop it back up on its stump?

One fucking button would have been pretty useful up there, I suppose. But buttons were for men like Joe Mouf-

freau. I guess that being a jack was something more ancient than that. The two forces were like lamp oil and river
water; they didn't mix, and it only takes a look from the
top of my mountain to see who won. Clear-cuts as far as
the eye can see.

THE LUNATIC,
WILD, JOLLY KIND

God doesn't build shit. Yeah, He creates stuff—the World,
the mountain ranges, all that—but any fuck with one eye
left in his head will tell you that He doesn't spend much
time fixing up all His crap. No, He made it, splinters and
snakes and all, but then He just took off, leaving the whole
goddamn thing for whatever carrion birds feast on dilapi-
dation. I hadn't been gone long, but after the whirl of skirts
and color, horn music and laughter that was The Lights,
Cordy looked like God's first, abandoned stab at a town. It
wasn't just that the facades had been torn away all down the
street by the probie agents. It wasn't just Peg's empty barbershop, either. It was like the soul of the town had passed
beneath a puddle of deep and solemn shade. The girls of
the Idaho Hotel and the gals of the Lady Appleton's were
still here, though they had gone silent, too, having set aside

their literary discussions and chess playing as if these things were flowers for a different season. In fact, the only face I saw in the whole town was Oral Avery's. He sat, trapped in the amber of his insomnia, looking out from the window of the Rooms Upstairs at the Bouley Tree, that giant lone pine in the middle of town, as if it had the final answer to his reckonings.

The little window by the door of Shorty Wade's was dark, and Ed and Shorty were gone, taken with Peg by the probies, but someone was still inside. I could hear Billy Lowground plunking away in a minor key as I made my way down the street to the shop. The door was standing open and a dusting of snow had blown inside, mixing with the stuff that was still all over the floor from when the probies tore up the shop looking for Dream. The snow had settled among the pieces of broken china tea sets and drifted up against the bedroom door. I went behind the counter and pulled out a pair of boots. They were too big for me, but they'd have to do. Same with the thick, waxed canvas pants. I kept moving, packing the clothes I would need, grabbing a few cans of oranges off the floor to eat on the trip into the mountains. I knew that if I stopped for a moment, I would second-guess the whole shitty idea. And it was a shitty idea. What's a thirteen-year-old going to do working a timber claim in the winter? Why should the jacks respect me? I owned the land, so I was their boss—in some way, anyway; how would they take that kind of development? Everyone said that kids were bad luck in the woods. Would they take me for a child or a goddamn man? And what about Linden Laughlin, who had tried to run me off? What would he do when he saw my skinny ass coming 'round the mountain? So, I didn't stop. I got everything squared away, pulled the door hard shut behind me and turned my face to the howling wilderness.

Like I was saying, God ain't handy when it comes to minor repairs, so whether it's a structure like the Serwalter trestle or Man himself, stuff tends to drift into mania and disrepair. Everything lists in the wind, and the St. Anne is a windy place. That's what I was telling myself as I stood looking across that desperate chasm, the river below just a distant trickle. Serwalter had disappeared into the trees, never to be seen again, the lucky fuck. He hadn't had his father's land to lose, though. So, I got gingerly onto the trestle and made my way across, as the whoosh of the wind in the trees faded and was replaced by a kind of roaring silence and the beat of my heart rose into my throat.

At the edge of the trees I stopped, but something told me not to look back. The life that I had lived up to that point was all behind me. What lay ahead, through that black cleft in the boughs, that was what was important now.

I found them halfway up the mountain, scattered through the trees. Cavuto and Holmberg, both shy and built thin and rangy like fallers ought to be, were standing on buckboards to either side of a giant fir, trading blows with their axes. Swedes are born fallers, and Italians are built for it, too, but for some reason most Italians I ever met in the St. Anne laid track or worked road maintenance. I think Ca-

vuto only ended up in the woods because of Holmberg.
Those two were fast friends, though neither one of them
could so much as fart in English, and who ever heard of an
Italian knowing Swedish or the other way around? Still,
they were friends and had been friendly with my father.
They were deep in their work and didn't see me, but I was
glad to see them. Up the hill I could hear Dollar Edwards
shouting out directions to some John Johnsons, and I knew
that Jack Nearing must be nearby, and Overland Sam, too,
if Linden hadn't fired him yet, or worse, killed him for talking too much. Peg Ramsay said once that Overland lived
outside because he ended up talking holes in a wall. Overland Sam walked everywhere, no matter how far, talking
to himself all the while. The Kaiser and Unto Sisson were
bucking a felled fir, working silently along different parts of
the trunk, each of them looking up into the treetops every
few seconds in the way that all jacks learn to do, watching
out for falling limbs. The Kaiser twitched his mustache at
me as I stomped by him, touching my cap.

If Unto gave the flick of a tail one way or the other that
I was there he didn't show it, but that was Unto. We'd all
gone to his wedding the spring before, after the log drive
had finished and before everyone had busted out for other
places. His wife was blind and the size of a corncob doll.
She was a smiling, laughing, pretty sort—the kind you find
in magazines eating an apple or drinking a milk. I think
she looked so happy because she couldn't see the man she
was marrying. For all his wife's prettiness, though, Unto's
heart beat only for the Witch, and he never once cracked a

smile through his own entire wedding. Later, when everyone was dancing, he sat to the side, smoking and drinking Dream and summing up the expenses for the whole thing with a grease pencil on a piece of wood.

Otto, big-backed as a buffalo, was hunkered over, working a pickax under a huge boulder, trying to pry it free of the frozen ground. Linden Laughlin was leaning on a shovel up the slope from him, his chin on his hands. His eyes were closed as if in a daydream, but he knew I was there. When he opened them, he was staring right at me and smiling, and I swear those goddamn eyes were full of things that only I could see: hot shards of glass, rusty tines, sick moonlight, fever, grandfather clocks, fish jaws and clumps of bear fur, headache and pond thirst. His eyes were also full of sorrow that I took to be for me, the fuck. With a grunt, Otto pulled the pick handle to the snowy ground and the boulder rolled free and crashed away down the mountain.

"Weldon!" Antti yelled, happy to see me.

"Antti!" My voice came out sounding like a small girl's as his big arms crushed me in a hug.

"Boy, what are you doing here?" he said.

Otto came over and tapped the handle of my father's ax, then put a hand on my shoulder.

"The Witch went back to—" I paused, thinking about how she hadn't wanted to say a thing about her family near Laughlin "—to the Cities of the Great Plains." The welt on her face where Laughlin had hit her had been red and shiny when she bought that train ticket east. By now it was probably turning blue-black. I decided to say nothing more to them about the Witch. She wasn't gonna be a picture in anyone's mind.

Antti frowned.

Without meaning to, I glanced at Linden Laughlin. Blood and blackflies looked right back at me.

"But, Weldon," Antti said.

"Careful how you address the little boss." Linden laughed. "Now he's here, he's liable to shake things into shape for all of us, hey, Cub?"

"I ain't here to do nothing but work the land that's mine," I told them all.

Slag metal, nausea, sunburn. "The woods are dangerous, Cub," Linden said. "Town is better. What do you say, can we work this timber to the mill and send the money owed to you and that little treat of a lady your father kept stashed away?"

I looked around the men for some goddamn support, but men are mostly cowards, or didn't you know? Otto's face coulda been carved out of moss and rocks for all the help he was throwing my way. Jack Nearing was studying the pool of kerosene he was pouring into his hand to get the pitch off. His whole body was steaming in the cold. Cavuto, head down, rubbed the back of his neck.

"I ain't leaving here," I told them.

"Go home." It was Unto Sisson.

"I ain't going anywhere," I told him.

"Go home to the Witch," Unto said.

"You go home," I said to him. "Fucking Unto."

Unto ripped his jacket off and bouldered toward me. He

was a big dumb prick with beard hair that grew up onto his forehead. It's always been amazing to me that lumberjacks—who cut shit down for a living!—can't seem to cut their own faces down more than twice a year. Antti stepped in front of him, but I stepped around Antti.

"I ain't leaving here. This is my land—" I pointed at Unto "—and it was my father's and it's all that I've got left of him and I'm gonna work it just like all of you. I ain't gonna fire nobody and I ain't gonna tell nobody what to do. I ain't that fucking stupid."

Unto snorted. "You're a baby."

"I'm fucking thirteen years old and I don't guess I'm as big as Otto or as fast as Overland or that I stink as bad as you, Unto. The only thing I ever chopped down was a tree as thick as my wrist. I got an ax I can barely swing, and I got boots so new they're giving me blisters. I can't cook shit, I can't sharpen a saw, I can't even use a crosscut saw. I can build a fire, but only if you give me a match and half a bucket of fuel oil. I'm cold and hungry and besides this land I don't have one single, lonesome, solitary red penny to my name. But I'm Tom Applegate's son, and he died on this land, so I'm here to do whatever needs doing as best as I can do it, and what I can't do I'll learn to do or die trying."

It sounded pretty good as a speech, but I delivered most of it at Unto Sisson's giant belly, which was standing right in my face. I nodded at it, then pulled my ax out of its sling on my back. "Now where do I start?"

It was all pretty quiet for a second. Then Antti started laughing and Dollar Edwards followed his lead.

"Where do I start," Jack Nearing repeated, and he broke out laughing, too. He stepped forward and slapped Linden on the back. Molding mushrooms, milk skin, rat bites. Linden gave him a look, then started laughing, too. He put his hand in his jacket pocket and pulled out a stick of peppermint, broke it and put half in his mouth, holding the other half out to Nearing.

"Bucket of fuel oil," Nearing repeated, putting the candy in his mouth.

Cavuto and Holmberg were laughing, too, even if they couldn't understand a goddamn word. Finally, even Unto gave me a twitch of a smile. He was turning when Jack Nearing made a strangled sound. His face was white, and his hand came down to clamp on Linden's shoulder. The tendons of his neck were stretching like skid-wire.

Dollar peered at him. Nearing was always a joker. "Jack?" Jack wasn't playing tricks. His eyes were bugging out as he tried to breathe around the peppermint in his throat. Dollar said his name again. "Jack?"

Antti shouldered Dollar out of the way, grabbing Nearing in a bear hug from behind and straining like he was trying to pull the wiry man in half. Nearing was turning all shades of sunset, from white to pink and red. It got very quiet as we stood there, all of us frozen to the moment and what was happening before our eyes. All of us, I should say, except Linden. While Antti strained and Jack Nearing turned the purple of a lazy summer evening, Laughlin stared at me, and believe me when I say that there was no half hate in his expression. Centipedes, dirty barns, carved stones, rune trees, horned men, half wolves, grease smoke; his dancing green eyes jigged in their sockets, lunatic and wild.

Linden snapped his gaze off me all at once as the peppermint stick went flying out of Nearing's mouth and buried itself in the snow. Nearing collapsed forward and hung from the circle of Antti's arms until Otto helped lower him down gently into the snow.

Dollar knelt down next to Nearing where he lay. "Jack? Are you alright, buddy?"

"I'll have broken a few of his ribs," Antti said.

Nearing lay there in the snow, his face still a peppermint shade of red. He shook his head back and forth. "You couldn't break these ribs if you tried, Antti. Linden—" he reached around in the snow for the stick of candy and, finding it, stuck it back in his mouth "—this is the worst piece of candy I've ever tasted, goddamn it."

Some guys helped him to his feet and there was general back slapping and cussing and all that kind of carrying on that happens when someone nearly dies and then doesn't. Unto stooped and picked up his jacket out of the snow. "You come and then this happens. You're bad luck, boy. Children are bad luck in the woods."

"Weldon stays." It was Otto, coming in kind of late to the whole discussion. He put his hand on my shoulder. "When he goes, I go." He was looking mean and big as fuck, and he wasn't looking at Unto, but rather at Laughlin. "Nothing happens to the boy."

A couple others, Holmberg and Antti, nodded their heads.

Linden examined me like a ladybug that had landed on his finger. He smiled. "Alright, then, the little boss has spoken."

I didn't say a word because I didn't have to. I took ahold of a bucked limb and pulled it through the snow to a pile of branches. I worked away in silence with the jacks, speaking when I had to, and thought about Tom and what he would say if he could see me.

LIKE A TALISMAN AGAINST DEATH ITSELF

Now, let me say that I've never been much of a cook myself, but I've always *appreciated* Marsha's cooking. I know she liked that. She liked making me food a whole lot better than she did making it for Joe Mouffreau. For one thing, I could pay for the good ingredients. Joe, in his big fucking whoop-de-do cabin with his four-wheelers and his debt, was far too poor to go around buying the nice meat. Really, though, she just liked the way I liked her cooking. She looked real fondly on me for that. Even the way she looked at me last night when I climbed into her truck, I could tell that she wished it was me she was going home with and not poor, dumb, ugly Joe Mouffreau.

Cooking is like any other art, and I get that. Some people have it and others don't. I don't. Still, whenever I make myself something real bad—and I mean real bad: tuna beans,

for instance, or sweet-corn Jell-O—I think back to that
first supper in the Lost Lot cookhouse and remind myself
that while I'm not the best cook in the World I'm not the
fucking worst. Alright Edwards's butler, Thorough, was
the fucking worst.

Night tumbled off the mountain just behind us as we
made our way down from the cut, hunger ravaging, so
that by the time I'd stowed my pack by the bunkhouse
door and stepped over to the cookhouse it was so dark that
the only light came from the sparks flying up from one of
Serwalter's crazy-ass chimneys. There was a lot of sparks.
Everyone stood outside the door, toeing the ground and
grumbling about belly-burglars and rubbing their hands
together in the cold a bit while they waited. Finally, Otto
peeked his head in the door. The smoke that poured out
was chalkboard black. Otto shook his head at us. There
was more grumbling and a few of the John Johnsons threw
their hats on the ground and threatened to quit or cursed
Linden Laughlin for a cheapskate until Linden appeared, at
which point they stopped doing all that stuff and just stood
waiting for the smoke to die down. This time when Otto
peeked his head in, he turned and nodded at us and we all
piled through the doorway.

The cookhouse had two long tables set with bread and
biscuits and pots of coffee. I sat down next to Otto and
Antti and made a grab at stuff before it was all gone. The
biscuits were gritty, the bread was salty and the coffee tasted
like it had been made with cigar butts. No one else seemed
to notice any of that, though, or else they were resigned to

it. There was smashed liver and butter for sandwiches, too, which might have been alright except that the butter tasted like liver and the liver tasted like lake mud.

Linden Laughlin sat in the corner of the room, his head leaned back, chomping on a piece of peppermint and drinking a bottle of Dark Corner, watching us all. He didn't touch the food. He caught me looking at him once and winked at me. Thorough emerged from the back of the cookhouse, carrying two piles of wet-looking noodles.

"I thought Alright Edwards was the best camp cook there was," I said to Laughlin.

"He was," Laughlin replied, sweet as you please.

"What do you mean, 'was'?" I said.

"Have you ever had a friend, little Cub? A true friend?" Laughlin asked.

I thought about Annie but pushed her out of my mind. "Where is he?" I said.

"In the ground, up from the riverbank a way." Laughlin whistled softly. "The ground was still soft enough we didn't have to take off work and drag him all the way down to the Lost Lot cemetery."

I couldn't fucking believe this. "How'd he die?" I asked.

"There are better things to do with the nighttime than tell ghost stories," Linden said.

"I don't want stories," I said, louder now. "I want to know what happened to Alright."

"He took sick after your father died," Laughlin said. "Perhaps he saw things he shouldn't have, or perhaps he was just too delicious for Death to leave on the plate. Who can say?"

"How did he die?" I was shaking, but with what I could hardly say. Here I was, only a day in the woods and already Nearing had nearly died and Alright Edwards was gone. It seemed as if the world I'd known was crumbling and disappearing around me. Linden smiled at me and leaned in close to speak into my fucking ear.

"He died howling, Cub," Laughlin said, chewing on the words as if they were beefsteak. "He died howling and burning. Lamp oil. Must have spilled it on himself and lit a match by accident. Or at least that is all we can presume to know. He was found by the river, but of course he couldn't put a fire like that out with water. He could have dived to the bottom of a lake and it would have been no use. He would have burned all the way down."

"You're wrong," I said.

Linden swept his arm across the room. "Ask the men that found him. Ask his manservant."

Thorough was moving between the tables with the noodles, looking about as crestfallen and beleaguered as a man can be. It didn't take but a look to know that Alright Edwards was gone and not coming back until the last trumpet sounded. Linden took another drink of Dark Corner. "The butler will do as a cook, right, boys?" He laughed a deep, old laugh, full of robust and merry evil, and then he winked at me again.

Russian Alex had taken off with Overland Sam to bring up his best team of skid horses, and so for the next week we felled and bucked trees in the deep snow. I worked just below the rest of the crew, using a hatchet to clear away the ninebark and thornbushes, mountain ash and young fir that could poke up through the snow and snag a log as it was skidding by, sending it, and whoever was skidding it, down the mountain.

We'd get up in darkness, eat in darkness and work in darkness until eight or nine in the morning when the snow would start turning dark blue and then gradually lighten and lighten until by around ten everything was a rosy pink glow. No one commented on it, but you'd catch a man taking his cap off and running a hand through his hair, looking faraway and appreciating how pretty it all was. Five hours later, things would get all rosy pink again for just a little while before the World lay back down in darkness. Men would keep track of one another by hollering out, but mostly we worked in silence. Blisters rose on my hands, popped and rose again, to be replaced by calluses and a satisfied kind of ache. I kept my head down, listened to what the jacks had to teach me and kept going.

For all his mythology, Linden Laughlin didn't seem to do a lick of work that whole time. Mostly he just gave orders from atop a splinter-jagged tree stump that reminded me of a throne. I say mostly, because sometimes he would move from man to man, talking, talking, telling jokes, singing bits of songs—"Beautiful Dreamer," "My Old Kentucky Home"—and some in other languages and with melodies so strange and wander-y that maybe he was making them up. His voice carried through the air in the weirdest way.

It wasn't like the voices of the other men whose talk came and went on the breeze, distinct or muffled, according to the needs of the job and nothing else. Wherever he went on the mountainside, I could hear his chatter, twisting from song to joke to old story to some foreign tongue and back again, every word distinct, the click of his tongue like bone on cast iron, his voice piercing the air like a nail in a tree trunk.

As it began to get darker, though, so would Linden Laughlin and his jawing.

"I have in my possession the letter a farm boy wrote to his mother when he knew that he was to die." His words would carry through the woods. "Someday I will deliver it. Presently I'm letting the tension build.

"The human heart can hold almost exactly one cup of hot tea. Did you know that? It holds roughly the same amount of milk, of course, and can accommodate sixty minnows if one has a mind to catch and pack them.

"Sally in the garden, sifting, sifting,
"Sally in the garden sifting saaaaaaaaaand.
"Sally in the garden, sifting, sifting,
"Sally upstairs with the hog-eyed man.

"You had a sister, Jelly," he said. "Your mother named her Sweet Tooth in the womb, but Sweet Tooth died in there and she never spoke of her to anyone ever again. Ha! Didn't you know that? Oh, I don't really know, Jelly. I don't really know if that's true or not."

Gradually the talking would trail off a bit and long, heavy pauses would settle themselves over us as we worked in the deepening dark, and I would know that somewhere up there on the mountain a man was working away, sweating in the cold, as Linden Laughlin stood by, all but invisible in the blackness, watching him blankly, breathing open-mouthed, once in a while raising a bottle of Dark Corner to his mouth until some strange notion tugged him along to the next man.

"The stars aren't on fire at all—they're balls of knives."

Finally, I heard someone say, "Laughlin, we calling hours or what?"

"Or what," Laughlin said, and laughed. "Or what."

So, we kept on working awhile.

"We done?" someone said.

There was a long pause in the night, so you could spend your time wondering if Laughlin heard the question or not, so you got the feeling that he was thinking about it, so you got the feeling maybe he was standing right behind you.

"YES!" he screamed, and then started laughing and kicking at the snow, slapping someone's back somewhere in the night.

He was still laughing as we trudged, solemn and tired, wet and cold to the bones, down to the bunkhouse. For a moment he would quiet and the only sound would be the rattle of branches and the creaking-pop of the trees and our boots in the snow as we made our way down the slope, holding to low branches for support, concentrating only on getting down to the bottom, down to the river, to the bunkhouse, to the dinner of liver and biscuits that was set out. Then, like white water, his laughing and his jokes would boil up again, all kinds of highs and lows, with nothing funny or friendly in them. The jacks let it all go, such was their respect, or fear, of him and their love of double pay. It was plain he was a real timber boss. The trees they had felled were beautifully cut and bucked, and ready to be skidded to the Serwalter chute. Any soupbones who would have ventured by, out of the foggy past, would have told you that the jacks on that mountain were first-rate and you don't get that kind of work out of a jack unless a woods boss has a knack. It wasn't just that he was a good woods boss, either. Linden Laughlin was famous for knowing which way a tree was going to fall, where the avalanche would sweep and if the log would jump the chute. The jacks treated him like a talisman against Death itself. Jacks are superstitious for good reason, and all available evidence to the contrary, they believed that Laughlin had saved enough asses in the misty past to justify trusting him with their lives. Still, there were times when it seemed that Laughlin didn't so much run the show as haunt it with his blathering and shenanigans.

I remember Cavuto getting a new handkerchief from Holmberg, but other than that I don't remember Christmas. We all pretty much had our heads down, working. And anyway, Christmas celebrated the birth of a child in a splintery old cowhouse, and jacks, if they had any kids at all, were mostly in the line of avoiding them, so the story of a pretty little baby didn't move them much unless they

were especially drunk and sentimentalized. The Christ
Child's poverty and low origins weren't much of a selling point with them, either. Of anyone in the World, a
jack knew what it was like to be poor and have to sleep in
stinking outbuildings. So, Christmas came and went, and
New Year's, too.

I was so tired most nights that I could barely make it
back from the cookhouse to the bunkhouse. Good thing,
too, for even with Serwalter Scott's splashing of whimsy
around the camp, it was plain once you walked in the door
that a jack's life was a squalid one. From the outside, the
bunkhouse looked big, but that was on account of the big-
ness of the logs that Serwalter had built it with. It had a
peaked-steep roofline what was made of cedar shakes so
that the snow would run off and not build up and collapse
the thing altogether. There were two chimneys, one in the
middle of the roof and the other at the back. The boards
of the porch were torn up by the stomping of spiked calk
boots, and inside you couldn't tell if the floor was any more
or less brutalized because it was so fucking dark. The only
light coming in was either from the grimed-over windows,
the stove in the center of the room or from the tiny cracks
in the ceiling where the chimney didn't set flush against
the roof so that the hot metal wouldn't set the whole damn
thing on fire. On top of the stove was the big oil drum
filled with water that was for washing clothes in. On either
side of the stove was five rows of bunks, which were three
narrow bunk beds stacked on top of one another.

I awoke in the night to find I no longer had a blanket. I

was shaking to my bones with cold, so I went over to my jacket and pulled it on and shoved a few more pieces of wood into the stove, then hunkered down there as close as I could to warm up. Suddenly, Laughlin was sitting next to me. By the light of the stove's glowing seams, his weird, long-fingered hands reached for a bottle in his coat and pulled it out. The Dark Corner within clung solidly to the bottom of the bottle as he tilted it to his mouth.

"Bad dreams?" he said.

I didn't answer him.

"I have dreams, Cub. Old as I am, there are more faces in my dreams than there are in my waking. Long before I could put words to them I had those dreams, resting 'tween my runnings through the forest. The only way to keep the dreams at bay was to eat. So, I ate. Long before I even knew what hunger was, I was gobbling away to keep the dreams from coming. Nothing rests a weary soul like a good meal, I say. Oh, Cub, I hovered in a hollow tree. I danced on a rotted log. Oh, I could caper. You should have seen me. Of course, you wouldn't have seen me. Nobody saw me, but they talked about me. I came for them through the mist, Cub, through the mist. One day when the ferns were at their highest and the thimbleberries were at their bloodiest, a tree fell nearby. A sword of sunlight sliced down. The blue jays went flying off in all directions. The deer ran. I hopped up on the trunk and did a jig all the way down to the torn-out roots and, waiting there at the bottom, was a feast of lumberjacks. And, Cub? They were delicious."

He offered me the bottle, but I waved it away.

"You're figuring on staying up here through the drive, aren't you, Little Boss?" he said. He tutted. "Your father—"

"I don't know if my father would have wanted me here or not," I interrupted him, "but he ain't here and I ain't asking. The Lost Lot is all I have left of him. If it was good enough for him to die on, then I guess it's good enough for me, too, not that I plan on it anytime soon. It's mine, and there ain't any part of it that's yours except what I owe you for labor as woods boss. So, I'll be right here until what fucking money that's mine is in my pocket and you're off my land," I said.

"You're sore," he said, grinning. "You're awful sore at me." He took another drink. "Well, you come for me then. You come for me. I know you, Little Boss. Peg Ramsay picked you out for me. Come on for me if you can." The Dark Corner made a sloshing sound as he took another drink. "I think that you're going to try to kill me," he said. "Yes, that's what I do indeed-y think." He set the empty bottle on the floor and shuffled into the darkness.

He came back with a set of blankets in his arms. "Here," he said, and dropped the blankets down onto my lap. They felt fresh and cold.

"I don't want any fucking blankets from you," I said, and let them fall to the floor.

He was at my ear quick as a snake. "You can do better than that, Little Boss. You can do better than pushing proffered blankets on the floor, can't you? You can't? Fine, then. Try for dreamland, Little Boss, but remember, I'm watching you and I'm waiting."

He melted back into the blackness and I sat there a few minutes more considering all his crazy talk. He was trying to scare me, and it was working. You'd be scared, too, goddamn it. Anyone would have been scared. Not one of the jacks sleeping and farting away all around me, no matter how big their beard or how huge their arms, would have relished the chance to sit up nights with Linden Laughlin.

I crawled my aching back into my bunk and lay there about five seconds before my goddamn feet started stabbing me in the joints from the cold. I rolled over and tried to pull the mattress on top of me, but the plank of the bunk was splintery and even colder than the air. Finally—and I fucking hated to do this—I got up and picked the blankets Linden Laughlin had given me off the floor.

Sometime in the night I began to itch.

We found Jelly Jacobson the next morning. One of the John Johnsons stepped out onto the porch of the bunkhouse to take a leak in the early-morning darkness and Jelly's boots had hit him in the teeth. He came in and duly made the announcement, and we all clambered out of our bunks to see for ourselves. There hung Jelly, frozen solid and straight, my missing blanket tied around his neck.

There wasn't any ladder about, but Otto held Jelly's legs as Cavuto used a hook and his spiked boots to climb the bunkhouse wall and reached over to cut him down. They laid him out on the porch. His eyes looked set to pop out of his head. The John Johnsons all milled about, trying to get a look at the dead man through the early-morning darkness, then they wandered off to eat. We stood around him in a circle, Antti whistling soft between his teeth. Unto caught me scratching myself and glowered at me.

"Fleas," was all he had to say.

Antti backed away a bit, and the others followed.

I looked down at my naked chest. The little fucks were everywhere on me, bumping around, skittering away like pepper popping on a hot skillet. Holmberg stood up from where he'd been undoing the knotted blanket from around Jelly's neck. He crossed himself and looked at me. I reached down and took my missing blanket and put it back in my bunk. I almost put on my shirt, then thought better of it and bent down to the glow of the fire for light to see by. The fleas were everywhere on my body.

Russian Alex showed up at the end of breakfast with his famous team of black Percheron horses. There was a silvery jingle to their tack, and their chuffing breath, so different from the breathing of a man, made it feel as if new and welcome strangers had come to the camp to lift everyone's spirits. Russian Alex himself was happy to be back in camp, at least for the first two minutes, time enough to take a sip of lukewarm piss-coffee, take a bite of salty pound cake and learn that his friend Jelly had just hanged himself the night previous for reasons unknown.

Russian Alex was a slight man, but he was tough as shit. He'd come from Russia, where he'd been born rich and then had to run for his life. He had been a sailor on the Black Sea, and a jack from BC on down. Where he met Jelly, and how the two of them had taken up acquaintance

I don't know, but he balled up his callused hands into fists and rested his forehead on them and cried like a baby at the news. We all sat there in silence with our caps in our hands looking at the floor, and occasionally someone would cuss under their breath, but except for that, the only sound was Russian Alex, sobbing.

"Everyone has fleas at some time," Jack Nearing told me quietly as he passed. "If this was summer they'd be eating everyone down to the bone, but it's winter, so all you gotta do is tough it out at night, got it?"

I nodded.

"I'd slap your back, Boss, but you have fleas. Chin up," he said.

Then it was empty in the cookhouse save for me and Russian Alex. After a while he calmed and then he looked up at me, his eyes all red-rimmed and tear-dry.

"Biters are slow in cold," he said. "Also, the clothes. Boil them each night. I give you clothes, too. You and I are the same body. Boil one clothes when the other clothes is dry. I put on the porch for you, but you stay away from my bed with your biters." He smiled at me. "Stay away from me."

Back in the bunkhouse I ripped my mattress and Linden Laughlin's blanket from my bunk and jammed them into the fire. He was sitting there, legs dangling over the edge of the bed. He looked at me without a smile, without a laugh. He didn't even blink under those black eyebrows of his. I reached up, all sore, and grabbed for my long flannel shirt and saw a whole tribe of those little bloodsucking assholes on it. For just an instant I felt as if I was going to throw up, but the moment passed, and I slid my arms into the shirt and pulled the collar up and buttoned it. A flea popped off it and landed on my nose. I grabbed him and held him close to my face. *Get me while you can, you bastard,* I told him to myself. *I'm coming for you.*

DEATH'S HOOFBEATS

"Your trailer is so nice and cozy, Weldon," Marsha said to me while we were buying the TV, "but I wish you had something for you to put your drinks on, or your dinner on. You can't just sit in the easy chair with your plate in your lap, can you?"

"I don't use plates," I told her. "I got cans and forks."

She shook her head and looked at the ground.

"Okay," I said, because I was tired and old and I wanted a bunch of beers at the Brothers Swede and no more fucking nonsense, please. "Okay, what is it you have in mind and can we get it really fucking fast?"

She clapped her hands. "A glass coffee table. Next door. You can even stay in the truck where it's nice and warm and I'll go get it. All I need is your wallet."

And you know what? I gave it to her.

Marsha had never done anything to make me think she was a crook. Most I could have said about her, besides the phony Christian act and the terrible taste in men who were Joe Mouffreau, was that she had maybe played with my feelings a bit. Still, back when I set fire to the rope bridge over the river between Joe's place and mine, she'd come over to see what all the smoke was about. And now that I had lost my license, she drove me around to places. She didn't have to do any of that. So, Jesus and Joe Mouffreau to the side, here I was in her truck, with a new TV and her sizing up my new trailer in her mind for the things I needed that I didn't have a clue I needed. Finally, I've known Joe Mouffreau a long-ass time, and I know just about everything real that there is to know about the man. One thing I do know is that he can't handle money for shit. I guess it made me feel good to know that when she opened that wallet, she wouldn't be able to help comparing him to me.

"Not more than three hundred," I told her. Then I winked at her, goddamn me.

Despite losing his best friend that morning, Russian Alex somehow had his two black Percherons fed and watered and ready to work before the sky had begun to brighten. I'd gotten so used to being hip-high to every jack in miles that it caught me by surprise seeing him standing there, barely up to the shoulder of those giant things. One little shift of those hooves and you'd have a broken foot. One quick kick and you'd be in heaven with no introductions. It was a wonder that Antti was as old as he was, given

how many geldings he'd been hired to stop the blood on.
Horses and men are all brothers when it comes to getting
their nuts chopped off.

Laughlin came out of the bunkhouse with the bottle
in his hand. He stood on the porch looking at us looking at him. Then, with one of those tricks he could do, he
stretched out his enormous arm and put his hand on the
roof beam that Jelly had used to hang himself. He ran his
hand along it a moment, then shrugged, popped a stick of
peppermint in his mouth and strode through the snow,
past me, past Antti and Otto and Jack Nearing and Dollar
Edwards and all of us who were trying to search his face
for something. He passed right by red-eyed Russian Alex
and his famous skid team like they were invisible. Maybe
they all were hoping to see an answer about Jelly in his expression, but I didn't need any answer from Linden. There
was no way that Jelly could have gotten himself up there
and tied a blanket around a roof beam and then around his
own neck.

The John Johnsons didn't give a holler and a hoot for
any Jelly Jacobson, or Tom Applegate or Alright Edwards
for that matter. They were promised great money and great
money can answer almost any difficult question. They followed after him up the hillside, like sparrows after a crow.
As for the rest of us, the ones who were up here because of
my father, we held back a moment. I don't recall anyone
saying anything. We all just stood there, throwing looks
around at each other, trying to say with our eyes what we
knew in our guts. It would have been a ridiculous scene

to walk in on, really, a bunch of tough motherfucking lumberjacks, all standing around making cow-eyes at each other because they're afraid to whisper for fear they might get heard. Three men had died already on the Lost Lot, and though no one had seen Laughlin kill them, it was him who had done it (or had just let it happen) each time. The only thing that had kept them here was the money, but even more ludicrous than the money he promised was the thought of sticking around, listening to him jabber on all day and waiting your turn to get killed. I saw it in their eyes.

"You can't go," I said. "You all can't leave me up here with him and them."

I got nothing back but blank stares and furtive glances up at the trees.

"Alex!" Laughlin's voice shattered the quiet of our circle like a boot through the ice. "We've had nothing but liver-meat for weeks. Shall we add horse to the menu, or are we skidding trees, what say?"

"Please don't leave me up here alone with him," I said, but I got no answer in reply save for the jingle of the horse tack as we turned and started up the hill after the voice.

Almost immediately it was clear that it had been a bad idea to bring horses up to work the Lost Lot. They were constantly getting mired down in the powder. Each one of those fuckers weighed over a ton and though they had big old hooves, in that snow, and weighing what they did, they could have been wearing skillets for snowshoes and still gotten stuck. It was just like the Bud Maynard movie where Tony gets trapped in quicksand and he's fighting like crazy with his front legs on solid ground, trying to pull his whole body up behind him. It was obvious how aggravating the whole ordeal was for them. Alex would step to the side and wait until they tired out and stopped thrashing and throwing those deadly hooves around, then he would coax them real slow until they were standing and pointed uphill again. They'd take a few more steps and their hindquarters would sink down all over again and the whole rigmarole would repeat itself except that the team was getting more and more tuckered out each time. Eventually one of them just stopped where it was and wouldn't move. Russian Alex came up around the side of it, talking to it, trying to get it going, but it just stood there, steaming and sweating in the blue light.

"I thought that these were *good* skid horses, Aleksandr," Linden said. "I've seen you with good ones before. I thought for sure you'd bring good ones with you on up here. Seeing as we're friends and all," he added.

"These ones are good ones," Alex said. "Everywhere. Everywhere these ones come with me. Too steep here. Too steep for them. The snow—" he pointed at the hooves "—caught up in the hoofs, so." He took out a long spike with a wooden handle and bent beneath one of the horses to lift its leg so that Linden could see the balls of ice that had formed beneath the hoof. He began to jab at the ice balls to break them free.

Linden took out a peppermint and held it in front of the horse's nose. Before the horse could take it, he drew his hand back a little ways. Russian Alex yelped and rolled away as the animal stumbled in the powder snow trying to get at the candy. Cavuto and Holmberg, standing just behind Alex, caught him and kept him from rolling down the mountainside. The horse fell, too, though so quickly and with such force that it seemed to bounce back on to its feet again and stood there panting and shaking. Linden put the peppermint back into his pocket.

"No more." Russian Alex threw his cap on the ground. "I take my horses back, and I take my hours back."

"I promised you good wages to bring good horses, Aleksandr. I don't know what you'd call these." He walked around the steaming animals, then bent and looked one in the eyes a moment before straightening and turning to Russian Alex. "Your sisters are dying," he said.

"These are my best horses," Russian Alex said, pounding his fist in his hand. Then he blinked at Linden Laughlin. "My sisters?" he said.

"Your sisters are being dragged from their homes as we speak. They will be killed, Aleksandr. You heard Death's hoofbeats coming for you from years away, didn't you? You rode a fast, gray horse to outrun him, isn't that right? That horse saved your life. That's the kind of horse that I thought you'd be bringing with you when you promised me your best."

The blood had gone out of the little man's face and the cords of his neck strung and unstrung as he struggled to find the English to speak. "My sisters. How do you know these things?"

"You might as well start forgetting them, Alexsandr," Linden said, and gave a wave of his hand.

Alex looked at the shivering horses and then down at the ground, then back down the mountain to where his best friend had been found hanging a few hours before. "I take my horses, take my hours and go."

"Back to Smolensk?" Linden clucked his tongue and shook his head. "No, Aleksandr. No more hours for you."

The small man began to cry.

The rest of the men looked around at each other. Cavuto not understanding a word of it all but rubbing his goddamn neck at raised voices like he always did. Otto, saying nothing but standing there with his mouth open at everything that was going on. Dollar and Nearing looked at each other, thinking that, Smolensk or no Smolensk, it was gonna be interesting days if we didn't have any horses to help us skid all these trees to the chutes. Not only that, everyone could see that those Percherons were the best pieces of horse that had ever been in the St. Anne. It was true that Russian Alex had more than one pair, but any other pair would have to have angel wings and unicorn horns to be any more beautiful than these two. They towered above everyone but Otto and Linden, all muscle and movement. I'm telling you those animals were gorgeous. Real lookers, and powerful. Each time one took a step it was as if water was surging beneath black velvet.

"Let him go, Linden." The words came out of my mouth fast.

"Quiet, Little Boss," Linden said.

"I'm saying to let him go," I said again. "I'll pay his hours after the drive."

"He brought you shit horses," Linden said.

"They aren't gonna work up here," I said. "Let him go. He tried."

Laughlin took the bottle from his pocket and took a sip and appeared to consider the matter. He put the bottle back into his coat. "Aleksandr, for old times' sake and for our friendship, and for the fact that your sisters will die in the next hour, and for the sake of getting this job done, let's work out the day and see how good they get at learning what's what. What do you say?"

Russian Alex's face was dripping tears onto the ground. He didn't look up when he shook his head.

"How about if Little Boss pays you triple for one day, just to try them out?" Linden said.

"Triple?" Russian Alex said, lifting his tear-welled eyes.

Linden smirked. "If it's alright with Little Boss," he said.

It killed me to see Russian Alex like that, a man who'd clawed his way across the World, living any way he could, escaping execution and crossing oceans, saving his money to buy the finest horses he could to do the worst work there was. And then my father had come along, and Linden Laughlin, and offered him more money than he could make in two years and who knows what dreams he might have allowed himself when he told them yes? Did he look off in the direction of home? Maybe he thought he'd send for his sisters. Regardless of all that he'd come through, and despite all those dreams that must have been his comfort through the worst of times, he had somehow arrived at this moment. He stood before me in the snow, his prized horses behind him and his cap in his hands, asking a thirteen-year-old for more money. Of course I nodded yes, but I wish to Christ to this very goddamn day that I hadn't.

I spent the rest of the day stripping the branches from the felled trees while Russian Alex was getting the Percherons somehow more comfortable working in the deep snow. He was angry as a hornet about it, but he was getting triple pay and so he kept his cursing in Russian.

Meanwhile I was getting eaten down to the bone by the fleas. My grandfather's ax was so heavy in my arms that raising it above my head and letting it fall was work enough. Swinging the thing side-on in order to chop the branches off the fallen trees was on a whole other level of effort, and as soon as I got down to work the biters got warmed up and started chewing. They'd lay off a bit if I stood real still, but as soon as I got to sweating and swinging that ax again, they'd sure enough get right back to the grindstone themselves, sucking me dry.

It was starting to get dark when Russian Alex and Linden got into it again. Linden had been drinking Dark Corner steadily since morning. After he'd thrown the first empty bottle down into the trees it wasn't but another ten minutes before he'd pulled another one out. The argument was about the horses, who'd been at it all day, dragging the logs with chains from where they'd been felled and stripped to the spot where they were put in piles, ready to be sent down the chute. That the animals had made it through the day and there'd been no accident was a miracle, but now they were refusing to move, shaking in the hindquarters, their heads down, their noses almost to their knees.

"Too dark," Alex was saying, and shaking his head. "Too dark now. I take them down now."

"We got two more loads and then you can take them to hell, for all I care," Linden said. "Worst horses I ever worked with," he added.

"No more," Alex said again. "Look." He gave their lead a tug, but the team was rooted to the spot.

Others heard them arguing and made their way over to where it was going on. "It's getting dark," Jack Nearing said. "Probably best to get them down while we can see."

"Get your own self down," Linden said.

"I might do that," Nearing said.

"Two more loads." Linden turned back to Russian Alex. "Two more loads, you little gouger. Little Boss is already paying you triple, so two more loads." This time it was too dark to see the empty bottle as he tossed it out into the night, but rising up from down below came the sound of it shattering against the rocks.

"He's done," I said. "It's too dark to work now, anyways."

Laughlin shook his head hard. "No, no, no. He's gouging you."

"He's finished for today," I said.

The little man stood quietly by his horses.

"I'm headed down the mountain, Linden," Nearing said. "That fine with you, Weldon?"

"Everyone's done," I said.

Russian Alex turned to unhook the load of logs from the skid lines.

"Not you, Aleksandr." Linden went to stand in his way. "You have two more loads."

"I told you, he's done," I said.

Russian Alex said nothing, took the pair by the lead and circled them around carefully in the dark.

"One of your sisters lies dead in a fruit wagon with a mouthful of broken glass," Linden said.

I felt my ax in my hand. Though I had been working all day with the thing and my arms could barely move, it felt easy in my hands. It felt calm.

His neck was too high, too small and far away. His chest or his stomach, then, I decided. I started to shift the ax, moving my hands down the haft. Was it my imagination or did the wood feel warm? Linden's hands dropped to his sides, though in the dark I couldn't tell if he was looking at me. If I swung the ax at his chest and he caught it, then I'd be fucked. His legs. I'd chop Linden Laughlin down. Russian Alex was speaking to the horses quietly, his voice calm and his words constant, like he was trying to drown Laughlin out. Around us in the forest I could hear the others gathering their things and picking their way down the mountainside.

"They hated you for leaving them," Linden went on. "They sold your things. Your father wanted a funeral for you. Your sisters spat on the ground and cursed him for a stupid old man. Still, one of your sisters died screaming for you to save her. One sister is still alive, Alexsandr, but not for long. Can you make it to her in time? Do you have a flying ship, you fool?"

Russian Alex said nothing.

"Do you?" Linden shouted, then screaming, "Do you? Do you? Do you? Do you? Do you? Do you? Do you?"

I let the ax fall to my side and began pulling it back. My aim was to do a slicing, sidelong stroke with it. When he was down, I'd crush his skull. There was no time. With the next instant came the merry, tinkling sound of the tack and then the great black shadows of those two horses rippled as they tumbled, ass-over-teakettle, down the slope, pulling Russian Alex with them.

GET YOUR LICKS IN NOW

I'd tried to go to the War, too, but they wouldn't take me on account of my hand. "It's good enough to chop down a fucking forest," I told them. "It ain't my trigger finger." But they didn't take me. Fuck them.

Anyway, here came Joe Mouffreau, Daddy Mouffreau's kid, fresh back, with all his slow shakes of the head and his stories. Still, he managed to drive around in a fancy red car and for a while there he was laying his aching head on every bouncing bosom he could find and sucking down free booze to boot. There was still plenty of people in the woods at that time, and enough of them that the bars got a pretty good turnover, so it was never hard for him to find an audience. Joe Mouffreau told those stories and drank for free at least through the end of the Korean War, and maybe into Vietnam.

Then, in the eighties, things calmed down quite a bit in the timber business. Daddy Mouffreau finally died, and Joe shut down the mill and sold the equipment off to a multinational. You stopped seeing new faces every time you came into the Brothers Swede. Joe had no one new to tell his stories to, but that didn't keep him from polishing away at them, anyhow, trying to keep them fresh and exciting for ears that had heard them a hundred times before. A lot of people had to perish to keep Joe's war stories fresh, but it was a sacrifice that he was willing to make.

At first, he picked off a few snipers here, a few there. Not much, just enough to lend believability to the whole story. Then he was sighting whole armadas and warning the admirals just in time. Once, he heaved a depth charge off the side of the destroyer, detonating a torpedo that would have sunk the ship. The numbers of enemy he'd killed and wounded (he was fighting whole onslaughts by this time) grew to a considerable enough size that most folks started to drift away, head home or escape outside for a smoke rather than let him tell the same story for the zillionth time.

More years passed and people died or moved away. The rest of us that didn't just got older and older. The woods don't grow young men anymore, and they can't keep grown men, either. You can bet, though, that if anyone new happened to wander in, Joe was tugging at their ear before the head had settled on their beer. When even those rare people stopped coming in, Joe called the *Spokane Daily News*.

He loves that I never went to the War. He thinks I tried to avoid it. It's all he has to say back to me when I remind him that he didn't raise the flag on Iwo Jima himself and that he's totally full of shit. Goddamn it. "If I'd known they'd be doing a finger count to get in to the next war, I would have held off," I tell him. "Then we'd have some real memories to tell the newspaper."

"Weldon," Joe fucking cajoled.

"Fuck you, Joe," I told him.

"Weldon," he said again.

"Fuck you," I said.

The point is, I've seen lots of poor fuckers die. I don't go telling stories after every single one. Russian Alex, Aleksandr, was the first one I was actually there for when they died, though. I can't say I actually saw him die, because it was dark, and the horses were black, and we were under the trees where no starlight could get. One instant Linden Laughlin was screaming at him and the next those horses just up and plowed right over the little man. One moment I was about to chop Linden down at the thigh, and the next there was powder flying up all around us as Russian Alex and four thousand pounds of horse tumbled through the trees, coming to rest with a crash somewhere far, far below.

Without thinking, I followed the path of the wreckage down through the dark, using my ax for balance as the slope got steeper and steeper and the snow shifted around my legs. I couldn't make out the trees until they were right in front of me, and every trunk that jumped up before my eyes was Linden Laughlin about to cut me down. The ax had been in my goddamn hand! Why hadn't I swung? The slope got steeper yet, and I found myself clinging to a sheer expanse of moonlit snow that was like a field tipped on its side. Here and there a few small ponderosas poked up through the incline and I took hold of them for balance. Rising up from below I could hear the soft, awful sound of Russian Alex and his horses dying.

Behind me, I could hear the other jacks struggling down the slope, as well. I was so tired. I wanted to sit down in that snow and put my head back and sleep until spring. I didn't want to see shattered little Russian Alex. If I sat there for just a few more minutes, maybe he would be dead and I wouldn't have to look him in the eye and tell him everything was going to be alright, or some awful bullshit like that.

I leaned forward to stand up, but the snow gave me no purchase and I had to sit back down again. As the jacks scrambled down, a little river of powder rolled around me to either side, running up under my arms and over my boots. I sat there waiting as the others passed me, then I reached for my ax and used it to help me stand. I made it all the way up this time before the snow rushed in to fill the space where I had been sitting. The force of it knocked my feet out from under me and all of a sudden I was being swept down the slope, riding the crest of an avalanche. Ahead of me, the shadows of the other jacks got jostled up with their shouting as they, too, rode the snow down the mountain.

I rolled over on my back and let it carry me, clutching the ax tight to my chest so that it wouldn't be torn from my grasp. Ahead of me a single pine tree jutted up against a field of stars. I threw my legs down into the flowing snow and planted them on a rock while at the same time swinging my ax as hard as I could. The bit sunk deep into the wood and I held on to the haft as the slide continued on past me, cascading and roaring around my legs, the ice crystals lighting blue and silver and gold for an instant as they crashed down the mountainside.

Gradually the slide petered off and my legs stopped getting bounced and finally my boots found the ground again. I hung there—half sitting, half standing—catching my breath, my fingers wrapped so tight around the ax handle that it was a miraculous miracle I hadn't broken them. When my heart had slowed, I pushed myself up. I made to pull the ax from the tree, but the bit was buried so deeply in the trunk that only the other half of the ax-head was visible. It shone out at me, a cold smile, a slivered moon. I smiled back at it. Only minutes before I'd told myself I wasn't strong enough to kill Linden Laughlin, and here I'd nearly chopped a big pine tree down in one swing. It took me five minutes to pry the ax out of that pine, and when I was done, I half expected the tree to fall off the cliff and crash down the mountain.

I picked my way down the avalanche slope slowly, careful lest I should set off another slide. At the bottom, the jacks were digging themselves free of the drifts and dusting themselves off. A single horse leg was sticking up from beneath a huge pile of snow.

Linden came up, a fresh bottle of Dark Corner in his hand, the steam rising from him thick and white in the light of the lantern hung on a tree branch. He was limping some, and there was ice in his mustache and dusted up and down his jacket. He took half a look at the hoof and turned to us. "Don't let me catch any of you putting this on Little Boss," he said to them. Then to me: "And don't let me catch you letting it worry your conscience, either, Cub. Accidents happen and it wasn't your fault." Then he coughed and bent over, fiddling some with his leg.

"I didn't do anything," I said.

Laughlin kept on with his leg in the dark, and the few faces I could see by the lantern light were doing everything but looking at me.

"They bolted," I said. "It wasn't— It was *you*. You fucking spooked them."

He stood up straight once again, with something in his hands. He held the skid hook up to the lantern light for all to see. "Got me," he said, and laughed. "Got me in the calf!" He laughed again. "I've been in the woods since Adam was a boy and I can tell you this has never happened before. First time for everything." He shook his head, looking at that bloody hook. "Well," he said, "it's not time to lay blame. Something spooked those horses, and that's all any of us knows."

"It wasn't me that spooked them," I said, though even as I was saying it I knew no one was listening to me.

"Anyone know anything about his relations?" Linden asked. Then he laughed. "Anyone know anyone who knows anything at all about Aleksandr, besides he had a bad day?"

His question was met with silence from all around. "Oh-ahh," he said. "Come, now."

"He's from Russia," Dollar Edwards said.

"Woman?" Linden asked.

"It was you who said he had sisters," Dollar said.

"Did I?" Laughlin tossed the hook off into the woods.

"Yeah. You said he had sisters, but they got killed today. How'd you know that?" Dollar asked.

"Oh, that. Alexsandr talked in his sleep. Seriously, now." He waited, looking around the ring of men. "Anyone?" He waited a beat more. "So it was just a sleep talker and his pair of stupid, useless horses?" He took a drink and started shambling down the slope. "Dig him out and get him down, then," he said. "Or just leave him here. We'll all sleep soundly tonight."

It took some doing in the darkness, but we dug Russian Alex out of the snow. The leather tack that he was tangled in had nearly severed one of his legs from his trunk, and his head lolled loosely on his shoulders like a broke-necked goose. We carried his mangled-ass body back to camp and laid it out on the bunkhouse porch next to Jelly Jacobson's, ready for Overland to take into town to be buried in the Lost Lot cemetery. I left the cookhouse in the middle of supper and went out into the snow by the edge of the frozen river. I listened to the water flowing beneath the ice. Come spring, this spot would be a raging torrent, but with the peaks all frozen up, the river was so low that you'd freeze to death before you could get swept away. I thought of Alright Edwards, thrashing around out on the river ice, trying to douse his burning body in the meager flow. Alright hadn't been tall, but he was burly. His beard alone must have weighed a pound. If the ice could hold him it could hold me. I chose a piece of heavy quartz from the riverside and after a few minutes managed to kick it free from where it was socketed in the frozen ground. I picked it up and shuffled out across the ice and heaved it. The rock hit the frozen water with a crack and skittered away, leaving a chip in the ice like a white star behind it. I went back to shore and got another rock and threw it down in the same place. The fifth rock crashed through and the water splashed up out of the hole.

I took off my gloves and jacket and hat, then unbuttoned my shirt and unlaced and took off my boots. The fleas had gotten all worked up with the rock throwing and what-not. They were biting like hell. *Get your licks in now, you little sons of bitches*, I thought, or something like that. Then I stepped into the hole and sat down.

IT'S ONLY A FINGER

"An idle brain is the Devil's playground," Marsha said when I answered the door. She was rattling a jigsaw puzzle in my face. "A thousand pieces," she said. The coffee table looked too big for the living room, but it wasn't so bad. It was good to have a place to put a beer or the remote control. She pushed the beer and the remote control out of the way and emptied the whole puzzle catastrophe onto the glass.

"So," she said, tapping the picture on the box, "they gave us a picture to follow and now we just have to follow it."

"Did they give me another hundred years?" I asked her.

"You," she said. "Always my Weldon. Look at it, though, isn't it a pretty picture? So much scenery."

It was scenic, alright. One of your standard run-of-the-mill scenic jigsaw pictures. In fact, it *was* a mill. A scenic old clapboard place surrounded by fancy, leafy fall-time trees, its scenic millwheel turned by the slow, gentle current of a scenic creek. I looked across the river at the desolation of Joe Mouffreau's mountainside and cursed the fucker under my breath.

"Now, Weldon, I know you don't agree with Joe about a lot of things. We both know he's not as smart as you, or as handsome," she told me.

"Fuck handsome," I said. "That ass cut down every last tree. I ain't got shit to look at but his goddamn Christmas decorations."

"You like them?" Marsha asked, excited. "Joe wanted to do something different this year."

"If you mean aggravating me into an early grave, he tries that one every year," I said.

She shook her head. "No, Weldon, the Christmas decorations," she said. "He just wanted his house to shine out bigger and brighter this year. Do you like the reindeer?"

Wire reindeer with Christmas lights for guts were stuck into the lawn that swept down to the river's edge.

"Where'd he get that shit?" I asked.

"We bought them," Marsha said.

"You mean *you* bought them," I said.

"Now, Weldon, we're not all as well-to-do as you. Anyway, all the decorating keeps him busy," she said. "An idle brain is the Devil's playground," she said again. Well, I guess she proved that one right.

I was so tired those days on the mountain that I wasn't thinking about anything else but how to stay—stay awake, stay alive, stay on the Lost Lot. I'd drag myself out of the bunk, drag myself through the day and drag-ass right back into bed when the work was done and Thorough had proven again how terrible a cook he was. Each night I took off my wet things—my little jacket, my pants with the waist so small Otto couldn't even have gotten his arm into them, my shirt—and hung them all on the hooks set around the stove so that they'd dry out as much as possible before the fire went out in the small hours and everything froze. My clothes looked so small next to theirs, like a child's. That wasn't the only thing that looked small, either, and you know what I mean. I was built like a ten-year-old. It wasn't always to be that way, you know, so I'm not afraid to admit it. I improved plenty on all scores, and that's the truth, but at the time I was just a kid.

I would get into bed as quickly as I could. It was a goddamn awful bed, made of rough board, with a fir-bough mattress that snapped like bird bones each time I lay down on it. There was no shortage of wood, so the bunkhouse was always piping hot; still, I kept my socks and long underwear on and pulled my blanket up over my head to stay warm as the fired burned low and the cold set in. I slept and I never had a dream but once, the night after Jelly Jacobson and Russian Alex died.

In it, I opened my eyes and saw my father lying there next to me. He was real in every way, save that in the blackness of the bunk he was somehow lit by moonlight and the steam of his breath plumed out against a pane of glass as he spoke to me.

"What are you doing here, Weldon?" he said. He had deep lines in his forehead, worry lines that he'd never had when he'd been alive. "Are you lost?" He seemed puzzled and lost himself. He seemed as if he didn't know what was going on, why he was awake. Why was he here on the Lost Lot and not back in Cordy in the cemetery with all the other luckless fucks? I wanted to tell him something to make those sad, worried lines go away, but I couldn't. There was nothing I could tell him to make him feel better.

"What's it like being dead?" I asked instead.

"It's the same," he said, and shook his head a little, before giving me the questioning look again.

"The Witch is gone," I said. "Annie is gone. Peg is gone."

"No one is ever gone, Weldon."

"Well, they're sure doing a fair impersonation of goneness," I said, but he, too, was gone. I rolled over and tried to fall back asleep, but something kept tickling my face. I thought it was still fleas, but when I grabbed at what it was, it bristled against my face. Whatever it was, I must not have noticed it when I climbed into bed that night. I got out of my bunk and went over to the stove for light to see by. Linden had yanked on the horse's tail so hard that there were bits of flesh where it had been ripped away. I threw the hair in the fire and went back to bed.

So, we'd lost our skid team and we weren't likely to get another one, either, given that Russian Alex and his horses had died their very first day on the job. Word of that kind of thing gets around, you know, even in the woods. Men don't like their horses getting smashed on rocks much more than they like the chance to get smashed on rocks themselves, so even though we had trees felled and bucked, we had no way to get them to the chutes. There was one whole day where we got up and scratched our heads at the situation. With the woods in full swing, there wasn't a donkey engine to pulley the logs within a thousand miles.

With no skid team we were forced to take down the trees that were closest to the Serwalter chute. Of course it was hard, terrible work and every toppling tree would near stop the heart, knowing that it might fall wrong and bust up the chute. Once a tree fell, we'd strip the branches and set the hooks and then it was all of us pulling on that great big bastard like Christ did His cross until we got it so's we could get it close enough that we might lever it up onto the chute. Linden was no help, busy as he was with limping around, drinking and burning holes in all with his bloodshot eyeballs. If anyone should ask him what needed to be done, he'd suck on a peppermint and look at them until they turned away. His general level of assholery to all should have been a good thing for me. After all, with all the weirdnesses he was performing, he was spending less time on tormenting me. Still, there was a whole lot of jacks getting up each morning wondering what it was we were gonna do with the daylight, and those who looked to Linden for some kind of guidance would walk away shaking their heads.

Since Russian Alex and Jelly Jacobson had died, everyone had gotten real sullen and no one spent too much time looking at Linden or listening to him. Sometime midmorning he'd limp off into the woods, hullo-ing and jabbering drunk, to assault the blue jays with some song he'd heard somewhere. By midday he'd finished a bottle and started in on another.

On the third day after Alex and Jelly died, Unto Sisson saw him start to trail off into the woods and went to block his way. "I want my hours," he said.

"I can't understand you," Linden said.

"I want my hours," Unto repeated.

"You'll have to speak more clearly, Unto, you big blockhead," Linden said. "I think you called me a liar. I think you said I wasn't gonna pay you."

"I didn't call you anything. I want my hours," Unto said.

"You don't think I could pay you right now if I wanted to?" Linden asked.

"Pay me, then," Unto said.

"No," Linden said.

By now everyone was stopping what they were doing and looking over at the two of them. Unto was a big man, and like I said before, he brooded. I could see it start to happen now, and so could everyone else. Even Linden could.

Linden laughed in Unto's face. "Get your money from Little Boss," he said. "Or don't. Either way, get out of here before I kill you." He limped around Unto and toward the trees.

Unto looked at us. His face was getting red and his chest was heaving in a way like you might see a baby do before they start to cry. He chased after Linden and pushed him forward, into the snow. Linden barked another laugh, his big, black boots scissoring the air as he rolled over to look up at Unto. Unto stood above Linden a moment, scowling down at him, but Linden didn't seem to notice or care. Instead, he just looked up at Unto and laughed and laughed until Unto finally turned around and barreled at me.

"I want my hours," he said.

Suddenly everyone was looking at me.

And what was I supposed to say? I hadn't thought that far ahead yet. I knew everyone was needing to get paid, and I knew they were gonna get paid with the timber we moved out of the woods. I couldn't pay him a cent right now, as it was, with just a big pile of logs sitting next to a rickety, ancient chute.

"I can't pay you now, Unto," I said.

He thrust his face at mine. Otto stepped forward, but at that point even paying Unto fucking Solomon's gold wouldn't'a made any difference at all. The Witch used to paint the front doorframe of the shop with butter each winter. When it finally melted it was spring. I say that because the brood ain't like butter that just melts away. The brood sets on you like rust on your jalopy, and once it's there it just eats everything down to the engine block and there ain't no way to stop it.

"If you've got to go, you can leave and I'll get you the rest of your hours to this point, soon as I can pay you," I said. "For now, you gotta trust me and know that I ain't gonna cheat you. I'm good for it. You get me, Unto?" The fuck.

I didn't have to look around to feel the other jacks shifting, but what was I supposed to say to them? We could all get paid if we could get this timber down the river, but I couldn't pay anyone anything at the moment, not with a bunch of logs scattered all over the mountain still waiting to be skidded.

I pointed to the felled tree in front of me. I'd been using a hatchet on some of the smaller branches, chopping away as much of the green boughs as I could so that a limber could get at the larger ones. "I don't have bills for you, Unto," I said to him. "All I got for you right now is this tree. If you want to take it down the mountain you can. Or you can stay and help me get it out. Or you can head to The Lights and drink what you got and wait for more."

Unto started to shake as a hundred gallons of blood went to his head. He looked off into the woods a moment, then balled up his fist and hit me in the shoulder, knocking me off balance. I fell backward over the downed tree trunk and landed hard on my back, the wind knocked out of me. Otto and Antti jumped forward, took Unto by the arms and pulled him back.

Linden let out a whoop of laughter. A few others standing around were laughing, too. It was an ugly, frightening sound. I lay there, looking up at that gray winter sky. It was heavy with more snow, and after that would come more and more. It would fall and fall and never stop. It would come up to our shoulders, it would fall around our eyes, it would bury the bunkhouse and keep on falling. It would be like Noah's flood, but a whole lot colder, a whole lot quieter, a whole lot lonelier. It would stop up the river, it would crush Cordelia and it would pile up around the trees until the whole valley was nothing but flattened fields of white.

"He's coming for you, boy," Linden said.

I looked at my boots, still propped on the tree trunk I'd fallen backward over. They looked so small. Well, they were small. And the hatchet? That was small, too. And me, as well. All my life I'd been small. I didn't have to prove to anyone that I was small.

The snow crunched around me as a couple men started down the mountain. A few others came closer. For some reason they weren't looking at Linden Laughlin. They were standing around me, looking down at me. No one ever accused lumberjacks of being brilliant minds, but it seemed strange. It seemed like the time to do something, but I didn't know what. I rolled on someone's foot as I tried to stand, and they kicked me away. There were more chuckles from the gallery.

All of a sudden I was so mad I couldn't think straight. "If you all want money right this goddamn second, then you're shit out of luck," I told them. "You all knew the deal when Tom gave you the work. If you want to fucking kick my ass down the mountain, then I'm right here. You all are big enough that I imagine if you worked together you could get that job done. But you know why you won't? Because you're all fucking fools," I said. "All of you, the ones I know, the ones I don't know. We're working on the side of a cliff. There's jacks dying. My own father is dead. Any of us could be next. And maybe fucking

Unto is right to get out while he can. He doesn't want to die, either. Maybe you'd be right to just go."

"Maybe *you* should go," Linden said.

"I won't fucking go, Linden, you fuck," I said.

"Just go," he said.

"This is my land," I said. "I'm staying right the here," I told him.

"Are you sure?" he asked me.

"Fuck you, Linden," I said, then I looked around at the others. "We're all too deep into winter to back out. You won't find work in the other camps unless it's washing dishes. No one else is hiring now, and you won't get hired by walking off a job, anyway. Not this late in the season." The hatchet head was streaked with pitch and grime. The bit was way past due for a sharpening. "My father was a fool to try to log this land. To those of you he hired, I'm sorry. To those of you that Linden brought on, I'm sorry for you, too. You all go back now, they'll call you what you are—fools, every one of you. But if you stay on with me and live, you'll get your money out of it, real money, double pay like my father promised. That's my fucking promise, too."

Linden laughed. "Her name is Sohvia, isn't it? She takes all kinds of callers, doesn't she, Little Boss?"

I tried to ignore him. "Linden?"

"All kinds of gentlemen callers, yes?" he went on. "That's how she met your father."

His hands were pushed deep into the snow.

I'd had enough of his jawing. "Linden Laughlin wasn't

born," I said. "He was made on the same day as measles. On the same day as beetles and fleas."

"Ha ha," he said.

"He can drink right through the bottle," I went on. "He can dance right through the floor—he can swing the girls around, make them beg him for a kiss, am I right?"

"It's been reported," Linden replied.

"You wouldn't fight twenty rounds with Jack Dempsey, would you?" I said. "He'd fight twenty rounds with you."

Linden had stopped his babbling and gone quiet, listening.

"Linden Laughlin eats the souls of jacks," I said. "Then he robs their families, and he does it all with a smile on his face and people fucking love him because he's the greatest lumberjack that's ever lived and he knows which way the trees will fall. He's as rich as the Devil, he can read minds, he can see across the World, he's as strong as ten men, has three rows of teeth and can chop a tree down in one swing. But I don't think he's got it in him anymore."

He studied me like a coyote studies a trap.

"If he's everything we're supposed to believe he is, he could get this timber down the mountain by himself and chew those trees to board feet. If Linden Laughlin is everything we're supposed to believe he is, he could jack this whole mountain by himself." I looked at him. "I haven't done any of the things Linden Laughlin has done. I haven't hurt or cheated anyone." I held the hatchet up for all of them to see. "I'm using this little thing half the time to get this timber out. You all have me chopping ninebark and

Christmas trees, but I understand, and I don't care. Still, I fucking bet that Linden Laughlin wouldn't raise a little finger to show he's serious about getting you all paid."

"Oh, now," Linden said.

"You won't," I said. "I will."

"I've made my promises," Linden said.

"It's only a finger," I told him, putting my hand down on the tree trunk. My heart was pumping but it all felt right. I felt calm. "Linden," I said, "look at me."

He was looking at the tree trunk, at my hand, my fingers splayed out.

"Look at me, Linden," I said again.

He wouldn't look at me. His hands clenched up into fists.

"Don't do that," Dollar said.

"No," Otto said.

Linden took a swig of Dark Corner and started up again on the Witch. "She's a wicked thing. She's—"

I chopped off my little finger.

Goddamn, but it was easy to do. For being so dull and battered up, the hatchet went straight on through and into the trunk, and my finger gave a little hop and rolled away to the side. It looked so small, so far away from home. When I looked up, everyone else was still staring at that little finger, there on the trunk.

Antti jumped forward, but before he could get to me I reached down and grabbed my finger and threw it at Linden Laughlin. If I'd have missed him I suppose it would have dampened the whole moment some, but I didn't miss him. My little finger hit that fucker square in the chest. It bounced off him and lay pointing at him in the stomped snow at his feet.

Antti had thrown his gloves down on the ground and knelt to take my hand into his own huge ones. They were purple with bruises and calloused and stained with pitch and saw oil. He began talking quietly in another language. The stump from my finger was shooting blood, just shooting it against the palms of his hands. He cupped them to catch the blood and said something to Otto over his shoulder, who was already digging hard into the snow with his ax.

There's my fucking promise, I wanted to shout at Laughlin. *That's* my *fucking oath, now where the fuck is yours?* But I didn't say it, goddamn it. I couldn't have gotten a word out if I tried. My goddamn teeth had started to chatter like twenty chipmunks in a shook-up box.

My legs decided I was going to sit down on the tree trunk. Antti was still holding my hand, although he couldn't hold all the blood. The sound of it trickling down onto the snow was the only sound on the whole Lost Lot. Otto brought the dirt, holding it in his hands for Antti. Antti reached into the dirt, into bits of old dry fern and pine needles, petals of squirrel-chewed pine cones, mica and the coarse sand of old granite, and he crumbled it between his thumb and forefinger and put the powder on the stump of my finger. Bits of dirt fell away, soaked with blood, and turned the puddle in his hand muddy. I was spinning now, feeling very white and cold. Whose clothes was I wearing? I tried to fasten back onto Linden Laughlin's face, but his outline was too sharp against the light. It cut my eyes and

I had to look away, back down at where my finger used to be. Antti was packing the dirt around it, mumbling away, his voice rising and falling. I was swaying, hypnotized as I watched him work and listened to him speak. And then, just like that, he turned my wrist over, turned it the other way, let go of my hand and stood. I held the hand up to look at it but was instantly dizzy. I held it in my lap and turned it every which way. In the blue light, the packed dirt was black with soaked blood, but the pulsing had quit. In the matter of a minute Antti had stopped the blood.

It was fucking amazing.

Well. It had been pretty quiet up to that point, but when I held the hand up for everyone to see, the whole clap-trapped tribe of them let loose with a mass eviction of emotion the likes of which might just go down in lumberjack history as the most talking, laughing, backslapping and general carrying-on that ever happened in one place. Because there was no balloons or pianos around, it was mostly swearing—your typical *sonofasonofabitch*'s, *holyhornymotherof-christ*'s, *lordthunderandjesus*'s, *shitfireandsavematches*, and all that kind of talk—but it wasn't *what* those big lugs were saying that pleased the hell out of me, it was *how* they were saying it. They were pretty fucking impressed, by the sound of it. Sure, they were amazed by Antti, who out of nowhere stepped forward and with some kind of sorcery convinced actual pumping blood to stop flowing with a little dirt and some magic-y sounding talk, but they were also staring at me, laughing and poking one another and pointing back at me. A couple of them jostled me and slapped me on the back as they laughed. After all, even in a lumber camp run by the fucking Devil, it's not every day you see a thirteen-year-old chop off his own finger to win an argument.

The mirth and malice were gone from Linden's face. All the evil wires that stretched beneath his skin had gone slack. He stared at my finger pointing at him from the ground, his eyes flashing and darkening, flashing and darkening like coins flipping in the air. He threw an empty bottle of Dark Corner down into the trees and limped away.

A fresh blanket appeared on my bed, I never knew from where. Cavuto fashioned me a work glove with no little finger. The stove felt a little warmer. Though it was still as cold as icicle tits, it began to get lighter a bit earlier each morning. Even the food started to taste better. Don't misunderstand me, it would still have choked a wild hog, but for some reason, maybe it was the practice Thorough was getting, or the tolerance I was building to it, I was able to swallow a little more of his food each day. The John Johnsons—some of them, anyway—were looking me in the eye when I sat down to eat. You wouldn't have called it any big thing, but to me it was.

Laughlin mostly avoided the cookhouse, coming in only to stand in the back of the room, suck peppermint and drink until the last of us had laced our boots and grabbed a biscuit to choke on as we fought our way up the slopes for another day. Then he'd limp along behind, quieter than he'd been, paler.

Back in the bunkhouse, a John Johnson who could do all

kinds of acrobatics walked on his hands and started hanging like a bat from the roof beams. Hanging by the feet from roof beams became the whole rage for a little while. Then it was *how long* you could hang by your feet from the roof beams. Sitting around the stove, Antti told all the stories the girls had made him promise not to tell. A John Johnson who claimed to be a Christian asked him to stop, but everyone else shouted him down. Otto still sat silently by, never saying either way whether all those stories were true or not, even when they included him.

Linden sat up in his bunk just like he sat on that stump, back straight as a rod, a merry expression constructed on his face, a bottle clamped between his stovepipe legs. At times he'd catch a talking spell and go jabbering away, but then sometimes, at some signal no one could see, he'd clap his trap and go quiet. I knew that he still wanted to kill me, but he must have known the jacks would come for him if he did.

The stump of my finger hurt like hell for a while, then it itched like fuck. I could work all day without it bothering me, for as long as I was limbing or clearing ground, but come nighttime and the warmth of the bunkhouse, its ghost would come back to me, all itching and burning and recrimination—just a pale white wiggle of a thing that never meant no one no harm. I'd scratch at the place it had once been, but it did no good. I wondered if I ever moved away if it would find me again. I suspected that it would. I suspected that goddamn ghost finger would come back, burning for me and me alone, to haunt me forever no matter where I went.

Linden Laughlin hadn't come out of nowhere to do the things he did without having done them somewhere else, I thought, lying there. He'd cut and hacked his way through the World, leaving the pieces scattered on the snow for the scavengers. He'd figured that I was gone, too, that he'd scared me off. Well, I'd come back, me and my little finger of Fate.

Spring began to come, as well. Not fast, mind you, but it *was* coming. We began to wake to the sound of the river as the beginnings of a snow melt rushed beneath the thin ice, a sound we had not heard all winter. The time to drive the timber was nearly upon us. The moment of goddamn truth, what I, what all of us, had staked our livelihoods and pride upon. I needed that goddamn chute to hold.

It was well understood in the woods that God, the Big Fucker, never made a chute builder who wasn't loony as a rooster. He'd get almost all the way there on creating a regular, decent human being, someone you could spend time with, have a beer with, and then at the very last moment, He wouldn't be able to control himself. "Here, boys," He'd say, picking up another piece of mortal clay, "this one here looks like he could have the brain of a back-East university scholar. And see this here? He'll have knowledge of facts and figures, and a keen eye. He'll be tenacious and crazy-eyed, just like Noah, who everybody laughed at when I told him to build a ship for all the World's animals. Yeah, I admit Noah was a giant asshole. He was just a gigantic one. He was a philanderer and an incestuous drunk of biblical proportions, but he also built the Ark that saved the entire human race one day when I was in one of my bad moods. Well, anyway, I see a little of Noah in this chute-builder that I'm making here. Let's see," God would say, "I'll make him love card games, horse racing and girls, like all the honest rest of mankind, but I'll go and make him miserable at all of them, just to see what happens. Oh, and he'll have the pride of a peacock and a chattery way of speechifying his grand delusions." God rubs his hands and says, "Yeah, this is gonna be great."

So yes, God would get going and do a fair job, then without fail He'd throw in some creative flaws and some trusty foibles, and yet another defective human being would be hurled into the World with a desire to build impossible things, a sweet tooth for the sauce and notions that were sure to get him run out of any God-fearing town by a mob.

Usually, they were men who started life with all the hoopty-do—silk pajamas, schooling, tea—and then, in strings of catastrophes brought about by their own general looniness, they would be disinherited by their families, cut off from their friends, scrubbed out of the society pages and end up living above some low establishment in some run-down part of town. If that run-down part of town was anywhere like The Lights, then they usually ended up meeting some lumberjacks, and the jacks, who are generally a bit more forgiving of personal quirks than the rest of the World, would take them in and give them something to eat. Or at least get them shit-hammered. Drunk is when the grand schemes would begin. These Noah-types, with all their know-how and strange visions, would listen to the jacks' sad recounts of logs needing to get from point A to point B down a steep gradient, plunk down their cadged drinks and, with a toothpick for a brush, paint for their audience castles in the air.

So that's how we got the grandly envisioned Serwalter chute. Built sometime at the end of the nineteenth century, it cut at a steep angle through the trees and trailed away down the mountain in long, wide curves, like the tail of some gigantic moon-colored dinosaur that had never made it to the Ark.

"It'll never go," Nearing said. "It's a waste of even one log."

Dollar didn't have to say anything in return. Everyone knew that without the chute we were fucked. We had to chute these logs and pray to anyone listening that the chute would hold and that was that.

The Kaiser and Holmberg and a bunch of John Johnsons had gone down to the river to fetch water. It hadn't snowed for a few weeks and the wood of the chute was rough and dry as old cow bones. They'd each taken two big buckets and headed down the mountain, fetching water from the St. Anne and humping it back up along the chute. Holmberg started pouring from the top, and the Kaiser just below that and then Cavuto below that, and on and on, every hundred feet or so until each section of the chute was as slick with ice as the one above it.

"Time," Linden said.

"Not yet," Dollar told him. "When we're sure we won't have a jumper or a stuck log, we'll go."

"Time," Linden said again.

Dollar pretended he didn't hear him and eventually Linden wandered off in the direction of the woods across the avalanche field.

Finally, there was no more putting it off and praying and looking at each other all nervous and then praying again.

"Nearing at the river," Antti said. "Cavuto halfway and Holmberg is quarter." He looked at me "Ready?"

I looked at Dollar.

"Ready!" came Linden's voice, mocking, from way off in the woods somewhere.

Dollar kept his eyes on me.

I gave it another moment. "Ready," I told him.

"Ready?" Dollar called down into the trees and nodded at me when the three *Ready*s came back from below.

We stuck the wedges underneath the log and upped it into the chute. Otto and Antti bent on either side to give it a first push and after that it was away. It started slow, kinda hoppy and jumpy as it gathered speed, but it evened out as it hit the ice that the Kaiser had been laying down, and by the time it shot past Holmberg it was just flying. He threw his arms in the air and gave a great big yell, but by that time it was almost to Cavuto. We all listened for the sound of it splashing into the slough at the river's edge, but it was at least a half mile away and it was some long, long seconds before Holmberg got the shout from Cavuto, who'd gotten it from Nearing, that the log had made it all the way and that the chute had held.

We were hats in the air over that. What with everything that had happened, the idea of getting any timber down from the Lost Lot was an impossible dream, but now we'd showed it could be done. Even Otto fished a grin out from someplace and cracked it open. The only one that didn't show anything was Linden. He stood there, looking closely at the bottle in his hands, as if puzzled by what he saw within.

I LET HIM GO,
BUT NOT FOR LONG

I love my new trailer. It's not fancy—not like how they live on the soaps—but believe me, if you've lived the way I lived most of my life, it feels pretty fucking fancy. I got it given to me as a gift from the Nature Preservers. They came up one summer day a couple years back, a whole car-load of them, and pulled up to my old bunkhouse. I was sit-ting in my yard armchair, drinking a beer. If you've driven the road along the St. Anne even once, then you know it's a winding fucking road, and it's steep to either side. You can't see the mountain until it's right on top of you. They came around the bend and pulled over in the gravel on the side of the road and got out, looking up. Me and my beer just watched them. It was a beauty of a day, and hot, too. They stood in the yard for two minutes at least before they looked at me. I didn't mind for shit. I knew that what they were looking at took a while to look at.

The kid's name was Jeffrey or Jeffries. I don't know. He was maybe thirty-five and he came over and sat down next to my yard armchair in the grass. "Holy Moses," he said after a while.

"You're goddamn right about that," I said.

"Stacey, let's have a beer," he said to one of a peachy pair of girls who were still looking at the mountain. They had a cooler in their car, and she came over and her arms were brown with sun and they were holding those cold cans against her breasts like a fucking litter of wolf pups and I loved her for it. She popped one each for me and Jeffrey and then for herself and turned to look across the river at Joe Mouffreau's asshole house and his fucking clear-cut. "Oh," was all she could muster.

"You're goddamn right about that, too," I said to her.

The clear-cut happened about fifteen years back, when Joe Mouffreau decided to retire. About seven in the morning there comes the rip of a chain saw cord, and then about six more joining in behind it. A few months later that forest was gone. Only thing they left was stumps and brush piles and Joe Mouffreau, sitting down there in his house looking out across the river at the glory of my mountain. It didn't bother him none, that clear-cut. He got to see my mountain. Somewhere in the middle of it all he tried to come across the rope bridge to talk to me about it. There's a lot of rope bridges stuck up here and there down the river. It's because there's precious fucking few real bridges and sometimes people have to have affairs or ask for a cup of sugar or come egg-sucking for beer and brag about how they cut down all the fucking trees on their land. I saw him coming and I went inside and got a can of gasoline and a lighter and set the bridge on fire. Seeing him hanging there with his fat ass in the water and screaming for help was worth it. Of course, Mouffreau called the police and reported me. They asked why I did it, and I just pointed up at that fucking clear-cut and told them he was lucky I never kept a gun.

The Nature Preservers stayed the whole afternoon. We walked along the river and then I went back to my yard chair and they wandered up into the trees and came out a few hours later with looks on their faces that made me happy I was doing what I was doing. The peach named Stacey brought me another beer. She didn't say anything but, "Thank you," and she bent down and put her arms around me and I smelled the upper forest in her hair, the moss and the sour citrus of the fir needles and the ponderosa sap and the vanilla of those great big white pines, those enormous white pines that are the last of their kind. It'd been a long time since a woman held me like that. I hadn't given much thought to getting old before then. I'd given a lot of thought to dying, which was why I was giving the mountain to the Nature Preservers, so that the Nature could be fucking Preserved, but I hadn't given much thought to getting old. She put her arms around me, though, so young and sweaty and happy, that I couldn't help but feel old, so I just let her hold me. If feeling old for the first time was the price to pay for that girl's skinny arms dangled around my old neck, happy as hell and me the cause of it, it was a fucking cheap price to pay.

After a minute of fucking bliss she pulled up and saw where I was living. Serwalter's old bunkhouse was all that was left of the camp. The cookhouse went unused for so long that it just drifted back into being forest. A couple broken spars poked out of the ground from what used to be a wall. The bunkhouse had seen better days that had themselves seen better days. The porch was fallen away, and the front door was covered in lichen and moss. There must have been a couple feet of pine needles on what was left of the roof. There was no running water or electricity, not like I cared.

Well, I told you I lived rough most of my life. I don't make apologies for it. I could have sold the Lost Lot and let them clear-cut it down to stumps and brush like Joe Mouffreau had done with his land. Even the Lost Lot was no match for the Modern Age, but I fought for that ground. I fought to hold on to it and, once I had it, I wasn't gonna let it go. It wasn't about the environmentalism of it or anything like that. I had my own good fucking reasons.

Anyway, God knows what daredevil was driving, but it wasn't two weeks after the Nature Preservers left that a huge truck rumbled around the corner carrying my new mobile home. So, like I said, I have a new trailer now and I like it. I have these real nice gold-colored curtains over the table that the mobile home man called the "breakfast nook." The light comes in there golden, like it's sunset every time of day. It makes you feel peaceful just sitting there in the big chair in the living room and looking at it. I have a shower, too, and hot water and a microwave that cooks things with just one button. My clothes go away now in my drawers and in the closet near the bed. It's still pretty tight, but I don't care. I know my way around, even in the dark. And it ain't like I'd live anywhere else. If I had wanted to get married I could have moved to the Cities of the Great Plains or elsewhere, but I have the Brothers Swede for socializing and I have my trailer for sleeping and pushing buttons in and I have my mountain for, well, I have my mountain for my memories, and for Linden Laughlin.

One morning, Billy Lowground came to camp. I hadn't seen him for a few months, and he looked pale as flour beneath that mop of golden hair. The circles around his eyes were blue as twilight on snow, but he was smiling and whistling a tune. It was strange not seeing him behind the piano. He stayed long enough to deliver a note and a crate. A jack read the letter to the fuckers during their breakfast:

Sirs:
The experience of being berated by the moral police and incarcerated by the real police has given me both perspective and the time to use it. The winter of the old year has well-nigh come to a close. A new year, a modern year, beckons. Come to my party. It's tonight.
All yours,
Peg Ramsay

So, Peg had gotten out of prison, and now the same sun that he could look upon freely was suddenly shining down

on the St. Anne, as well. I pried the top off the crate and
pulled out one of the bottles nestled inside. The liquid in
the bottle twisted and turned upon itself, but I wasn't thinking about how it would taste, no, I wasn't. Fresh Dream
meant that Annie was back in Cordy.

Outside, the morning sky was full of dark clouds that
could only mean rain. Spring was here and the forest was
dripping, but no work got done that day. Instead, everyone used their time in gussying. Goddamn *combs* came out,
and actual soap made an appearance, worked into a furious
lather by frigid jacks in the glacial flow of the rising river.
The whole bunkhouse coulda been filled with beauty con-
testants for the amount of primping and preening going on.
Cavuto pulled out his collection of handkerchiefs, and the
Kaiser worked his mustache till it looked like you could
hook fish with it. Jack Nearing and Antti and Dollar Edwards were caught up in the festivities already, practicing
the dancing they were gonna do. Even Otto seemed to
be looking forward to the party, rolling and unrolling his
sleeves up and down his massive arms.

Then we trekked the fuck down to Cordy, goddamn
woodsbeasts to the man.

There's a word we used to use that no one uses anymore
called *stakey*.

"Stakey" was that feeling of being cooped up in the great
outdoors and needing to see more than just the ten or twelve
faces you've been seeing for the last long while. You wanted
to drink the booze, you wanted to eat new food in a new
place and you wanted to see women. Getting stakey was like

getting horny, but for everything. Getting stakey was like getting the brood; once you got it, it just ate away on you until you just had to get it out. Overland Sam was called Overland Sam because every time he got stakey he'd just put down his peavey or his ax and walk down the mountain and head off somewheres new for a while. He had the stakey as bad as Unto had the brood. Anyway, because of the roads being thawed out considerably, and because everyone was so goddamn stakey, we were down the mountain by about five in the afternoon.

We started hearing the sounds of the party all the way from the Lost Lot cemetery. Whatever kind of soiree Peg had ever held before, it must have truly taken freedom from incarceration to make him wax this generous. I'd wager that all the Cities of the Great Plains themselves couldn't have drunk more in a night than Cordy was about to. People were dressed up; you could tell that much in the dying, stormy light because dirty clothes don't glow out like clean clothes.

I looked in the high-up windows of the Rooms Upstairs for Sleepless Oral Avery, but he was nowhere to be seen, until some of the jacks started pointing up at the spire of the Bouley Tree. There he was, high up in its branches, dressed in what would pass for Sunday clothes, hanging on tightly to the tippy-top of the trunk. He had a smile on his face, Oral Avery did, and he laughed down at us, gaping back up at him. He had a crosscut saw in one hand, and while we watched, he swung it crazily up into the air, brandishing that long, metal blade at the stormy sky, and practically *willing* the lightning to reach down and smack him out of his skin. Oral Avery, the lumberjack even God didn't want.

That's how everyone knew it was set to be a party.

It'd only been a few months but being back in Shorty Wade's place felt different to me as chalk from cheese. Used to be I thought it stank and was dark and had all kinds of big fuckers that fought loud and drank louder and laughed loudest of all. Back then, I still thought Bud Maynard, with his huge white hat and his ritzy-titsy horse was the only thing going. Back then, I was still dreaming about working the Lost Lot with Tom and Otto and Antti and Linden Laughlin, the greatest jack who had ever lived. Back then. It felt like a whole lifetime away to me, standing there in the doorway of Shorty Wade's place. It still smelled, Shorty Wade's did, but even so it wasn't anything like on a level with the smells you got from a bunch of men dressed in wet wool with one pair of boots each living in a clammy log box with no ventilation and no running water and a stove and a pot for boiling the fleas and lice out.

We left our axes by the door and went through to the back to throw our heavy coats down with everyone else's on the big iron bedstead, then came back out again where the dance was just starting. The floor was strewn with cornmeal, which made it slicker to dance on. Billy was already set down at the piano, his curly-gold hair flopping all around his ears. There was heat and light and laughter and boots stomping. The girls from the Idaho Hotel and the gals from the Lady Appleton's were all there, dancing with whoever swung them up, and whenever there wasn't enough girls, the men would dance with the other men. I saw Cavuto and Holmberg swing each other around so many times they collapsed and had to lean up against the wall by the coffee and sandwiches. Through it all, in and around it all, the air was salty-brown with the smell of steak and onions and potatoes frying in big skillets and the misty spike of Peg Ramsay's Dream.

Dear Lord, how it all tasted like a picnic at midnight in heaven to me. I dived into those sandwiches—huge slabs of crusty white bread crammed with chunks of ham and wedges of sweet, white onion and nothing else. I tore into the coffee, too, stirring spoonfuls of sugar into it and gulping it down scalding hot.

Shorty Wade poured me a glass of Dream so full to the rim that a little spilled over and the first wave of it hit my nose warm and smelling of juniper and ripe thimbleberry. I told myself that I wasn't gonna list sideways like I had before, and I drank that stuff *slow*. Somewhere in that space of time I saw Linden Laughlin had come in. One minute he wasn't there and the next he was propped up against the bar, speaking with Pink Mame as easy as you please. By the light of the lamps he didn't appear half as pale as he did up in the snow, and it looked like he'd run a comb through his black hair. He lifted a torn-open tin can of something that wasn't Dream or Dark Corner to his lips and sipped at it, took another sip and another. Then he leaned down once more and whispered something in Pink Mame's ear, and whatever it was he said just blanched her out. Those little pink spots on her cheeks disappeared, and one of her curls seemed to give up and fall lank against her face. When he looked across the room at me, through the swinging and shouting and arms and legs, it was like he didn't even know me. Around him the dancing went on, but we all knew he was there—that tall, sharp-featured man, quieter now, wary, a black stick of stillness in the revelry.

Annie plucked the glass from my hand and drank the Dream down in a swallow, her cheeks flushed and her hair already hanging damp around her face. I'd known she was there because of the Dream, and I had been thinking all day what to say to her when I saw her. *If* I saw her. She probably didn't want to see me, anyway. I had been thinking myself in circles and then, as if by magic, she was there, and I found myself surprised to see her.

"Annie," I said, "I…"

She took me by the arm and dragged me into the middle of the floor. I was almost as tall as her now, I realized as she put a hand on my back and took my other hand in hers. I put my hand on the small of her back, too, and we started dancing.

"How the fuck?" I said, and then, remembering my language, "Where'd you go?"

She laughed. "Here, there, The Lights awhile. Wherever people go with broken hearts."

I felt bad as shit. "I'm sorry, Annie. I'm sorry Peg brought you back. I'm sorry that you have to see me."

"Silly goose," she said. "It wasn't Peg that brought me back, it was you."

"Me?" I said.

"It was your letter," she said. "I had to come. I knew you were in trouble. And as for heartbreak—" she took a deep breath and I could feel her sigh "—it wasn't you that broke my heart." She gestured around the room as we danced. "It was all this."

"What do you mean?" I asked.

"It's all ending, Weldon," she said. "Peg was right. 'A new year, a modern year, is upon us.'"

Overland Sam had pulled out his fiddle and was playing along with Billy. They were playing fast, sawing away on that song like they were trying to cut the damn thing down, but as we danced, the music seemed to slow down in my ears. It was like the moment was pressing itself in around her and me, squeezing us close together, getting ready to shove us out through some small doorway, past which was the whole entire Future.

"I can't believe you got my note," I said.

"Estelle told me a young man was looking for Rotgut Annie," she said.

"The old lady?" I asked.

"She owns the boardinghouse I stay at," she said. "Her and Peg go way, way back, as far back as you can go."

"Where is Peg, anyway?" I asked.

"Catching up on business down at the shop," she said.

We danced a moment in silence, then she said, "It's strange not seeing a line of jacks stretching out of your dad's shop to get their fortunes told."

"A lot of stuff has happened since I saw you last," I said.

"I'm sorry, Weldon. I'm sorry that I couldn't be here to help you when you needed it," she said.

"Don't ever be sorry," I told her. "I'm the sorry one. I treated you bad in front of everyone that night."

"Your father had just died," she said to me. "I understood."

"I want you to know that I'm sorry," I said, "because you're special to me."

"You're special to me, too, Weldon," she said.

Goddamn. I was so goddamn caught up in that girl and our dancing that Linden Laughlin seemed to appear out of nowhere at my elbow. He had the kind of smile on his face that would fool a man of the cloth, but it didn't fool me. He leaned down over us.

"May I have a dance off the young lady?" he said.

Annie looked at Linden and looked quickly away.

"We're not through," I told him. "Can't you hear the fucking music?"

"Come now, Cub," he said. "Step aside and let the pretty thing share a dance with me." He put his hand on my shoulder as if to excuse me. I flinched and knocked it away, then tripped on my own feet and fell to the ground in the slippery cornmeal.

Linden Laughlin was the greatest lumberjack to have ever lived, so he wasn't slow. He grabbed Annie up in his arms and drew his nose along the nape of her long, pale neck. As she struggled in his arms, he pulled a knife from his jacket and swept it through the air. When he drew his hand away, Annie's thick, honey-colored braid hung tightly in his grip and a rank look of triumph was on his face. The music was still galloping away, but people had seen it happen, and now everyone was looking at me, sprawled on the floor.

I struggled to my feet and dusted off my hands as the room fell silent. Something deep down began to melt away from my heart. It ran in rivulets and cascades until the shape exposed beneath was as terrifying and craggy and deadly as the Lost Lot itself. Annie stood there in shock above me, her eyes on that twist of hair in his hand, as Laughlin turned his back on us and began to walk toward the door. I let him go, but not for long. He had stepped out into the night by the time I was at the door. My grandfather's ax was in my hands. Linden's back was still to me as I pulled the ax behind me then and swung it sideways at him. He was turning to face me when the blade caught him, burying itself into the flesh and bone of his side. He didn't scream, though his breath came sharply through his gritted teeth.

The first thing that I felt as the blade sunk in was surprise. I hadn't really thought that Linden Laughlin was *real*, let alone that he could be chopped down. I suppose that I had at least half expected my ax to go sailing through thin air, the handle sweeping through empty black clothes. Also, I'd never tried to murder anyone before. I wasn't fully prepared for the whole procedure. In my shock at having caught him in the hip, I let go of the ax. Linden took a step backward, the blade still buried deeply in his side.

I've heard that when you're about to die for good that your whole life and everything you've ever done comes rushing before your eyes. That sounds to me like a whole

lot of rushing, but I expect that there's moments come back
to you for sure. I wonder what they were that came back
to Linden. How many men had he killed or allowed to die
in the woods? Did their faces return to him now, one long
trail of blood and guts and depredation? The ones he had
swindled, the ones he had robbed of pride, the whole host
of unfortunates with whose paltry deaths he had filigreed
his own legend, just as their money had lined his pockets.

Linden grunted and tried to pull the ax from his side, but
I jumped forward and grabbed the handle, jerking it free
and pulling it away. He winced, but he straightened himself up like his dignity had been hurt. I think it was Shorty
Wade that came forward from the throng and went to
grab me and pull me back, but Unto Sisson was a big dirty
motherfucker, and I guess he was still pretty pissed off that
Linden had made him look like a fool. He knocked Wade
to the ground and stuck his fists up at the John Johnsons
and anyone else that might have tried to stop me.

Linden, beginning to wobble a bit, tut-tutted.

"Come, Cub. You're surely not in the killing way, are
you? It was only a little joke." He held the braid up to the
sky and then brought it down to his nose, breathing in the
scent of Annie's hair as if lost in Paradise. The huge fucker
had his eyes closed in bliss until the moment I chopped that
arm right off his trunk. It fell into a puddle with a meaty
slop. After a life of fame and malevolence, it looked like
Linden Laughlin's time in the woods was at an end.

Almost.

Laughlin twitched at the lip and his eyes began to tear,

but he broke out in a spittle-rich fit of laughter that made everyone back up a foot or two before he bent down into the muck to retrieve his lost arm. He swung the thing upward at me, catching me in the face and knocking me off balance. He drew himself up and limped toward me, holding the severed arm by the hand and swinging it in a wide arc that hit me in the head once more, knocking me to the ground. He fell on me then, bleeding freely from the place where his arm had been, and sinking his teeth into my thigh. He shook his head furiously back and forth, as if he was trying to bite my leg off. I dug my fingers into his nostrils and twisted him off me. You can bet that he shrieked then, goddamn it.

He was still on his knees and remaining hand when I scrambled to my feet and kicked him in the head. He dropped to the road like a pile of shadows, and what was left of his mocking expression was knocked free from where it hung in his eyes. You could see it fall in a heap of broken parts there at the bottom of his sockets.

I went to stand above him where he lay bleeding in the mud, outstretched, clasping his own severed arm by the hand, looking up at the stormy sky.

If I'd thought things were quiet before, they were deathly silent now. I knelt down so that both my knees were on his chest, and I put that ax handle up under his chin so it was lying full across his neck.

He was already almost dead, but I looked down into Linden Laughlin's eyes, anyway, and I saw him down there, past all the evil and the madness and rage, and I held him there as I pushed the handle down on his windpipe. He bucked a few times, but I didn't let up one bit. When he went still finally and his eyes went fixed, I held him down for another minute more, then I rolled off him onto the ground at his side and just lay there.

Annie wasn't done, though. She was the first to move, shoving her way into the circle of gapers and picking up the arm. The dogs of Cordy clustered around her, yipping and nipping at each other to get closest. They pawed up at her in her too-big trousers and suspenders as she held the arm high above her head.

She stood there for a moment, then spun in place a few times before heaving the dark, spidery thing off into the trees behind Shorty Wade's. The dogs took off after that arm like it was a lamb chop, and we listened to the ensuing riot and woulda gone on listening to it, save for the crack of thunder and a blast of white light. An ax blade of lightning sliced down from heaven, striking Sleepless Oral Avery where he had climbed with his crosscut saw high up in the spire of the Bouley Tree.

His body fell, hair ablaze, through the roof of the Rooms Upstairs, and you could see the light of the fire twinkling cozily away for a few minutes as the flames decided where to go next. Then they decided to go everywhere.

ALL YOWLING DARKNESS

For all the time he said he spent in the South Pacific, and for the number of dead men he was up to in his stories by the time he got it into his head to kill me, I don't think that Joe Mouffreau understood what a dirty fucking job it is, killing someone. He must've watched too many Bud Maynard movies.

It's hard killing a man. It's messy stuff. Bud Maynard's gun, whatever model it was, musta shot magic fucking bullets, because when he shot you the bullet didn't even leave a hole. Maynard never missed. He just pointed at you and there was a puff of smoke and next thing you knew you were rolling around in the dirt or falling off a balcony or some such ridiculousness. When Bud shot at you there were no parts that flew off you. What I'm trying to say is that actually killing a man is as dirty a thing as can be done. No matter how they make it appear in the movies, it always looks clean compared to what it actually is. If you don't believe that, you can spend a little while thinking about Linden Laughlin's arm lying there in a puddle of mud.

Actually, it was fucking Bud Maynard we were arguing about last night when Joe Mouffreau decided to take his own shot at murdering someone. Bud came back through the St. Anne in the late thirties. He was doing promotional work for Ralston Feed Company then, and though he wasn't doing movies anymore, there was a radio program put on by Ralston every week that was like *The Lone Ranger*. I wonder if Maynard thought it was funny that he started in silent movies where everyone could see him but not hear him talk and ended up on radio where no one could see him, but everyone could hear him talk. I was working on Marble Creek then, and we all went down to get a look. There's been presidents came through here, but none of them got the crowd that Bud got. He arrived in one of those fine, brassy trains they save for senators and millionaires to ride in, and the curtains were red velvet and drawn against the light. A big crowd of us waited in the hot sun there for him to come out, and when he did people gave a big cheer. He looked just like he had in the movies, but saggier. His eyes were still shiny and black as buttons and he still had a big white hat on and flashed that big white smile. If he'd stopped there it would have been good. It would always be good to see an actual movie star, but here was Bud fucking Maynard, the original cowboy of the movies, and there wasn't a man, woman, child or dog in a hundred miles that didn't know that he'd lived here for a piece before he was in the movies. Wherever else he said he'd been, he'd been here, and folks loved him for that.

Then he opened his mouth and started to talk. Some folks afterward said that it was he was drunk. Others said that it was he was nervous. I think both. Plus, a few years ago I got dentures, and it got to be so I could recognize that those goddamn teeth of his were too white even for a movie cowboy. Fact was, that even if he was nervous and drunk and had dentures rattling around in his head, no one really wanted to hear him say anything. The spell was broken the instant his high, nasally voice started peeping about Ralston and how it's the only feed to feed and what-not. Then he gave a wave of an arm and Tony the Won-derhorse stuck his head out the train car window. He was beautiful and golden-colored, with a white blaze on the nose and the same dark in his eyes as Bud had; still, there was something about the way he appeared in the window that seemed like he had done it about twenty thousand times already. A kid jumped down from the train and held the Ralston feed up in a sack for Tony to eat and Tony took a few bites and everyone cheered and Maynard looked on like the whole thing was just the tits.

We were all expecting him to say something about how good it was to be back and how he had lived here and wasn't where we were a special place or something like that, but instead he just started into the benefits of Ralston over other feed. Then he turned around and went back inside the train car and Tony ducked his head back in, too, and that was the last we saw of either of them ever again.

"Tony was a chestnut, Weldon," Joe said. "I know because I was there."

"You and the entire Western World was there that day," I told him.

"I was thirteen when he came through," Joe advised me.

"Maybe you were," I said.

"I was," he said.

"Then your mind's going because Tony was a golden with a white blaze on the nose," I said.

"That's just not so, Weldon," he said.

"Fuck you, Joe," I said.

"Listen," he said, and reached around to his back pocket for his wallet. "I'll bet you—" he opened it up so I could see what he had inside "—I'll bet you twenty-seven dollars—" he counted it out on the bar "—that Tony was a chestnut. Do you have twenty-seven dollars, Weldon?"

Did I have twenty-seven dollars.

It was about four in the afternoon. A football game from the nearby college was on the television above the bar. Outside was just as white and cold and dreary as the light coming off that fucking TV set. I ain't the drinker I once was. I'd been drinking the same goddamn beer all afternoon. I ordered two whiskeys off Paulette behind the bar and took my wallet out to pay for them. It was the way Joe was talking to me, maybe. He never talked to me like I was a child before, but when he started seeing Marsha, he all of a sudden started talking slow and loud at me, like

I maybe couldn't understand his brand of pap. He knew how to get on my nerves, the fuck. I paid for those whiskeys with a hundred and gave Paulette the change. "Have a whiskey on me, Joe," I said, and knocked mine back. "If you've only got twenty-seven dollars we can bet with that or, if you like, we can double it and you'll owe me later." I held my wallet out and let Joe have a good, old gawk at what was inside. "You fuck," I said, "Tony was a golden."

"Forget it," he said, and drank the whiskey.

"I don't forget anything," I said. "Especially not the color of Tony the Goddamn Ritzy-Titsy Wonderhorse."

"It doesn't matter," he said.

"It does so matter," I told him. I can't say why exactly it got me so mad, him saying that it didn't matter, but it did. I ordered another two whiskeys and we both drank them and pretended to watch the football game. There was snow falling on the field and the announcers were going on and on about what difficult conditions they were. Joe got up to use the bathroom and on the way he stopped at the phone.

"I think I'll be heading home soon, Old-Timer," he said when he'd come back out again. "Wanna wait outside with me, see if a couple old codgers can pick up a ride?"

"Fuck you, Joe," I told him, but it was dark outside and you could hear the wind in gusts against the windowpanes. That wasn't any kind of weather to be out driving around in, and anyone that *was* out driving around was probably the only one out driving around. I coulda let Joe Mouffreau just hitch a ride all by himself from whoever happened to come by first, but it was fixing to be a long time between trains, if you know what I mean, and I wasn't in the mood to end up standing around by myself for another six hours until Paulette locked the place up. Fuck that. So, I decided I'd go with him, but I was gonna wait at the bar and finish my whiskey rather than standing out there in the cold with Joe, rehashing the surrender of Japan.

"Weldon," Paulette said when Joe had stepped out. "You'll never guess who it was I saw at the Indian casino last Wednesday. Marsha Leeds."

"You don't fucking say," I said.

"Yup," Paulette said. "She was with Joe, and by the looks of it, they were in deep."

That was no surprise.

"Oh, yeah?" I said.

"I had to give them money for gas," she said.

It wasn't but fifteen minutes before a truck pulled up, the fog lights coming through the window of the front door and painting themselves against the ceiling. I could hear the engine, low and loud. I said good night to Paulette.

"Weldon," she said, and leaned over the bar.

I went back over to the bar.

"Be careful out there tonight, alright?" She leaned in close and gave me a peck on the cheek and what did I smell on her but Dream? After all those years, centuries it felt like, to smell those crushed juniper berries and forest mulch and swirling mica. Maybe it was a trick of my memory, but it was a magic trick.

And then I was in the howling outdoors and the snow wasn't snow anymore but spun crystals of sand and rock, and Joe was out there with me in the road waving his arms so that Marsha would see us through the gale. Yeah, it was Marsha and Joe that I was gonna have to get a ride home with, and it was almost enough to make an old man trudge back inside and wait for better company, but Joe was already climbing in the tight back seat of the pickup and Marsha was waving at me to get in, get in, get in, and I got in.

"Brrrr!" Joe said from behind me as the door shut. "If it's not cold I don't know what."

"It's ten below already," Marsha said. "And it wants to go lower."

"I guess it'll figure some way to go lower, then," Joe said.

"I guess it will, at that. Weldon," she asked, "will you be warm enough out in that little trailer?"

"It's cozy enough," I told her.

"No satellite reception tonight," Joe said. "It might get mighty lonesome."

"Lonesome ain't one of my problems at the moment," I said.

"Well," Marsha said, looking in her rearview mirror at Joe, "no one knows what's in our hearts but Jesus."

"I reckon I know my own heart just fine," I told her. "I reckon I could tell Him some stuff that might surprise Him."

I might have known that something bad was about to happen, the way she kept looking back in that rearview. Joe wasn't the kind of starlet to go platter-eyed over, but she couldn't seem to stop giving him meaningful fucking glances in the back seat of the pickup. Maybe I shoulda been a little suspicious, but you know how it is once you get in the habit of not being afraid of someone. It's as hard a habit to break as any.

We crossed the river and pulled slowly along the road. With all the trees gone, you have to be careful of avalanche, but the mountains were as frozen and solid blue as icebergs. Ahead, though, you could see the vast, dark patch of blacking right up into the night sky that was the Lost Lot, and below it was my trailer with the little gleam of golden warmth in the window where I had left the breakfast nook light on. It made me happy again just to see that little light and to know I was gonna be inside and snug soon, and draw the curtains so that I had that light all to myself, and let the wind blow outside and the dark pines on the mountain above whoosh and shoosh away in the blizzard.

You can get rich all your life and it doesn't mean a thing if you don't have a feeling like that. I guess Joe knew that. When he came home these days, all he had was a hill of stumps, an empty, cold house that he couldn't afford to heat it was so big and goddamn Marsha all the goddamn time with her God talk and her Indian casino debt.

Marsha heaved a big old sigh as we pulled up to my trailer. "Anyway," she said, a bitter scoop of fatalism in her voice, "so long, Weldon. Remember to say your prayers."

Joe didn't say anything. He didn't even get in the front seat when I got out. I said so long and thanks to Marsha for the ride, nodded once at Joe and slammed the truck door shut. She turned around slow in the road as I stomped off my boots and went inside. It was good to be back home.

I went to the cabinet and poured myself a whiskey, then went to the breakfast nook window to draw the curtains. Outside it was all yowling darkness and I held there a minute just feeling it all. It was a bit like falling into white water—all fury and roaring, but inside your head, as always, only stillness. It's the roaring that makes you hear the stillness in your head louder. I imagine that when I die it's gonna be like that. There's gonna come a big, white sound, like spring rapids or avalanche, and it's gonna sweep me up into it, but it ain't gonna carry me away, no. No, it's gonna make me a part of it. In that moment, when I'm dying for good, I'm gonna *be* that white water. I'm gonna *be* that avalanche. Yes, I will. I know how it's going to be. Those last few moments I'm alive, I'm gonna dive down deep into that roaring and I'm gonna swim through until I find the stillness at the raging heart of it. And then it'll feel just like it did, standing at my trailer window, about to draw the curtains on it all, the wind shrieking down the blackness of the road, the temperature dropping and nothing but peaceful stillness here inside.

I was about to pull the curtains when something way down the road glowed red in the darkness. They blinked once again, and I saw that they were brake lights. It was like Marsha was starting and stopping over something. Then they came on for good and sat staring redly at me through the window, and I started to think about what the fuck I was gonna do.

All of Cordelia burned that night, save for Shorty Wade's, as it was on the extreme edge of town. The rest of it?

Whoof! It took a couple hours, of course, but the fire devoured Cordy without even seeming to touch it. From the moment it engulfed the Rooms Upstairs, it was clear that the flames had been pent up in the wood of town for a long, long time, and all it needed was Oral Avery to release it. You can't keep fire like that back. It's a stampede.

Annie and me and the rest of us stood out in the middle of the street watching it all go back up to heaven or wherever Peg Ramsay had summoned it from. Peg himself appeared from his barbershop, a bottle of Dream in his hand, and yelled, "Raise a toast, you dirty, homeless, shiftless bastards, raise a toast!" He held high the Dream. "It has been a pleasure to walk and work among you. May your hearts leave this place lightly and may there always be a home in your memories for the St. Anne and Cordelia and all that once was." He took a huge swig and tossed the half-full bottle through a burning sill. Blue fire exploded from within. Then we were all throwing our bottles into the blaze, and all of Cordy took on the iridescent blue of a beetle shell.

Seeing as the Rooms Upstairs and my father's shop and the whole goddamn thing was burning to the ground, Pink Mame and the gals of the Lady Appleton's pulled all their mattresses and bedding, quilts, carpets and dresses out into the street. The girls of the Idaho Hotel, realizing a good idea when they saw it, followed suit. Jacks helped, picking up silk pillows and velvet curtains under their arms and carrying them down the street, careful to keep them out of the mud, following Peg Ramsay out of town and toward the lilac grove at the railroad spur.

Everyone in town slept out that night, wrapped in perfumed blankets, beneath the petals of fresh-blooming lilacs. Ed Kleinerd and Shorty Wade and Peg Ramsay were there, Billy Lowground and all the gals and girls, plus a couple hundred jacks from the nearby timber camps, all pressed together for warmth.

Annie lay beside me, wrapped in a jacket, her head on a small pink pillow. I fell asleep in the glow of the distant fire, thinking about how goddamn glorious it was to see her again, thinking on what she had told me just before Linden had cut off her braid: *It wasn't Peg that brought me back, it was you.* I slept, and there were no dreams, or if there were, they were like the deep swimming of rainbow trout whose tails left sweet, fragile ripples in their passing.

THAT'S HOW ORNERY I AM

I stood there at the little window in the breakfast nook maybe ten seconds more, watching for Marsha's glowing red brake lights to blink and go off as her and Joe Mouffreau decided that there was some other way they could get the money they needed than robbing it from a ninety-nine-year-old man. Christ, though, when I think about it, what the good Christ could be any easier than taking money from a ninety-nine-year-old man? I was a bonanza for those fuckers. I'm so wrinkled and shrunk-up and weak that you'd have a harder time eating a cracker than robbing me. And there I'd been, flaunting my fucking life savings around the Brothers Swede, the whole entire time rubbing Joe Mouffreau's nose in it, letting him practically smell the hundred-dollar bills in there. No, there wasn't an easier way for them to get the cash. The longer I watched those brake lights staring back at me, the more I knew it. I took my grandfather's ax down from above the doorway and stepped out into the blizzard, pulling the door shut behind me, blocking out the light and covering me in darkness.

I don't have motion sensors or glowing reindeer, so the only light that was cast came from Joe's goddamn house, and that was a million miles away, across the river and through the gale. I mean to say that it was goddamn *dark*. I didn't fucking care. Counting my years and years in the woods and a season or two in the silver mines, I've spent more than half my life in darkness. The cold wasn't bothering me any at that point, either. Unless your feet are blue, what is cold?

Like I said, Joe hates the dark. Scared to death of it. So, he musta gotten out of Marsha's truck, took a few blind steps into the blackness, then got terrified and just started running. In any event, I watched his shadow blunder by me and collide with the corner of the trailer by the breakfast nook. He lay there in the snow a moment, then I made out his shadowy form rising, and I followed him to my front doorstep.

I have to say, it wasn't like Joe to try to kick in a man's door in the dark on an icy step, but that's the course of action that he took. He flailed around a fair bunch for an old guy, but he caught his balance on the doorknob and in so doing realized that the door was unlocked. As he pushed it open, I could see by the light from within that he had Marsha's .22 slung over his shoulder. I'm not young, you know. I can't actually swing an ax anymore, so I used my precious fucking resources and summoned the strength to reach the ax up the steps and trip Joe with the ax-head as he stepped across the threshold. Joe fell, shattering the glass coffee table. He rolled in pain on the broken glass, doing six kinds of screaming. You would have thought for a second that he'd met the Witch, the kinds of curses he was laying down.

"You won't find what you're looking for in there, Joe," I yelled at him. "I keep my money on me. You want it, come take it, you desperate piece of worm shit."

Then Joe rolled over and shot me here, in the fucking hip. That pain was fucking terrible, and you can write that down. I fucking crumpled to the ground. Jesus, it was a disgrace.

Joe rustled around a bit on the threshold and I knew he was getting up. Soon, he stood on the steps above me looking down, swaying, one eye blinded with blood from a gash on his forehead. He slipped off the top step and bounced hard down the other two and onto the ground next to me.

Sometimes you get lucky and the fucker trying to kill you falls down the stairs and dies. No such luck in this account. Sure, he moaned and groaned as well as any useless fuck, but not for long. He scrambled for the gun and I scrambled for my father's ax and we made crazy snow angels in the powder for a while as he or I got the upper hand. I haven't fought in ages, but unlike Joe I always *could* fight. Still, he was fifteen years younger than me, and I'm no spring chicken. After the shit I've been through, fighting this ugly was a disgrace. The jacks would have laughed their asses off to see it.

I grabbed his glasses and flung them into the woods. We struggled some more, and I managed to get on top of him. I was gonna tell him that he was a piece of shit and had been his whole life, and that he turned every single fucking thing he touched to garbage in the instant that he touched it, and that he could go ahead and have the money that I had in my wallet if he could promise me when he shot me that he'd do the job right rather than half-assing it and fucking it up like he'd done to every other thing every chance he got. I wanted to say all that, and maybe I did, too, but I can't remember too well. What I *do* remember yelling, as he threw me over and stumbled to his feet, was, "He wasn't a fucking chestnut brown, you ass. Tony was a golden with a white blaze." He leaned back a little as he pointed the gun and shot me again.

Right in the fucking head.

I don't know how long we were there, but it couldn't have been long. A few more minutes and we'd both have been frozen to death. The pain in my hip was a fucking disaster. It took me a moment, lying there, to remember that Joe'd shot me in the head, too, but when I did, I put my hand up to it real slow. It came away all covered in tacky, sticky blood. I was glad that it was so dark. You live a full life, there ain't no more of a kick in the teeth than having one last, good look at your brains on your fingertips before your heart stops. But there weren't any brains on my fingers, just blood. I felt around for the hole but there wasn't one—just a long furrow here, on the side of my noggin.

Joe'd tried to shoot me in the head and kill me, but with his glasses off he couldn't see well enough to finish the job.

The trailer door was swinging crazily on its hinges and the snow was drifting in. Joe was trying to crawl up the steps, but he'd seen better days. I crawled after him through the snow and caught his boot, giving it a pull hard enough that his head knocked against the stair. This time he was all mine. I rolled over and grabbed the ax, and then, real slow because I was getting light-headed, I rolled over on top of him and felt the bit sinking into his chest, through his heavy clothes. I used my weight to push down on it a few times, ugh, ugh, ugh, and felt the warm patch spreading beneath his jacket. Joe didn't have anything left to say on the matter. He coughed once, a bloody cough that got all over my face, but I kept pushing the bit deeper and deeper. I rolled off him and watched for the fucker's chest to move and show me that he was breathing, but if he was, he was taking about a year between breaths.

If you want to know what pain is, try being ninety-nine sometime. Then get yourself shot in the hip and the head on the same night. It doesn't matter if it *is* a .22. Fucking use a peashooter. Use a marshmallow gun. It doesn't matter what you get shot with when you get this old. Still, if you're gonna die, it shouldn't have to be next to a paltry fuck like Joe Mouffreau.

The phone was a long way away, up on the counter near the refrigerator. I didn't think that there was a chance in a million that the phone line was up, it was blowing so hard outside, but that phone was the only thing keeping me from dying next to that asshole, Joe Mouffreau, so I made a decision to try to get to it. I pulled myself up the stairs, dripping blood, until I was lying on the floor of the trailer, out of breath and almightily fucked up. I had to crawl through the broken glass of the coffee table to drag myself up to the breakfast nook bench and peek through the window. Marsha's taillights were gone, which of course was no fucking surprise. I bet she was wishing she got Raptured.

My one leg didn't work for shit, seeing as there was a bullet lodged in my goddamn hip. There was a slick of blood all up and down one side of my head, a bit of my own earlobe waggling around free enough that the goddamn wind coulda blown it away. Not only that, but my left arm had been broken somehow when I fell after Joe shot me the first time. I reached over toward the phone on the counter, thinking to myself all the time what I was gonna say to the emergency operator when they asked me what the problem was.

The ice crystals were like tiny stars being carried along whose job it was to catch up whatever light they could and bring it to somewhere else. These ones carried the kind of cold, blue light that was the light I had grown up with and walked out into each morning and clapped my gloved hands against. It was the kind of light that was so hard at the edges that maybe you'd think it was cruel or something, but it wasn't cruel at all; it was familiar. It was like those glints of light had come to take me back out into the cold with them, like they had come to take me home, except that I *was* home.

Still, there was fucking Joe Mouffreau, dead at the foot of my stairs, looking dumb, peaceful and self-satisfied, and as much as I wanted to go with the light, there wasn't any way I was gonna let myself get found dead next to such a pig-faced lush and lie-about loser. After ninety-nine years you oughta be able to choose the way you die, goddamn it. The phone was attached to the wall, but it had one of those long stretchy, coil-y type cords that they like to give to old people for some reason. I hated the goddamn thing because it was always getting tangled on itself, but I was glad for it now because I was able to reach up and pull on it. The cord stretched and stretched but the phone didn't come. It was caught on a something up there and I knew what it was and I fucking cursed Linden Laughlin, that bastard, one more time.

EVERY SWEET THING

A river drive is a goddamn sight to see, if you've never seen one. The last one that I was on was 1931, and it was mostly a lark by then, because by that time there were trains reaching far into the mountains and roads and trucks reaching wherever the trains couldn't. It was a Daddy Mouffreau idea, to river-pig a herd of about fifty trees. They thought to do it as something to grab some press. They were always doing that sort of thing—longest lumber train, all that kind of shit. The logs were runty things, no more than a foot and a half through at the most, and terrible hard to ride seeing as they spun so fast and had no real dignity to the way they bounced around in the rougher water. There weren't many men who river-pigged by then, so a lot of the guys they got riding those things were young harvest hands hired part-time from over in the farmlands. They looked the part:

tough and husky for the cameras, save for that their faces were clean-shaven. There were some soupbones there, as well, old-timers like Jack Nearing, who by then had been in enough close scrapes up in the timber shows that it looked like most of him was scraped off. Dollar and Holmberg were both dead in the woods by that time. The Depression had sent folks scattering to the four winds and no one kept in touch much with anyone else.

I wasn't more than twenty-one then, of course, but I was out of practice with river work by that time, having been top-loading logs on flat cars for almost four years. I hadn't been down on the river much at all. One of the things we were supposed to do as part of the drive was to get the logs jammed up so's they would hold and people from all around could come out and see what a log jam looked like. Then someone from the Mouffreau mill would take some pictures and we'd bust up the jam with some dynamite. The pay was good, even for stingy Daddy Mouffreau and the indignity of working for him, so we were all in.

Before we started, a man had come up from a magazine and asked where was Wandering John at, and hadn't he heard that we always started the drives by going and putting a rock on his grave to keep him in the ground? The last time, his pine box had ended up floating all the way to the sawmill, which was where they caught it up and brought it back and buried it again, everyone laughing and telling stories about it up and down the St. Anne. I remembered laying a rock, a piece of raw, white granite, on his grave myself before we started the drive from the Lost Lot. But it had been eight years since then, and hard ones, too, and no one had been laying any rocks on anyone's grave or any such nonsense since at least 1927. I looked at Nearing and he looked back at me and shook his head.

"Well, maybe if you could show me about where he was buried the last time you saw him," the magazine man said, and next thing you know we were making a pile of river rocks and standing around and posing, and a few of the farm hands were twisting daisy chains and laying them on the stones and whatnot. Fact was, there was no one left who had any clue where Wandering John was, and it was most likely he got swept downstream and was in the ocean by now, with his feet up on a sea turtle.

The drive was a pitiful little thing, and Daddy Mouffreau, who had wanted a big jam-up to begin with, was too cheap with his good-ass timber to give us logs that were big enough to jam up in any kind of believable way. We got a few centered up on a sandbar in the middle of the river, but the other logs would push them off and they'd go bobbing merrily away, bouncing like a little girl's pigtails as they toodle-ooed. When we finally did get them to knot up, we prayed they'd hold long enough for the shutters to click.

In the water the farm boys were useless as bull tits. Mostly they just ate up the sandwiches and wrestled around on the bank and pointed at fucking deer and moose like the animals had escaped from a zoo. It was mostly Bill and me and a couple other older-timers that got the whole jam jammed, but when the time came, not a single one of us wanted to be caught dead or alive in the goddamn picture with such tiny logs and we all said as much. So, they got the farm boys out there on the bank and took a picture of them all big and beefy and then they sent one out with a peavey to stab around in those logs until enough floated free that the jam would come undone. You have never seen the like of it. That farm boy was square-shaped and flat-footed, and as I had suspected, transfiguration was beyond him. He couldn't stand up for shit on those logs. Every time it looked like he was gonna catch his balance, he fell into the water. They sent another fella out to break up the jam. Same thing. Finally, I got tired of watching and all the sandwiches were gone. I grabbed a peavey from the dolt sloshing out of the water.

"It's a mighty tough one out there," he said. "You might could use a stick or two of dynamite to bust 'er loose."

I ignored him and hopped on out to the middle of the river on the logs.

Well, all it took was a single little jump in the right place and the whole jam started to move, and suddenly I was the only one in the river. I jumped aboard the biggest log I saw and squared up, pulled my peavey from out of the current and poked away at a few other logs so's I could get free of the mass of them. It was a beautiful day, and the sunlight sparkled on the water. I'd learned to ride the river that first spring on the Lost Lot, and it all came back to me. I was still a smallish man, but like they say, I was catty. It wasn't hard for me to keep my balance, even on these barky broom handles that Mouffreau had given us to work with. I rode that thing all the way to the mill itself. You can see the picture of me doing it, somewhere.

The papers all called it a day to remember and I guess for me it was; still, I wasn't sorry to see the river drives go any more than I was sorry to see the days of horse skidding timber go. I guessed that meant I wasn't a jack, after all. In fact, the only real reason I remember that day any more than any other day was that it was the first time I went back to visit the grave of Linden Laughlin. All this talk of Wandering John, and the fact that it'd only taken us a few years to forget where the fuck we last put him, got me to realizing how easy it might be to forget where it was that we'd put Linden. There wasn't anyone else around to remember but me, and I was the only one who cared at all to begin with.

"I have something to show you," Annie told me as she was ladling stew onto my plate one night during the river drive. In the days after I killed Linden Laughlin, she had come up to help Thorough cook and not poison us.

"What is it?" I asked.

"Later," she replied.

The St. Anne doesn't have that kind of watery dark but for a few weeks each year, in full-roaring spring. The last of the ice is gone from the air, and instead it's freighted with the good, groundy smell of soaked brown pine needles and moss and rotting wood. She walked ahead of me a bit. "Branch," she would say sometimes, and I would put my hand up so I wouldn't get whacked in the face.

"Be careful of the roots here. There's a step down. Duck under." She gave me directions and then she had slowed and was beside me and took my hand. "Guess," she said. Her hand was warm, almost hot, and she threaded her fingers through mine.

"What is it?" I said.

"Look," she said.

It was a tiny cabin, no glass left in its window and no door or roof, either. The frame was still standing straight, though, despite the elements.

"It's Bud Maynard's cabin," she said, and we looked at it for what felt like an eternity, the pulse in my blood going wild.

"How'd you find it?" I asked her finally.

"Just out walking," she said, though something told me she had known its whereabouts all along.

"Have you been inside?" I said.

"Yes," she said. "Would you like to see?"

Whatever size Bud Maynard was in movies, he was short in real life. The doorway was small enough we almost had to duck through, and once inside you could have touched the ceiling, had there been one. He'd carved his name above the doorframe, the self-important fuck.

She swept away the last of the snow and laid a blanket out on the floor of the cabin and then sat down cross-legged on the floor and beckoned to me. "Sit."

I sat.

"Are you afraid, Weldon?" she asked me. I *was* shaking a bit, I guess. Hell, if you can't remember the first time you were with a woman and how nervous you were, then maybe you're too old to keep living. When memories that good slip through your fingers, then what really is the point of staying alive? Me, I remember every sweet thing about that moment in time. And it *was* sweet. All of it. I have the unimproving type of memory, and there is no way that Annie could be improved upon.

"I'm not scared," I lied.

We lay down on our backs, looking up at where Bud Maynard's ceiling used to be. It flashed before me what if he had stuck around and never gone on to the movies. He'd probably still be living here, taking handouts, and I wouldn't be lying down on a blanket in his abandoned cabin with Annie. Everything we had was soaked with melting snow and mud. She was wearing boots, too, and thick wool pants and a heavy sweater that smelled like sheep and girl all together.

I could tell you all kinds of stuff about what she looked like to me then—not just her long, pale neck, and the ragged crop of hair, but other stuff, too, if I wanted to. I have it all in my goddamn memory. You know the first time that love happened to you. You know what parts were different from how you thought they'd be, how much like a child you felt in the instant and how much like the whole enormous starry sky she was when you were with her. I can't tell you anything that can improve your own memory of that kind of thing, any more than describing it to you could sugar up my memory of how beautiful Annie was, lying there with me.

I've lost count of how many women I've been with. There's been moments with some that were almost that good, and there's been some that I only remember because it was all wrong. There's been some, like Marsha, that weren't bad or good but more just something that could happen that was better than nothing happening at all. I'd be willing to bet that not all of them have thought, or are gonna think, about me on their wedding nights or on their deathbeds. I do know this, though. If I'd sold the Lost Lot and gone, that night would never have happened. When I've sat up sometimes, thinking about the past and looking at that great big mountain stretching up to the sky behind my house, there hasn't been once that my mind hasn't gone to Annie and that cabin. If I've thought about selling the Lost Lot and moving somewhere else a thousand times and a thousand times haven't done it, it's at least a little in part because of her and us and that night. And I'll tell you what, if this is my deathbed, and it looks like it probably is, then you can leave off wondering what it is I'm thinking about when the white water finally sweeps me up.

We lay in the dark and didn't say nothing, just let the feeling settle in around us and over us and I felt the wish of her eyelashes against my cheek, her breath warm in the crook of my neck. Maybe we both slept a little, I don't know. All I know is that sometime in the night she was gone, this time for good, and when I woke in the early gray light of morning, the cabin was empty as a cupboard.

I followed our tracks back through the mud and slush to the camp, and I only ever went back inside that cabin once, some years back when I heard that she'd passed on. I went up there to see if maybe a little of her was still there. Bud Maynard's cabin was empty. Annie hadn't died on this land. She'd moved on up into Canada and met a farmer and married and had children. If her spirit was anywhere at all, it wasn't there in that little wreck of a cabin; it was with the man and land that she made her own. Still, she'd left me a little piece of her heart, I told myself. I sat on the empty floor of that cabin where once we'd been together and I knew that it was still there, beneath blazing starlight, that portion of her love that she'd meant for me alone.

ELBOW TO ELBOW

It specifically *wasn't* that I was putting off taking that rock up to throw on Linden Laughlin's final resting place. One thing I never did in the years since the last drive is *forget* to put rocks on top of his grave. It wasn't like what you might expect, that I was afraid he was gonna get washed away like Wandering John was. We buried him too high up on the mountain for that. All Marsha's Rapture yammering would have to come true a good three or four times in a row for the floodwaters to come lapping at Linden Laughlin's grave. It wasn't that the rocks would weigh down his soul or anything, either. A few rocks aren't gonna keep a spirit from rising out of the ground, I know that. If I thought there was a chance they would, I wouldn't'a started piling them there. No, I want Linden Laughlin's ghost up and walking around. He isn't gonna stray far.

I started putting rocks on his grave because I just didn't want to lose it. Bodies molder in the ground. Everything falls: pine trees, snow, rain, night, Cordy. Memory is no different. Things you thought you'd never forget come loose from places you can't imagine they ever would. Beneath all of that, it's easier than you might think to lose a grave in the woods. Some years I'd just put one rock up there. Other times, like when Antti sent the letter that Otto had died, I'd pile on three or four, just to make fucking sure the fucker knew I was still kicking. When you look at his grave now, you could be forgiven for thinking that Linden was closer to me than most of the living people in my life. Now that I'm as old as I am, it's a fact that he is. He'll be closer yet, if you do as I say.

Anyway, it was agony but I gave another good pull on the springy phone cord that was caught up on the counter, and with that the cord came free and the rock that was holding it back came off the counter and gave me a crack on the fucking noggin. My head was just taking a beating.

I dialed the emergency number. "Joe, you fucking, lying, misbegotten, pony-sucking, piece of clay-colored dogshit," I screamed at him as it was ringing.

"Nine-one-one," the woman said, her voice crackling down the line. "Is this an emergency?"

"Not anymore," I yelled. "Come and pick me up. You fucks took away my license so I can't drive myself to the hospital. Plus, fucking Marsha Leeds and Joe Mouffreau just tried to kill me."

They took me here because it was closest. They said that
the only reason I lived after Joe shot me was that I was so
weak from being drunk and cold and ninety-nine. They
said that even though I was bleeding from the bullet hole
in my hip and the one along the side of my head, that my
heart wasn't strong enough for me to die from blood loss.

But it ain't having a weak heart that lets you live as long
as I have. It ain't even *living* that makes you live as long as
me. All that shit about living a "full life" and all that. You
can make love to all the women you want, make millions
of dollars or eat out of a Campbell's soup can most of your
life like I have. It doesn't matter for shit. What matters is
outliving. Choose something, or someone, to outlive and
there ain't a thing that can kill you. Look at Joe Mouffreau
for a fucking object lesson. What did he have to outlive? I
outlived Linden Laughlin before I was even fourteen years
old, and after that there was nothing more to do but keep
on outliving him.

I wanted Linden Laughlin buried on the Lost Lot. I had
my reasons. At first, as the jacks and I dusted off our hands
and walked away from his grave, I thought there wasn't any
way that I could live without being able to kill him again
and again. As time went on, though, the hatred changed.
I worked timber jobs all over the St. Anne. I fell in love
with girls and fell out of love with them. I had dogs and I
took care of old cars and I drank and drank and drank. I
hid Peg's Dream on my land, and when word came a few
years later that Peg had died in The Lights, at old lady Estelle's boardinghouse, some of the jacks and me went up

on the mountain and dug up all the bottles from where they were hidden and we waked that rangy, mean, good-hearted, conniving bastard of a barber down at Shorty Wade's for bringing us all together somehow. Even Jensen and Webb, the prohibition agents that had first arrested him, came and doffed their caps to him and said they reckoned he was alright and not the worst soul to ever prance God's green Earth.

Those of us who were left to finish the season on the Lost Lot all made a tidy bundle of money. Even with Daddy Mouffreau being as chisel-cheap as he was, I was able to pay everyone double and then walk away with more cash than I suspect most thirteen-year-olds could ever dream of. Antti and Otto bought a set of donkey engines that could do the work of ten horses in a day. Cavuto used his share to partner with some other Italians and buy a pool hall in The Lights. Unto (fucking Unto!) took his hours and moved him and his too-sweet-for-Unto wife to the Oregon coast, where she found work in a school for the blind. The Kaiser bought a motorcycle.

With all of that going on, it never left my mind that I was outliving Linden Laughlin, and the hatred started to fade some. He wasn't a shadow dogging my heels. I went away and worked in Wallace driving a truck at the smelter. Shorty Wade died and Ed Kleinerd moved to Miami Beach. I have a postcard to prove it. For a while there was no good place to drink, then Paulette came and bought the building and Shorty Wade's became the Brothers Swede. Who the fuck the brothers are, I've never thought to ask.

Most people have gone or died. I don't mourn them like you see on television. I don't brood over what's gone by. I keep ahead of the brood by swearing, drinking and knowing that all of them, living or dead, are wandering around somewhere on the patch of ground where they put themselves. My father is in the Lost Lot cemetery, long since grown over and returned to scrubby forest that will itself be clear-cut soon. Peg and Dollar Edwards are down the road in the cemetery of the burned-down church. Nearing disappeared, Holmberg got laid out over in the Moscow cemetery, right behind a mall. Thorough moved on, too, but not far. He was hired by the elementary school to feed the kids in the lunchroom. Given his culinary abilities and his love of children like the birds with their tiny goddamn faces, I'd say he did just fine. He gave me his little brass binoculars to keep as a final farewell to the woods and the time that we had shared.

Otto and Antti are buried in St. Paul. I visited them there once on a failed search for the Witch. Their gravestones seemed pretty companionable in the winter sunlight. You could feel that they were contented there. For a moment it seemed like I could lie right down there with them, but it wasn't for me to be buried there.

I think about the Witch every day. Things back then weren't like they are now. A hundred years ago, when you said goodbye and left for the great, wide World, that was it. Sometimes they even held a funeral for you before you left. The last time I saw the Witch, she was framed in the frosty windows of a steam-powered locomotive. I never saw her again and, though I tried, I never found out what became of her, or whether she'd finally found her sister. She'd come from Finland, but she may as well have stepped out of a fairy tale, so wild were her eyes and her savage pride, so strange were her forecastings and cures and desolate keenings. Once gone, it was as if she had been subsumed back into the epics from which she had first emerged. In that way, I suppose she never died at all; she just went back to join the host of other stories that are passed from mouth to mouth during the fireside hours. The Witch, who saw the Future and hated any man with whiskers. I like to think of her, some somewhere, dragging the burlap sack with her possessions in it along a rocky stretch of coastline, the mist from the sea jeweling the hem of her dress, her pale eyes set on the smoke rising from the chimney of a far-off cottage. The birds aren't forest birds, but reeling gulls, and the whoosh of breeze through the pines is replaced by the hollow buffet of the wind goddess. The door of the cottage opens, and a face looks out. Then the door opens wide, and out comes a black-haired and fierce-faced woman who runs toward the Witch and gathers her up and pulls her close.

Those trees that we cut were the only ones I ever cut on the Lost Lot. It's not as if I went through all I did for the trees. I ain't a tree hugger and I don't give a beetle's butthole for the kids that climb up in trees like monkeys so's no one can come and cut them down. After Linden died it just felt better to leave them standing all around than to cut any down.

I left the trees standing because I wanted for him to

wake up from his ghost nap every day and the first thing he saw to be all those big, huge things that he wasn't able to get his hands on. I wanted them to whisper to him on the breeze. I want him to smell their sap in his ghost nose. I wanted hikers and health nuts and hunters and whatnot to roam around his ghost grave, just as vital as you please, taunting him with their ability to feel pain and loss and love and beauty. All that living that he can't kill. There's been times I've sat up there, high on the mountain rising up behind my home, and I could feel him ranting and raving around me, circling me, spit-mouthed. He hasn't had anyone to talk to in a while. I expect he's more than a little pissed off, but that doesn't matter to me. We'll have the rest of Forever to fucking rehash. I expect I'll enjoy that a whole hell of a lot more than he will.

Take the river road east from Cordelia and watch the curves. The truckers hit them hard and I haven't lived this long just so my corpse can get dumped in the St. Anne. I'm no Wandering John. Take the road thirty miles. You'll know the Lost Lot when you see it. Everything around it has been cut. The trees are giants and the clouds still get caught up in them. Linden Laughlin's grave is about three-quarters of the way up the slope. It gets steep so bring boots or whatever. It might take some time to find it, but you'll know the spot by the big pile of river rocks.

Just plant me right there next to him. Mind you, not "down the hill a little ways," and not "off a bit where old Weldon will be peaceful." I want you to lay me right the fuck down next to that fuck. I mean, *right next* to him.

Elbow to elbow. All this time he's been waiting for me to
die so that he can have the mountain all to himself. If that's
what he thinks, he's got another think coming.

★ ★ ★ ★ ★

ACKNOWLEDGMENTS

I have been fortunate to have all kind of adventures in my life, but none of them has been as joyous, hair-raising and death-defying as being with the amazing Haley Tanner. Not only that, I am indebted to her fantastically close reads, her encouragement and her certainty that Weldon Applegate's story was worth the telling. I don't know how I got so lucky.

A huge (and long-overdue) thanks to my parents, Bob and Sue Ritter, for making the decision to live in northern Idaho in the first place. The magic of that place has shaped my life and my imagination in ways that I am only beginning to understand. Thanks go as well to my brother, Lincoln, who was out there in the woods with me and was a part of all the adventures, real and imagined.

Mom, thanks for putting up with all the swearing in this

book. I will make sure to tell everyone that I didn't learn it from you.

Thanks to the Tanner Family for being so gracious and good to me. I love you all.

A huge thanks to my hero and literary agent, Lucy Carson (and all at the Friedrich Agency), for accompanying me through the foothills and up into the crags of this novel. I feel profoundly fortunate for her belief in me and in Weldon.

Thanks to my musical family, who has seen me scribbling furiously away in hotel lounges, airplanes, vans, backstage, before and after shows, in parks and behind festival tents. I love you crazy bunch of wild people. Darius Zelkha, Justin Taing, Nicole White and all at Brilliant Corners, Mike Leahy and all at Concerted Efforts, Doug Rice and Jonathan Horn, Carla Sacks, Louis D'Adamio, Asha Goodman Trebing and all at Sacks & Co., Lynn Grossman and all at Secret Road. Also to Josh Kaufman, Zack Hickman, Sam Kassirer, Ray Rizzo, Mark Erelli, Justin Carroll, Liam Hurley, Katie Muldoon, Rachel Hanley, Bernie Guerra, Justin Tamplin and Kenneth Mednick. Thanks as well to Matt Fleming and Scott Hueston, and to Pete Frostic, Tevin Apedaile and all at the Greenroom Resource, and to all the folks at Thirty Tigers.

I feel so fortunate to have gotten to work with Peter Joseph at Hanover Square Press in bringing the world of the Lost Lot and the St. Anne to life. Great thanks to him, as well as to Grace Towery, Christine Langone, Ingrid Dolan and Eden Church for this adventure. I'm loving every minute of it.

Anyone who enjoys a good rollick and a fascinating read

about the lost world of the lumberjacks should pick up *Holy Old Mackinaw: A Natural History of the American Lumberjack* by Stewart Holbrook.

Finally, profound thanks to Beatrix and Moxie for making sure that I got up really, really early every morning to write this book. If there is any pure lightness and love and laughter in this story, it is through their auspices and example.